Two Feet off the Ground
By Suzie Carr

Edited by Trish McDermott

Also by Suzie Carr:
The Fiche Room
Tangerine Twist
Inner Secrets
A New Leash on Life
The Muse
Staying True

Keep up on Suzie's latest news and projects:
www.curveswelcome.com

Follow Suzie on Twitter:
@girl_novelist

For My Honey Bun – Thank you for coloring my world with your love.

Chum – Thank you for the journey.

Chapter One

The second I met Paula McKenna I knew I was in deep trouble. Not the kind of trouble that would land me in jail or make my twelve-year-old son, Owen, question my moral integrity. More like the kind that forced me to look inside myself and realize I had a lot of growing up to do if I was ever going to be happy.

We met under the belly of the Sling Shot ride at Roller Kingdom Amusement Park. Owen introduced her as his soccer coach. She was more of a bronzed goddess to me. She shook my hand and thanked me for being a chaperone. Her skin felt like silk and she smelled just like Zest soap.

She was so commanding and smiley. As our group herded forward, I studied her from a few paces behind. She pounced around the park sniffing out adventure like a happy-go-lucky puppy dog afraid of nothing but the day ending.

I liked her instantly.

She was fearless, a complete and perfect blend of fun and confidence, and I secretly envied people like that. Some thought I was crazy because I've never been able to climb a ladder more than three steps, careen down a roller coaster with my hands raised up to the sky, or fly in an airplane since I was young enough to get away with wearing pigtails. I was that person who hung back, holding everyone's pocketbooks while they went off and had fun. That day at the park was no exception. I sat like a chicken on a bench all day, holding everyone's stuff in my tote bag, smiling like I was having a grand ole time.

If Paula didn't have such beautiful curves for me to admire all day, I would've been pissed off that I had wasted a perfectly good Saturday in amusement park hell. As a hairdresser, Saturdays were everything to me, especially to my pocketbook. It's when I double-booked and made all my spending money. It was how I could afford to buy Gucci and Prada. That day may have set me back an outfit or two, but it also granted me a front row seat to glimmering beauty.

Paula and I first really connected at lunch time. I watched her bend over to pick up an apple core she dropped. Her hips sloped at just the right angle, sculpted like a work of art. When she scooped back up, she caught me staring at her.

Our eyes locked and time just froze. That's when I first suspected that Paula McKenna was going to be that one woman who was capable of challenging me in ways no one has ever been able to do before.

* *

On my way into work two days later, I called my boss and best friend, Aziza, to find out my schedule for the coming day and to see if I'd need an extra-large coffee to rev me through to lunch. If Flo was still my ten o'clock cut and color, I'd need two. That woman zapped every last drop of energy out of me the minute she pounced at me with her scratchy voice and probing questions. I had to admit that there had been a few times when I had to bite down on my lip to keep from whacking her over the head with the bristle brush. She just didn't know when to shush her mouth.

When Aziza answered the phone and immediately asked how my day at the park had gone, I couldn't help but smile. "I had the best time."

"Let me guess," she said. "A brunette?"

6

I think of anyone in this world, Aziza knew me best. Actually, better than even I did sometimes.

"Like milk chocolate with swirls of caramel."

"I want details when you get here."

I smiled and must have looked like a sunflower in full bloom as I gunned it through the coffee shop parking lot. I couldn't get to the salon fast enough. "I'll bring a couple bagels."

"You better bring more than a couple. It's gonna be a long day. Flo's already fidgeting in your chair."

Clients like Flo seriously made me wish I'd listened to my mother and become a librarian instead of a hairdresser. "I'll be there in a few."

"I'm going to stick her hands in paraffin wax to keep her busy," Aziza said.

"Tell her I'll bring her a glazed donut. That ought to make her happy."

* *

I first met Aziza when we were eight-years-old. She moved into my neighborhood and instantly bonded with everyone. I'd lived there my whole life and failed to befriend most of them. She waltzed right in and attracted them to her like ants to a sugar cube.

The only reason any of them ever paid attention to me finally was because Aziza insisted they could and should. So, there I was, twirling batons and kicking up my heels alongside them all thinking I was queen shit now because I had a whole nest of friends. Then, the unthinkable happened. Aziza's family decided to uproot to the other side of town, a heart wrenching fifteen minutes away. Her family's station wagon hadn't gone as far as the sycamore tree on the corner of our street before the snobby girls turned their backs on me and ran off to play Barbie dolls without me.

For years, I played solo in my front yard, mourning for those sunny days with Aziza. I don't think flowers bloomed on Third Avenue for the three whole summers we lost touch.

Then, one day, my deadened world blossomed again. In fact, I wouldn't be exaggerating if I said a whole garden of roses, carnations, lupines, and daffodils bloomed from the cement cracks and smiled up to the sky on that day. It was my first day of middle school, and my knees shook so hard that I swore the sidewalk would crumble beneath me. I walked up to the towering stairs in front of the main entrance to the school and just stood there trying to look cool with my new corduroys. I had no idea how I'd survive three whole years at this school. That is until I saw Aziza, with her long, silky black hair, gliding up to me with a posse of pretty girls behind her. I could tell that they would become the popular girls of Woonsocket Junior High School.

I took one look at their matching jackets and decided I'd do just about anything to make them like me. Hell, I'd even jump out of an airplane if need be. Thankfully, I never had to because for starters, Aziza was too kind to do that to me, and secondly, she did something that most unpopular girls dreamt someone popular would do for them. She invited me to her slumber party.

My moment of acceptance into the group came that night when I proved I could smoke a cigarette. I lit the first one up and then puffed away all night long, even though I had to run into the bathroom every half hour and puke. Anything to fit in.

I clicked so well with the group, that by Monday morning a few of the popular boys started to sneak notes into my locker, just like they did to the pretty girls. On weekends, Aziza and I would sleep over each other's houses and call the boys all night long.

She and I became inseparable. I looked up to her like she was a celebrity. I could tell that she liked having a protégé like me who adored her realness and loyalty. We just worked. Aziza knew my deepest secrets and I knew hers.

Well, all except for one.

In our senior year, I had dragged her under the bleachers to tell her I had sex with Dean King, the captain of the football team, in that very spot the night before.

Aziza topped that.

She confessed that she kissed Annie Brown, one of the prettiest girls at school, and liked it.

A funny thing happened to me when I pictured the two of them kissing. I was turned on to the point that if I hadn't started to break out into a nervous laughter, I would've had an orgasm right there in front of my best friend.

It wasn't until Owen—who was born nine months after that night under the bleachers—was out of diapers that I finally confessed to Aziza I, too, longed to tangle up with a woman.

Since that pinnacle moment, the two of us shared everything together, even the stuff that cut deep—like many years later, the day Aziza dropped the key to the new Bella Day Spa in my hand— a year before we planned to open it together.

"You can open and close it anytime you want. I can make you salon manager, so it can feel like yours," she said to me.

I guess I couldn't really blame her. Her parents forked over a two–hundred-thousand dollar gift and she ran with it. She transformed from my best friend to boss overnight. The thing that really pissed me off about this though was I'd never get to see my name next to hers on the incorporation papers like we'd always dreamed about since the day we both enrolled at Rhode Island Beauty Academy. *Ms. Lauren Woods* should've been sitting right up at the top of that paperwork alongside *Aziza Asibandi.* Instead she had cut our dream into a million little pieces and threw the broom at me.

It took a few years and several hair splinters later to get past the envy and sting of being just one of the employees. It didn't help at all that *Elite Magazine,* the go-to resource for everything and anything in the spa business, featured Bella on the cover of their "Most Luxurious Spas" issue and touted Aziza as the most successful owner of the decade. When I read that, it cut through me like a pair of dull shears.

She glowed in the article, and it annoyed me. Each paragraph applauded her artistic approach to decorating and how she skimped on nothing. Even, Deogie, the salon's white Boxer mascot, wore silk on her back to remind clients that fashion ruled.

These were all my ideas. I picked out the patina design for the back wall, the recliner seats for the sinks, the lacy curtains for the romantic effect. I even managed the staff, the appointments, and the public relations that got us on the cover in the first place.

I was so jealous. I wanted to take out a full page ad in the magazine so I could announce to anyone who cared that Bella's success was largely due in part to me. You know how I finally got over this jealousy? I woke up one morning not feeling at all like facing my twenty clients and called out sick. Just like that, picked up the phone and told Aziza I wasn't going in. Instead of getting mad at me, she simply said to me, "I envy you."

No one had ever envied me.

That's when I cut my leadership reins and let her carve out Bella's path for herself. And, when I did, I have to say, I enjoyed my freedom and watching her fumble a little. I found myself rearranging my schedule to suit my needs instead of Bella's. And I loved this. Take the past Saturday at the amusement park for instance. Aziza was back at the spa sweeping up hair and cleaning dirty sinks, while I got to lounge in the sun and fantasize about a doll named Paula.

"So did you flirt with her," she said to me that night after we closed up shop.

"We were chaperoning."

"That didn't have to stop you." She came up from behind me and laced her fingers through my hair and twisted it up on top of my head. "You need to trim your ends. They're brassy."

"Just massage my scalp, please."

I closed my eyes as she circled her fingers around my head. The pressure of the day's stressful load slowly erased. "Do you think it'd be a bad idea to ask her out for a drink, being that she's Owen's coach and all?"

She slid her fingers down the back of my head and rested them on my shoulders. "Maybe it's better if you just forget this one."

"It's too late now." I couldn't stop thinking about those curvy hips and her mysterious mocha java eyes.

Chapter Two

One of the wisest pieces of advice my grandmother gave to me before she died was to make sure my baby knew I loved him. That first week I brought Owen home, she'd lie in bed with him on top of her and hugged him so hard I swore her frail bones would break all over his little body. She'd looked me square in the eye a few times and said, "Raising a great kid requires a lot more than luck. You need to give him structure. Otherwise, he'll turn out to be one of those screaming brats you see in the toy aisle pissing all over everyone's nice shopping day with his tantrum."

Five days later, she died of cancer right on our living room couch. I was multi-tasking, eating macaroni and cheese while feeding Owen a bottle, and she was taking a nap. My mother carried her pills over to her, and when she wouldn't budge, my mother started shaking her frantically, yelling at her to wake up. When she didn't, my mother ran down the street in her silk nightgown screaming that her mother was dead. Selfishly, instead of running after my mother, I just sat numb wondering who was going to help me teach Owen how to crawl, walk, talk, and recite his alphabet. Gran was supposed to. That was our big plan.

My parents couldn't. They both spent more than fifteen hours a day pleading their defense cases to judges, and then came home to unwind with a couple of martinis and piles of court papers.

I remember looking down at Owen at the moment of her death and apologizing to him for the terrible life he was going to have now that Gran wasn't there to make sure I didn't screw him up.

Poor kid flew right into the inept arms of a clueless seventeen-year-old. I was just a kid myself. How was I supposed to understand the complexities of a newborn baby? The first time I changed his diaper after my Gran died, he peed right in my face. I screamed like someone had just thrown spiders at me. I handed him straight over to my mother and begged her to save me. She simply placed him back in my arms, tossed her messenger bag over the shoulder of her tailored suit and dashed out the door.

Those first few days alone with him I spent wallowing in self-pity. I hated the smelly diapers, the screaming, the throwing up, but more than anything, I was repulsed at the way my body looked. My boobs were so swollen that at moments, even walking across the room brought tears to my eyes. I had to trade my tight jeans in for baggy sweatpants just so I could breathe. I looked like a bag lady thumping around my parent's house, running from the microwave to the changing table to the basinet. I needed roller skates to keep up with the hectic pace.

I just wanted my normal life back. I wanted to hop in Aziza's Jeep Wrangler and race wildly down to the beach to meet up with the rest of our friends who were partying before heading off to college in the fall. Instead, I was stuck cleaning spit-up from my extra large t-shirts.

Life would never again be normal for me.

After about a month of this self pitying, Aziza came to my rescue. I had called her up in hysterics one night because I couldn't stop Owen from crying. The boy wouldn't sleep. I had circles so dark under my eyes that I looked like I spent the last month getting clobbered like a punching bag. She whizzed over and handed me a cassette of Baroque classical music. "Trust me," she said. "My mother swears on her soul, that this will do the trick."

She plopped the cassette into a portable player and the room filled with French horns, trumpets, and clarinets. I could hear them all, even over Owen's screams. She lowered the overhead lights and we sat on the edge of the bed together. The smell of baby powder mixed with her flowery scent to create a calming effect. A few minutes into the song, Owen stopped crying and started cooing. Aziza and I stared down at him, and I swear he looked like a little angel.

Night after night, I'd prepare his bottle, sit in the rocker by his crib, and feed him by nightlight to his favorite classical music. He would just stare up at me with his big blue eyes with his little fingers wrapped around mine.

I fell in love with him, my baby boy, and realized over time how lucky I was that my life never returned to normal.

Now, twelve years later, I loved that Owen still craved our bonding time as much as I did. In fact, he was the one who started our Tuesday night ice cream date. On his third birthday he asked to go to the mall to get ice cream. He liked how the walls of the creamery were painted with the same spots as cows. That first night we took turns calling out familiar objects we saw in the spots. Owen had discovered one that looked just like a soccer ball. He named it Oliver.

Oliver still hung on the wall all these years later. As we stood in line to order that night, I could see him peeking out at us from behind a new smoothie machine. Owen ordered a banana split with two scoops of crazy vanilla and a handful of crushed snickers on top. I finally decided on pistachio ice cream in a cone drizzled in chocolate.

We sat together on a bench in silence overlooking the carousel ride. I chased a drip sliding down the side of my cone. It got away from my lips and sped down my fingers. I kept chasing it and suddenly the cone imploded like a demolished building. Bits of cone and gobs of green ice cream smashed to the shiny floor. Miraculously, it just barely missed my new lace edged capris I'd bought from Ann Taylor the week before.

Owen jumped to his feet and threw his wad of napkins down on it. I knelt down beside him and helped him smear the squishy pile from side to side. With the growing tower of napkins between us we must have looked like a couple of Neanderthals huddling around a campfire.

"So, coach is throwing a party next Saturday," he said. "And, she's inviting us."

"Us?" I swallowed the exclamation point that threatened to jump out of my throat.

"Yeah, everyone's going. There'll be like a hundred people there. She's having a pool party."

A pool party meant bathing suits, no makeup, no hairstyle, and—I could only assume with the kids being there—no alcoholic beverages to take the edge off meeting her again. I was not going to this party. I'd figure out another way to meet up with her.

Logic cranked tighter in my brain as I smeared the ice cream into a bigger mess. I shouldn't even consider Paula in any other context but on a soccer field blowing a whistle. She was too much of an adrenaline junkie anyway. I definitely didn't need to put myself through that kind of torture.

"I've got way too much hair to cut to take another day off, sweetie. Maybe you can just go with Jake."

He shrugged his shoulders, and then scooped his arms around the sticky napkins. "Whatever," he said. "You're going to miss a great time."

Nothing new there.

* *

I came home from a grueling twelve-hour shift at the salon the next day, and discovered I had a voice mail. I pressed the button to retrieve it. "Hey, Lauren, it's Paula. I talked to Owen at practice today and he tells me you're not coming to my party. I was really hoping you would. Any way that I can change your mind?"

I kept the phone against my ear for several seconds after to give her question a moment longer to marinate.

I slowly closed my cell, and then placed it on the counter alongside the loaf of bread I forgot to put away that morning. A line of crumbs dotted the granite. I took a deep breath, grabbed a paper towel, and brushed the crumbs into the sink. My heart pounded and I loved every refreshing beat of it.

I needed to tell Aziza. I grabbed my phone and called her. "Do I go? It sounds like she really wants me to. But, she's Owen's coach. Is this unthinkable? Or is it unavoidable?"

"Take a breath. It's a freaking pool party. You'll lob a volleyball back and forth across the pool and maybe, if you're lucky, get to slam dunk her later on."

"Okay, so say I go. What do I wear? My pink bikini or something more modest, like a tankini or a one piece?"

"You're not wearing a one-piece."

I shot towards the kitchen and poured myself a tall glass of wine. I gulped a mouthful. "I haven't put on a bathing suit in eons. This means I'll have to get a bikini wax, and you know how my skin swells. I'll look like I placed a beacon between my legs that screams out to everyone, *look at what I did*. And me, in a crowd of people? I'm not going."

"Get drunk."

Down a few vodka cranberries, and I might even be able to climb on top of Paula's shoulders and whack the ball across the net not caring if my c-section scar fell out of my bikini bottom. I gulped another mouthful of wine. "You're a big help as usual."

"Just tell her the truth. Tell her you're booked solid that day and can't go. Hook up with her later."

How could I possibly cut hair that day now? "I'll let you know what I decide."

"Right, like you're going to go soak in a relaxing tub right now and forget all about this chick," she said. "Call me when you're done talking to her, darling."

"Of course." I hung up and paced the living room with my near empty glass. A field of butterflies were taking up flight in my stomach. I felt just like I did the first time I kissed a girl, high as a kite. I floated from one end of the room to the other feeling nothing but air under my feet.

I stared at my cell willing for it to make the call itself.

Eat the Frog.

This was Gran's famous phrase. I could hear her whisper in my ear, "Imagine if you were told that you had twenty-four hours to eat a frog. Wouldn't you rather just eat the frog in the first minute of the day rather than agonize over it for twenty-four hours?"

I stared harder at the cell.

Time to eat the damn frog.

I dialed her number. Before I pressed the send button, I breathed deeply one last time. Okay, maybe more like five more times. But, finally, I stepped on the edge and took the leap.

It rang and my heart jolted.

It rang again and my heart bucked like a bronco.

It rang a third time and I could no longer swallow.

Just when I thought I'd lose consciousness, the familiar click of voice mail sounded in my ear and I felt like kissing the ceramic tile at my feet. Thank God for voice mail.

Her voice sounded like a gentle breeze on a warm summer night, so cool and welcoming. "Hi, it's Paula. Leave a message."

I paused, perhaps for longer than I should have. I wanted to sound sexy, like Angelina Jolie. "Hey Paula, it's Lauren. I'll be there."

I hung up the phone and finally exhaled.

* *

Floating around a pool on inner tubes and noodles didn't exactly call for glam, but I wanted Paula to take notice. Of course, I didn't want her thinking I spent the entire afternoon primping for her party. But I also didn't want to show up with blotchy skin and ratty hair.

I leaned over my sink to get a good look at a new freckle that popped up on my forehead overnight. I hated my freckles. I rummaged through my makeup bag and pulled out some concealer, then plopped a generous amount onto every one of them that I saw. Then, I pulled out my eye shadow and started spreading it over my lids.

I spent the better part of my teenage years analyzing models in magazines to see if any of them shared the same misfortune I did of having fair skin and close-set eyes. Most of them were tanned with almond shaped eyes. They wore smoky, sultry shades that swept their tiger-eyes up in the corners. The problem with my complexion was I couldn't go too dark or bold because I'd look like a cheap whore. I also couldn't go with pastels because then I looked like an Easter egg. So, I always played it safe and went with neutrals.

I've always thought applying makeup was an annoying little routine. It's like one of those things that once you start you can't stop. People I know have actually pulled me aside to ask if I was sick when I wasn't wearing any. I became a slave to it at thirteen when I covered up a pimple on my chin with a glob of foundation. I'd never felt comfortable rolling out of bed and greeting the day with naked skin since.

Once I was finished with my makeup, I moved onto my hair. I wound sections of it around my extra wide curling iron to create a mass of soft, glossy waves.

After an hour, I finally emerged with fly away ends sealed into oblivion, and just the tiniest tickle in my throat from the cloud of hairspray dust I left wafting behind me.

I looked at the clock and was shocked to see I had wasted a whole hour getting ready for a pool party.

Imagine an actual date?

* *

"Mom, that was it. You just passed it."

Sure enough, I had sailed right past her street. "How am I supposed to read the street sign when it's all mangled and faded?" It looked like someone put it through a garbage disposal.

When I had a clear shot, I made my big risky move for the day and pulled a u-turn in the middle of the busy, narrow East Side Street.

Finally, we arrived on Arnold Street. Each house looked like it was straight out of the pages of *Better Homes and Gardens*, with pretty, arched front doors and pitched roofs. I pulled up to Paula's, an immaculate yellow Victorian. Plump impatiens of every color smiled at us from below her front windows. Her lawn, a lush, thick carpet of green, looked like something I could take an afternoon nap on. Cars spilled out of her driveway and onto the street, lining both sides.

"Where are we going to park?" Owen asked.

"Apparently not here. I hope you're ready to walk."

I drove around in circles for another ten minutes finding us a parking spot. I had to settle on one four blocks over.

I made a mental note to never again complain about the noise of the crickets outside my window on a summer night, or the smell of timber burning in the nightly community bonfire on the lakefront, or the sap from the weeping willow trees that ruined the paint on my Beemer.

Owen and I walked down a lopsided sidewalk. Big oak trees were growing from out of the cracks. My sandals crunched against the crushed cement, which drowned out the squeals of a group of kids playing on a swing set in a front yard. I could smell spaghetti sauce seeping from the house's open windows.

I carried a bowl of lentil salad, and by the time we made it down to the end of the street, my wrists were starting to cramp. I honestly thought of ditching the bowl under a berry bush we were coming up on, but I braved onward with it.

Finally, we arrived at Paula's front door. Owen pressed the bell and it chimed.

We waited.

I shifted my feet a few times.

He rang it again.

I tapped my fingers against the plastic bowl.

Still no answer.

Owen twisted the door handle.

I swiped his hand off it. "We're not going to just walk right in."

"It's locked anyway," he said.

Good. None of this felt right anyway. Who walked into a pool party with shiny lips and glistening eyelids? I wanted to run. I wanted to clear the white picket fence before anyone saw us. We could go back to our condo and pop a few bags of popcorn and watch movies all day.

"Let's just go." I spun on my wedged sandal and flew down the walkway cradling my bowl of lentils like a baby. I felt like a mother running for her life, trying to save her family from certain disaster.

"Wait," he called out after me. "Do you hear that?" He twisted his head to the left.

My belly somersaulted when I heard the faint sound of voices and splashing coming from the backyard.

Owen ran over to the gate like he was sprinting towards a finish line. I clung to my bowl and ran after him. I wasn't about to go in there alone.

His hand reached up for the latch. Through the crack I saw blurs of skin and bathing suits, of people enjoying a day in the sun without a care in the world how they looked or what Paula thought of them.

How lucky for them.

He pushed the gate open and all the blurry people came into focus.

Rich, green shrubbery circled the property, like sentinels keeping the city outside at bay. A fountain and a gazebo sat next to a carp pond. Intricate masonry decorated the patio. Each stone fit with the next like a jigsaw puzzle. In the center - the kidney-shaped pool. Thank God I chose to shave instead of wax.

Paula had managed to squeeze the entire soccer team and their parents into a twenty-by-fifty-foot hole in the ground. Everyone, aside from one pretty brunette standing at the grill, lounged in the pool. A man with a funky two-foot hat played "Piano Man" on a keyboard, as others sang along out of tune in between sipping on drinks. The air smelled like hotdogs and grilled chicken.

I latched onto Owen's arm and walked ahead with him. He weaved us through the maze of folding chairs and end tables littered with soda cans and beer bottles. I'd be needing several of those.

A Frisbee whizzed by us, skimming the top of Owen's head. He scrammed over to it and flung it right back over to the deep end of the pool towards a hefty man sinking like a whale. When the guy reached for it, pool water gushed out and onto the interlocking stones of the patio.

Owen threw his backpack on the ground and dashed off to a herd of kids by the diving board, leaving me standing alone. One skinny kid shot up in the air like a rocket and slammed his tucked knees into the last ten square centimeters of water that was free from rowdy partygoers.

I tucked my bathing suit strap more securely under my sun dress. No way in hell would I be getting into that pool with all those people. Where would I fit anyway?

The sun beat down on the patio, making it feel like I was standing on top of a fire. My skin already felt like it was getting crispy. I shaded my eyes with my hand and scanned the area. I spotted Paula perched on the top rung of the pool ladder prepared to jump into a circle of blonde mommies. I didn't remember seeing them at the PTA meetings.

She radiated confidence. She wore a navy bikini. Her skin was perfectly tanned. Not a freckle in sight. Her body, toned, curvy. She arched her back, and swan-like, dove in without making a splash. She surfaced and the sun danced across her shoulders, making the water droplets look like glistening diamonds on her skin. Someone tossed her a Frisbee and she caught it with one hand.

I stood alone on the patio in my polka-dotted sundress, oversized tote bag and bowl of lentils. I wanted to blend, to become as indistinctive as one of the stone puzzle pieces below my feet. I dug out my water bottle and chugged some lemonade. I should've spiked it before leaving home. What the hell good was sugar water from Trader Joe's going to do me at that moment?

The people clung together like maggots on a grain of rice. We all clamored to breathe the same air. How could there possibly be enough? I opened my mouth wide to take in a deep breath, but couldn't. Suddenly, the yard began to shrink. I looked towards the pool and the scene blurred as if bound in saran wrap. Then, the people in the pool, the trees, the fence, the keyboard man, even the sky, thudded towards me like a bowling ball slated to strike me down. My vision tunneled and in the center of it all was Paula pointing the Frisbee at me.

God not now. Not here. Not in front of all these people. Not in front of Paula.

I panicked and the adrenaline pumped into overdrive. I couldn't stop the anxiety attack now. It blew me off balance like an F-5 tornado, spinning my mind backwards and forwards and flicking my heart beat in and out too fast to keep up with. I tossed my water bottle to the ground and clutched my chest. It pounded like an out of control jackhammer. I broke out into a cold sweat and then my body started to tremble like I took one too many amphetamines.

I drew a breath, long and deep enough that surely I must've vacuumed up all the air left. I curled my eyes back towards the pool trying my best to ignore the flood of prickly needles scratching through my body. I looked up just in time to see Paula launch the Frisbee at me.

"Heads up!" she yelled.

It flew towards me at train derailment speeds. To my surprise, I actually caught the damn thing, lentils in hand and all. The crowd cheered me on like I'd just won a gold medal at the Olympics. If I didn't throw my hand up in front of my face when I did, I would've been spending the next week on the couch with a bag of frozen peas on my face.

In a mad attempt to escape still dignified, I raised the Frisbee above my head and purposely overshot it back to Paula, then turned and bolted towards the gate. At first I heard Paula yell out at me and when I turned back to see her, her mouth opened like a guppy snacking on goldfish. She waved her hands in front of her like she was signaling the start of a drag race. Her words garbled and fell short of my ears.

I just smiled over my shoulder at her and kept running forward like I was having the time of my life, then wham! I smacked my shin right into the cast iron fire pit. I shot up in the air, still hugging my lentils. I could've eaten an entire hotdog and swigged a can of beer in the time it seemed to take me to reach full height. Then, just like a popped balloon, I deflated and fell to the ground, my chest pounding into the cement like an angry hammer.

My body was squashed up against the hot patio like a sizzling hamburger over a charcoal grill. My arms tingled and it took a few seconds for me to feel my injured leg. I lifted my head to find Owen. He stared at me in horror with his hands covering his open mouth.

I looked to the pool and watched my bowl of drowning lentils float away.

It took a few more seconds for my leg to come alive, and when it did, the pain ripped through it like a cheese grater. I rolled over and squeezed it to my chest.

Paula landed by my side first. Drops of water trickled down from her arms onto my skin. She yelled out to the brunette still standing at the grill, "Can you get us some ice?"

She placed her hand on mine, soothing me better than Aloe.

"I tried to warn you," she said. "But you were too quick. What were you running from?"

"A bee," I said. I was so good at lying. Truth be told, though, it did feel like a million of them were piercing my leg with their stingers. I had to grit my teeth to keep from crying. Blood pooled around the fresh cut. I couldn't look at it. I started to shiver in the hot sun. "Is the bleeding bad?"

"We may need a tourniquet," she said, smiling.

I imagined blood squirting out of my leg and gathering in pools below me. I wanted to throw up.

The brunette handed Paula a first aid kit and an icepack. First Paula plunged her hands into a pair of latex gloves. Then, she poured peroxide onto some gauze and delicately patted it against my skin. I winced with every pat.

Aziza was going to love this story. The irony in it was so typical. I prayed for Paula's hands to be on me, and my wish was granted, alright.

When all the blood was clear, she wrapped up my leg like a slab of beef.

"Let's get you up on a lounge chair so you can elevate your leg," she said. "Owen, can you give me a hand?"

Owen jumped to my side and helped her launch me off the ground. She propped several towels under my ankle, then pulled up a chair. The brunette headed back to her grill, spatula still in hand. A few others jumped back in the pool to swim with the lentils. Some refilled their drinks and munched on chips. Me? I sat there looking like a soldier wounded from tripping over a rock on her way to battle.

"Hey, how about a beer?" she said reaching behind her into the cooler. "Or would you rather have some wine? Or maybe some straight grain alcohol?"

"Beer is perfect." I couldn't reach up for it fast enough.

She leaned back, took a swig and laid her eyes on mine. "I warned my brother not to put the fire pit in the middle of the patio. And look at him over there." She pointed to a handsome blonde look-a-like on the diving board. "He doesn't even realize you almost broke your leg on it." She straightened. "Let me call him over—"

"No. Don't do that." I wrapped my hand around her arm and I swear I felt a current pass between us. I think she felt it, too, because she curled her eyes up at me. "I'm fine, really," I said to her.

Suddenly, a pretty girl wearing a bright orange bikini walked up from behind us and draped her arm around Paula's shoulder. "Hey, sweetie, we're going to need some of your special Margaritas soon." The girl then flung her red hair over her shoulders and straddled the lounger next to Paula, like she was staking out property in the Wild West.

"When did you sneak in?" Paula asked, bending over to give her a hug.

"Apparently not in time to enjoy the show." She skimmed over me and smiled. Her hair was perfect and her skin like a china doll. I felt like the ugly duckling next to her. *God, please let her not be Paula's girlfriend.* They'd make such a pretty couple. I immediately diverted to the icepack.

The girl came to my side and cradled the icepack to my leg. "I haven't seen you around before. Are you a friend?"

"I'm just one of the parents," I said.

I looked down at her finger and saw a diamond ring as flawless as Paula herself. Its brilliance poked me in the eye like a lance. Pretty, nice, and possibly marrying the last perfect lesbian on earth. I hated her.

The brunette over at the grill called out to both of them. The flame-headed girl stood up. "We'll be right back," she said, grabbing hold of Paula and yanking her away from me.

Before I had a chance to readjust the icepack, Paula's brother had dashed up from behind. He slid onto the edge of my lounge chair and lifted the icepack. The blood had seeped through the bandage already. "That's going to leave a nasty bruise."

"I'll be fine. It's doesn't hurt that badly." I smiled and straightened up in the chair.

"At least you're not wimpy like my little sis over there." He nodded to Paula and her perky fiancé at the grill. His smile accentuated his chiseled face. "She took a bad fall on a bike ride down Mount Washington last summer and nearly passed out when she saw the blood flowing down her leg."

I needed to hear more. "I'd never guess that about her."

He stood up and his quads instantly flexed. "Don't let her fool you. She acts all tough in front of the kids, but she's really a softy inside."

"Well, that's a good thing because she was pretty mad at you for putting the fire pit where you did."

"Did she blame that on me?" He narrowed his eyes.

"She was ready to give you hell."

"She's the one who put that thing smack in the center of the patio." He scoffed. "Look at her over there playing miss innocent to all the pretty girls."

I rolled my eyes over to Paula and her sexy little girlfriend and scoffed along with him. "Who's that girl with her? Is that her fiancé?"

"Her fiancé?"

"Yeah, the pretty redhead next to her," I said.

He turned back to me and opened his eyes wide like something really important just dawned on him. "You have a thing for my sister, don't you?"

He wasn't shy.

"Don't be ridiculous." I felt like a dorky teenager.

He stared at me for a moment before breaking into a cocky grin. "Then, why did your face just turn five different shades of red?"

I decided to ignore his question and readjust the icepack. His swaggering grin circled around me like an annoying gnat. "Would you mind getting me another beer?" I asked him.

He walked over to the cooler, plucked out a beer and handed it to me. "Just in case you really want to know, the fox next to her happens to be *my* fiancé." He then turned and walked towards the grill.

My heart twirled in the wake of his words.

Chapter Three

By the time I arrived at work on Tuesday morning, I was still in such a good mood that I actually thought I could rub some of it onto Angie, the shampoo girl. As we stood side-by-side at the shampoo bowls, I asked her, "Did you have a nice weekend?"

She just nodded and continued to scrub the client's head. She wouldn't be winning any service awards with her frosty personality, but she sure could put the tingle down your spine with her rigorous massage.

Angie was by far the most serious apprentice I'd ever met. If she wasn't shampooing someone, she was folding towels or sweeping dust bunnies. She'd foil a head without gloves on if she thought it would impress Aziza. Little did she realize, Aziza didn't give a damn what she was doing. In fact, Aziza begged me at least once a week to fire her because of her disastrously dull sense of style. Angie wore her mousy brown hair tapered into a bob and this bugged Aziza.

Angie didn't realize it, but I was her only ally. Her work ethic impressed me. In fact, if I owned the place, I'd hire twenty of her type just to have an army of clean freaks on hand so I'd never have to break another nail digging down the drains or scrubbing color stains off the floor. I couldn't stand some of the early airheads Aziza had hired. They tramped around Bella in their tight jeans and three inch heels, talking nonsense about reality television and what club they'd be hitting that night.

Aziza had no clue how to run a successful business. It was only successful because I cranked the wheel behind the scenes. And, the only reason I bothered to help out was because I didn't want to work alongside stylists who believed smoking cigarettes while working on a client was cool or that it was okay to wash out a dirty plate in the same sink where I washed my clients' hair. And, most importantly, I certainly didn't want to be associated with those old-fashioned stylists who still thought it was hip and trendy to perm the hell out of someone's hair and call it a style.

My future was in Aziza's hands; she didn't have a clue what to do with it. If it wasn't for me creating strategic plans in the backroom, Bella never would've drawn in the million dollar revenues it did every year. I was the one who attended the management workshops put on by our suppliers. I was the one who read every marketing book on the shelves of the bookstore around the corner. I was the one who came up with the whole employee development plan. I was the one who pushed the stylists' skills to star-quality levels. And, I was also the one earning eighty-five percent of every penny that my chair brought into that salon.

The money went a long way with me.

Every beauty school graduate wanted to work for Bella because of what they thought Aziza could do for them. If left up to her, she'd still be hiring a bunch of hot girls and letting them paint their nails and snap bubble gum at the front desk. Basically, she'd let them do whatever they wanted.

I was the one who made sure each apprentice started out with the same rules in hand and methodically followed order. She'd start out as shampoo girl, where she'd sweep floors, shampoo clients, and fold towels. Then, when I thought she was ready, I'd graduate her to blow-out level where she'd get her chance to show off her stuff. This whole process took about two years. By then, if I felt she was Bella material, I'd give her a haircutting test. If she passed, I promoted her to junior stylist. From there, her fate depended on how well she could build up her chair. The more she profited, the faster she'd move up to the coveted reign of senior stylist. At that point, she could charge outrageous prices and profit from some of the highest commissions around.

Bella offered the best of everything to a budding stylist. Great pay, benefits—which were unheard of in a private hair salon—education, sliding scale commissions, and a herd of clients trampling through the door on any given day to pamper themselves silly.

We had our clients trained. They learned early on that if they wanted to be clients, they had to be patient to get an appointment, especially with a senior stylist like myself. My clients had to plan their haircuts like they were scheduling a wedding. This was no walk-in-clinic that accepted emergencies. My book filled up six months in advance. The only one that came close to that was Aziza, who still trailed behind me by about two months.

Angie wanted to succeed. I was almost ready to let her start blow-drying my clients. She certainly had the shampooing down. I watched her as she stood beside her client scrubbing her head like she was doting on the Queen of England, even though she was only an orthodontist from down the street.

I just loved her ambition.

I circled around back of her to grab a towel for my combs and accidentally bumped my bandaged leg against hers. I winced and she freaked, dropping the hose from her hand and letting it squirt all over the client. She wrestled the hose like it was a cobra, and the client ran around in circles desperately trying to escape the geyser raining down on her. Both were screaming, and I couldn't help cracking up. Poor Angie would be mopping up that floor all afternoon making sure every nook and cranny was bone dry. She was as red as the fresh blood soaking through my bandage again.

Aziza came running up to me all breathless, completely ignoring the drenched duo standing beside me. "You have a walk-in."

"Since when do I do walk-ins?" I asked.

She shrugged and smiled at me in a sneaky sort of way.

"I can't do it." I looked down at my watch. "I have a foil in 15 minutes and I'm booked solid for the rest of the day. Give her to Terry."

"She asked for you."

"Who is it?"

She curled her finger up and motioned for me to follow her. I bounced my heels in sync with hers as we made our way past the pedicure loungers and through the maze of stations on route to the front desk. When I entered the reception area and saw the back of Paula's head, I skidded to a halt, leaving a scuff mark the size of a small airport runway on the hardwood floor. I would've recognized the back of that head anywhere.

"Paula?"

She stood up and twisted her body around to see me. "Hey you."

"Well, isn't this a nice surprise. What brings you by?"

"I mentioned to the team I needed a haircut and Owen told me you cut hair. So, here I am."

I loved my son so much. He'd be getting an extra half hour of computer time that night for his good deed. "Well, I'm sure I can squeeze you in. I've got a few minutes." I said this as though all my appointments for the day magically erased themselves from my book.

"Great." She smiled and her whole face lit up like sunshine. "Chuck and I are flying out to Vegas tomorrow for a little getaway trip and I'm starting to look a little haggard."

She talked about flying so casually like she was taking a spin around the neighborhood on a scooter. "I don't think you look haggard at all."

We stood face to face smiling at each other by the new hairspray stand me and Aziza put together the week before. "How's your leg?" She eased her eyes down to my bare shin.

"It's still attached and working, so I guess that's a good thing." I shook it a little for effect.

She leaned down and touched it. "You might want to get it checked out by a doctor. It shouldn't be bleeding still. You might need it stitched."

Just then my scheduled foil, Meredith, sashayed through the front door with her Jackie O sunglasses and surgeon-enhanced cleavage. I wished I could've just brushed her away like a pile of dead ends, but, her daughter was getting married in two weeks and she had scheduled her foil a year ago. She hated to wait.

I nodded at Meredith. "Hello."

"You're not running late, are you?" She asked, breathless like she just ran the last one hundred yards of the Boston Marathon in her linen suit.

I turned a weary eye towards Paula. "Sorry, it might actually be about an hour before I can cut your hair." Actually more like two, with a high-maintenance bleach-head like Meredith, but I'd rush through it if I had to.

Paula bowed backwards and waved for Meredith to walk on by her. "Go right ahead, ma'am."

The two of us stood like honor guards watching her royal highness pass between our bodies. Paula winked and I just about melted into a pile of mush right there on the floor.

"I'll just sit and watch," she said.

Watch she did. She watched while Meredith bitched about the cape being too tight around her neck, about the coffee being too strong, and about the hot water scalding her precious head.

But, best of all, when I finally got to the cutting stage of the ordeal, I could feel her watching me like a cat would a mouse. I wouldn't disappoint. I cut into Meredith's hair the way Picasso would slide his brush along a canvas, deliberate and in complete control. I sculpted the hair with animated slices and flicks, and as Paula's stare intensified, so did my artistic flair. I was totally in my element and showing her my best moves.

By the time Meredith walked out the door, most everyone in the salon, aside from the few people with their backs to my station, gushed over my chic creation. When I finally walked over to Paula with twenty minutes to spare before my next appointment, my confidence was fully stoked.

Her golden flecked eyes twinkled under the track lighting. "You're fun to watch."

"Wait 'til I get started on yours." I winked.

"I'm ready if you are, babe," she said.

My face flushed, so I spun on my heel and waved for her to follow me to the shampoo area. Angie assumed her position at the side of the sink and readied a towel to wrap around Paula's neck.

I nudged her aside, suddenly annoyed with her employee-of-the-month behavior. "I've got this one."

Paula slid into the seat and I placed the towel around her neck. It had been quite a long time since I'd draped and shampooed a client, but I was quite sure, none had ever turned me into a puddle of warm syrup the way she did.

I leaned her head back and soaked her hair down with warm water. Then, I poured a glob of our most expensive shampoo into my hands and lathered it into a ball of suds. I steadied myself, and then placed my fingers into her hair. A zap of energy shot from my fingers to my toes. Her eyes closed and she let out a slight moan. My heart began to race as I massaged her scalp. Knowing I was actually touching this woman—giving her pleasure—could've given me an orgasm right there in the middle of it all—alongside Angie folding a pile of towels, Terry refilling shampoo bottles, and someone getting her eyebrows waxed.

I circled my fingertips round and round, all the while examining her striking features. Not a wrinkle on her clear face, high cheekbones, and a full set of moist pink lips. I snuck a peek down past her face and admired her toned shoulders and chest. I fixated on the rise and fall of her breasts, as her relaxed breathing deepened.

Then, she opened her eyes and chuckled. "I'm going to have to start charging you if you keep doing that."

The blood rushed up to my face in a flash. "What? I was just admiring your shirt." *And the perfect roundness of your boobs underneath it.*

"Yeah, just like I was admiring your shoes when you were cutting that lady's hair."

My lower body flared. I laughed a little to disguise how turned on I was. I had floated up so high I could've cleaned the ceiling fans and replaced the burnt out light bulb while up there. I doused her head with water again and rinsed all the bubbles down the drain.

By the time I got her to my station, my coloring returned to its usual pale ivory self. "So, Vegas, huh?" I asked her.

"Yeah, I travel quite a bit, especially in the summer."

"That's the biggest perk of being a teacher, right?"

"It'd be hard to ever work a summer again," she said.

I drew a comb out of the Barbicide and wiped it down. I had no idea how I'd get through this haircut, I was trembling so badly. "I imagine it would be."

"I dabble in some personal training at a gym a few mornings a week, but I wouldn't consider that work."

"Personal training, huh? Maybe I should stop in and get a few lessons from you. Maybe I'd be able to keep up with Owen, then."

"Yeah, he's quite a ball of energy. He's the best player I've got on my team. He's got talent and he's disciplined."

"Disciplined?" I asked. "I'm not sure how you get him to do things for you, but I'd like to know your trick."

"On the field he's got it more together than most of the girls on my adult soccer team do. But, off the field, he's just as forgetful as the next kid. I'm still waiting for him to return his release form for the D.C. trip coming up in a couple of weeks."

I combed through her tangled hair. "D.C. trip?"

"He didn't mention it?"

"It's not ringing a bell."

"We're chartering a bus and heading down to see some of the museums," she said. "He was supposed to ask you to chaperone. But, apparently, he never did."

"That's my disciplined boy for you." Forget the extra half hour of computer time.

"We need one more chaperone. Are you interested?"

Was Donald Trump not rich? Were there not twenty-four hours in a day? "I'll take a look at my schedule and let you know." I went through my "schedule": Lifetime movies, grocery shopping, laundry…

Aziza coughed from over at her station. She pretended to clean her countertop with a rag. When I looked at her, she smirked at me as if transported back to middle school again. She obviously approved.

I spent the next twenty minutes whizzing my shears in and out of her hair, and praying it wouldn't end. I cut her hair into chunky layers and when I was finished, she looked even more beautiful than I thought was even possible. I could've spent the rest of the afternoon running my fingers through her tousled new haircut, but, my next appointment was fidgeting by the front desk, putting her fingerprints all over the glass shelving. So, I brushed the little hairs off of her face with my soft feathery brush, and whisked her up front.

"What do I owe you?" She reached into her Nine West pocketbook and pulled out a pink checkered wallet.

"Nothing. Don't worry about it."

"What? Why not?" she asked.

Suddenly I felt more foolish than if I'd just told her the going rate of fifty dollars. "Let's just call it even this time around. You know, the barbeque and all."

She thumbed through her bills and pulled out a twenty, then dropped it on the counter. "At least accept a tip."

I reached out and took the twenty and flushed again. "You're going to have to let me put some red lowlights in your hair sometime. Maybe we can swap training sessions for highlights."

"Whenever you're free," she said picking up a card and a pen from the holder on the desk. She jotted something down and handed it to me. "Don't be a stranger." Then she turned and waltzed out the door.

I looked down at the card and beamed when I saw her e-mail address. E-mail was so much safer than a phone call.

* *

The reason I'd never settled down had little to do with my picky taste or ability to give love, and more to do with my knack for always dating people on the opposite end of my wavelength.

I lasted a whole whopping three weeks with my last girlfriend because every other minute she lit up a joint. I refused to take Benadryl because I hated the way it spun my head, let alone smoke pot. The girl before her performed stand-up comedy and finished every story with a joke. I couldn't even remember the time of day Owen was born, so punch lines were out of the question. Total disconnect on that one, too.

The one and only time I did actually date a girl with a matching panic disorder didn't go so well, either. In fact, it didn't go anywhere. The girl had bigger problems than I did. At least I could go out in public or for a walk without breaking down. This girl freaked out the second I suggested we go get a pizza at the mall. I wiped my hands of that one really fast.

Aziza always talked about my anxieties as though they were something tangible that I could crinkle up into a ball and toss out of the car window on my way to the mall. She didn't see how anybody would put up with them. I knew that she was dead wrong on this one. I had everything in the world to offer a woman. With every second that passed since I first laid my eyes upon Paula, I wanted more than anything for her to be the one to finally accept me for who I was.

She searched *me* out even after seeing what a clumsy fool I could be. That had to mean something.

"She is absolutely adorable," Aziza said, rolling her words out nice and slowly.

"Oh my God, I know, right?" I climbed into the pedicure chair next to her. I inched my feet into the scalding water, gritting my teeth as they disappeared into the bubbles.

She handed me a champagne glass filled with Bella's signature drink, Jolie Bella, which consisted of orange juice, champagne, cherry juice and a squirt of lime. "I think she likes you."

"Really?"

"She was totally flirting with you," she said.

"She's probably got a girlfriend."

"I know for a fact she doesn't," she said.

"This must be one of your 'vibes,' right?" She was so full of crap.

"No. I went with more conventional methods. I called Kristen and asked."

Kristen Phelps was the Providence lesbian circle gossip queen, aptly nicknamed, "The Drama Llama." She knew everyone's business—who was dating whom, who was sleeping with whom, who had broken up with whom. Kristen couldn't be trusted, yet everyone wanted her around. She stirred a lot of trouble, dishing out more scoops than Ben and Jerry's on a hot summer night.

"You didn't?!"

"I did," she said.

I dropped my jaw.

"What's the big deal?" she asked.

I kneaded my fist against my palm not sure if I should actually pick it up and hit her with it or hug her. "You need to tell me before you launch a covert operation without me. What if she found out you were snooping around for me?"

She looked away. "Well, if you don't want to hear anymore, that's fine."

I grabbed her arm. The only thing in the world I wanted was to hear more. "I'll pinch your arm if you don't start talking."

Aziza leaned towards me, smile returning, ready to dish the dirt. "She's totally unattached. The last girl she dated is that folk singer, Tania West. You know, that chick who we saw play at Pride last year. And, actually I just saw Tania last Friday when I was helping Jen at the Arts Fundraiser downtown. She is so hot. She was totally flirting with me." She stopped to giggle. "Anyway, Jen knows Tania from her days playing the local scene. Apparently, she and Paula broke up a while ago and Paula's been free ever since."

Tania West. Yes, I remembered her flat stomach and the way her oversized belt buckle topped her low-rise jeans. She was hot. Last I had heard, she was about to go on a fifty-city tour. Great. "Wow, I feel completely adequate now."

Aziza, apparently done with the conversation, flipped open the latest issue of *Fashionista Magazine*. "Look at this outfit. Who would wear this out?"

I grabbed the magazine from her to get a closer look and tossed it back in her lap. "I'd never let you drive my Beemer again if you let me walk out in public with that on."

"I think this model is so hot." She leaned across the arms of the pedicure chairs and shared the view with me.

"No way. Too thin."

She remained stretched across the chair's arm, snuggled up against me. She continued to flip the pages and stopped at the top ten fashionistas of the month. "You can't tell me you don't find Chelsea sexy?"

Maybe if a stick figure with big hair turned me on, I would. "I love her shoes," I offered.

She scooted back against her own seat and poured some peppermint oil into her bath before turning on the massager. Then, she closed her eyes and drew in an exaggerated sniff.

We sipped our Jolie Bellas in silence, swirled up in the delicious minty world. Working at a day spa had many perks. If we weren't detoxifying under a creamy facial masque or unwinding on the massage table under the gifted hands of our award-winning masseuse, we were relieving tension in all sorts of other pampering ways. To me, the greatest benefit was soaking my tired feet in a luxurious bubble bath, alongside my best friend at the end of a long day.

"She asked me to be a chaperone again," I said.

"Where will it be this time? Diving from a fishing boat off the coast of Block Island?"

"D.C."

Aziza shot up in her seat. "An overnight?"

I grabbed hold of her hand and squeezed it. "Better than that." I sat up taller. "Two!" I shook our entwined hands in the air in victory and then the brand new magazine tumbled down and plopped into her foot bath.

We both watched it ride the bubbles for a few seconds.

"Well, that really sucks." Aziza plucked the magazine out of the water and watched it drip. "I wasn't done reading it." She tore a towel off the stand and swaddled her precious magazine like she would a newborn baby.

"Screw the magazine. It'll dry," I said. "This is much more important."

"How are you going to deal with her being so out there?"

"Out there?" I asked.

"She's wild you said. What're you going to do one day when she asks you to jump out of an airplane? Or glide down Mount Washington on two sticks? Batting your long eyelashes at her will only work before you sleep with her. It's never going to work in the long run."

"That's mean."

"It is what it is." She put her magazine down and began scrubbing her foot with a pumice stone. "I heard her mention she's going to Vegas this week. Gee, that sounds like something right up your alley."

She could really irritate me. "Could you please just stop with the sarcasm, already?"

"Am I wrong?"

"Seriously, stop," I said.

She scrubbed her feet some more. "You'll need to either become really good at hiding your fears or change if you want this one to go anywhere."

I jumped up and tore my feet out of the water, flooding the floor with mini puddles and soap bubbles. I scooped up my flip-flops and marched to the bathroom to get as far away from her as soon as possible before I lost complete control and slapped her across her miss-know-it-all pretty face.

I wished for once she could support me instead of challenge every step I took towards happiness. The only thing she could do better than I was dig herself under other people's skin and annoy them, like a splinter, only much worse.

* *

Later that night after Aziza and I shared make up hugs, I stole the laptop from Owen when he went to get a snack from the kitchen. He spent so much time glued to his MySpace page that a five-minute hiatus from it wasn't about to break his online social status. Okay, well, five minutes turned into thirty before I checked and rechecked and triple checked my e-mail draft to Paula. But, Owen would live. He munched on salt and vinegar chips and watched a rerun of "Wipeout."

I settled on: "Hey Paula, I've been thinking about getting some personal training sessions and wanted to know if you're up for one more client? Let me know, Lauren."

I hit the send button.

I knew I had better get in shape, fast. For a brief second, I wondered if I should've consulted with a personal trainer before my personal training session with her. I didn't want to show up at the gym, out of breath, lightheaded, and on the verge of a heart attack. I twirled off the seat towards Owen. "I feel like going for a run. Want to join me?"

"You don't run." Owen shoved another chip in his mouth and crunched down.

"You can coach me. Wouldn't it be fun to run a race together? We could run every other morning and then sign up for a few of those five-mile runs." I had my new exercise lifestyle all planned out in a minute. This would be easy.

"Five Ks, not five miles."

"Ks, miles, who cares? Let's get started." I ran off down the hallway towards my bedroom, yelling back over my shoulder. "I hope I still have those running sneakers I bought a couple years ago when Nordstrom's was having that sale."

I rummaged through the pile of shoes and sandals on my closet floor, tossing them to the side as I dug deeper. I searched the entire collection, and came out empty-handed. I might've donated them in the spring when the veterans sent that folded up plastic bag to my mailbox asking me to fill it and leave it on my doorstep.

First thing in the morning, I would trek to the mall and outfit myself properly. I returned to the living room and Owen had already slid back in front of the laptop. He reached into the bag of chips again and grabbed a handful. The way he crunched down on them could have woken a sleeping bear out of hibernation. Honestly, when did he learn to eat with his mouth wide-open like that?

"You got an e-mail," he said, dribbling a few crumbs to the floor.

I sprung forward and scanned the screen. An envelope sat in the bottom corner edge of the monitor, sending my heart fluttering. "Well, move over." I nudged him off the chair and he rolled back towards me to read it with me. "Do you mind?" I looked up at him and pointed my eyes towards the couch.

He huffed away. "Don't close out of my game."

Too late. I had already clicked on the x in the top corner of the screen. He had the rest of his life to play another game. I had about five seconds left in me before I passed out from a lack of oxygen if I didn't read the message.

"How's Sunday, nine a.m. at Fitness USA? I'll meet you at the front desk. I'm taking off for Vegas in a few hours, so if I don't hear back from you, I'll assume I'll see you then."

Okay, this was big. Of all the things Paula would have to do after getting home from a three day trip to Vegas, she chose to be with me. Definite interest!

I would not disappoint.

I had four days to prepare. I'd need a new outfit, new sneakers, waterproof mascara, and some Red Bull if I was going to have any chance at lifting anything more than a ten pound dumbbell.

Chapter Four

The last time I had stepped into a gym was a few weeks after I gave birth to Owen. Back then, I had a three-inch muffin top of baby fat to lose around my belly before I had a fair chance in hell of fitting into my size two jeans again. So, not surprisingly, I was all fired up back then and expected to spring right back to pre-pregnancy shape. I walked into Brick and Mortar Bodies, the hippest gym around. This was the type of place where young girls pranced around in spandex, and men drooled at them like vultures from their weight benches. I was determined, and I must say, equally impressed with the sales pitch of one very eager and very convincing fitness account manager named Georgina. I sat across from her and she sketched out my fitness plan, promising to take her sweet time training me. Each time she'd look up at me from the paperwork, her sexy, smoky eyes tickled me like a feather.

She had mentioned they had a daycare center that catered to newborn babies. For a small fee, of twenty-five dollars a session, Owen would be entertained for as long as I had the strength to whip my butt back into respectable shape. The best part, if I joined as a lifetime member, I'd get a free smoothie every visit for the rest of my life. So, out came the pen and a small chunk of my lifesavings for a down payment.

It didn't take me more than one day to realize that being a lifetime member really sucked. When I strutted into Georgina's office decked out in my black and red spandex biker shorts and matching top, only a pencil, sharpener and empty rolodex sat on her desk. I was told by another worker that my voluptuous personal trainer skipped town and was heading to Hollywood to act. I was stuck with Ralph, a red-headed kid who looked like he'd be more interested in playing with matchbox cars than training me.

Even the smoothie guy had packed up his blender a few weeks later and headed off to bigger and better opportunities somewhere off the coast of Florida. With my incentives gone and my baby fat melting away miraculously on its own, I threw in my gym towel.

Twelve years later, I still had yet to step foot in that meat-market of a gym, and yet, I still mailed in my twenty-two dollars and seventy-one cent membership fee every month.

Judging from Paula's athletic physique, I could only guess she belonged to a gym the likes of a Brick and Mortar Bodies. I imagined that the only way she created those toned muscles was from frolicking around a sanitized fitness conglomerate, kicking up her cross-trainers at all the ogling men. Which is why, when I pulled into the gravel, bumpy parking lot of Fitness USA, the rust spilling down the sides of the brick building and the dusty haze on the windows shocked me.

Walking in, the smell of sweat smacked me in the face instantly. A hairy man with a goatee and a body of tattoos greeted me from behind a grimy glass counter, which housed an army of trophies. He stood up and when he gripped my hand between both of his, I swear his biceps flexed to the size of redwood trees. "Welcome, doll," he said to me. His hand felt like sandpaper and the thick hairs fleeing from his nostrils shook when he spoke. He needed a hot shower, a shave, and some cosmetic dentistry.

"Hi," I backed up a foot or two. "I'm meeting someone here for a workout." I peered behind him to look out for Paula. The gym looked like my mechanic's twenty car garage—tall ceilings, bright lights, and gigantic garage doors towards the back, which opened halfway and offered a view of the backside of a Harley Davidson shop. Mirrors lined one wall completely, and on the opposite wall hung pictures of bodybuilders flexing. Grunts belched from every corner. And the place smelled like a wet sneaker.

One skinny guy wearing a Def Leppard faded shirt smiled at me as he ran on an elliptical machine. Ozzy Osbourne played over the loud speakers, masking the ear-shattering clanking of weight plates. Men were lifting barbells the size of Mack truck tires, and then dropping them on black mats. I could only imagine the stench of these mats after years of soaking up the sweat from these monster men.

Where were the women? Where was Paula?

"First timer?" the guy asked.

"That obvious?" I asked.

"We hardly ever get any women as dainty as you in here." He scanned me from head to toe with a pleased smile. "Paula was right when she said you were a pretty little thing."

"She said that?" I stepped closer to him fully willing to risk my life to hear more.

He ran over my question without flinching, rambling on about stuff I didn't care about. "I also want to warn you, we don't have yoga or spinning classes or any of that girly stuff here. But we are going to be starting a Boot Camp class in the fall. Paula's going to be teaching it to those wimps back there. Speaking of, she's in the can and will be right up." He reached under the counter and offered me a folded towel. "Want one?"

I grabbed it and he tugged back on it, jerking me forward.

"Come on. You have to be stronger than that," he said.

I surrendered and he flew back a few steps, banging into a shelf with even more trophies.

"Paula's going to have her work cut out for her with you. You're going to have to build up those arms if you ever want to survive a workout session with her. She's tough."

I looked down at my skinny arms and just then, Paula emerged from behind me and grabbed the towel back from the hairy man. "Hank's just a wimp. He thinks because he can't handle my workouts that no one can." She placed the towel back in my hand again. "Let's warm up first."

She turned and marched ahead like she was on a mission to save the world. I followed her, suddenly afraid if I lagged too far behind she'd make me drop and give her fifty pushups. She strutted across the floor like she owned the place. Her legs opened up to a wide stride as we charged towards the mat in the far corner of the room. Her ponytail bobbed from side-to-side. Beads of sweat threatened to trickle down my temples already.

When we got to the mat, Paula turned on her sneaker to face me. She folded her hands behind her back in true coach fashion and cleared her throat as if ready to send me off for the highest stake game of my life.

"So what'll it be coach?" I asked playfully. "Sit ups, abs, go ahead and throw it at me. I'm ready."

She swayed her head to the side and looked past me and narrowed her eyes. "Seems you've got quite an audience here."

I stole a peek behind me and discovered that all the muscle heads, aside from one body slamming a punching bag, were watching us.

"They act as though they've never seen a pretty girl before," she said.

She thought I was pretty. My heart twirled. I loved the way the word just rolled off her tongue so cool and casually, like *'Hey it's sunny outside today'*.

"I'm sure they're just trying to figure out what I'm doing here." Everything down to my pink shoelaces spelled girly.

Her eyes sparkled, even under the harsh glow of the florescent lights. "I'm the only lady they're used to seeing in here. With two of us, they're never going to get the proper workout."

I giggled like a school girl.

She handed me a jump rope. "Why don't you jump for about one minute? I'm going to get a step block."

I attempted to jump over the rope, but every time it circled my head, my ponytail caught it like a spider web. It took me about ten times before I got into a rhythm and could skip over the rope and make a complete revolution with it. By the time Paula came back to the mat, I struggled to catch my next breath. It's very difficult to look sexy and be halfway to passing out at the same time.

"Time for some step-ups," she said.

Step-ups? I'd be lucky if I could walk ten more steps on the mat.

She set the block down and stepped up and down a few times to demonstrate the move. "Do that for about five minutes and I think you'll be ready to get started. You never want to work cold muscles. You'll pull them and regret it for days."

Oh, I knew the pain. I once pulled my hamstring on Johnson's Pond trying to get up on water skis, of all things. If stretching beyond a split mid air and slamming face first into fifteen feet of water wasn't enough to instill a lifetime of fear into me, then nothing could. I couldn't walk on my leg for a week.

"Let's warm up my muscles, then," I said. I stepped up and down and eventually sweat began to run down my face and threaten a mascara leakage. Even though I wore waterproof mascara, it never protected from raccoon eyes. At the two minute mark, I stopped dabbing my eyes with my towel and focused on preventing a complete meltdown of my respiratory system. Breathe in twice, open up the diaphragm, release the breath, pull in the diaphragm. I read about this breathing technique in the salon's copy of *Fitness Today* magazine. I repeated this mantra for the next three minutes, praying it would keep me from passing out. I wouldn't give up.

When her watch beeped, I buckled to my knees and fell into a stretch. I bent forward and attempted to touch my toes. My fingertips flirted with the point right above my ankles. Oh, the stretch felt good. My muscles ached already. If she forced me to work this hard for the next hour, I'd be shoveling aspirin into my mouth that night for sure.

"Do you belong to a gym?" she asked, scooting next to me to stretch, too.

Admitting I bought a lifetime membership to Brick and Mortar would be more humiliating than not belonging to a gym. "No, but I have a few exercise DVDs that I workout to." I only half lied. I did have a few exercise DVDs from the late nineties. No need to mention they existed under five layers of blankets in my closet with their wrappers still unopened. "They're a good workout." I must've sounded like a real jock now.

"What about free weights? Do you have any?"

52

Well, that would've been a big *no*. I jotted down a mental note that right after my workout I'd drive directly to Wal-Mart and buy some. "Yeah, I have a couple lying around my living room so I can work my arms while watching TV." I just kept plucking the lies out of thin air.

"What weight are they?"

"Oh, you know – hmm, the cute pink ones."

"Two pounds, five pounds, ten pounds?" She raised her eyebrow at me.

"I think I've got all of them." Owen was going to be so thrilled to see me walk in the house later with an armful of the weights he'd been begging for since his birthday the year before.

"I'm going to show you some exercises you can do at home with them." She slid up in front of my outstretched legs. "First, we'll start with some abs." She placed her hands on my ankles and pushed them forward so my knees were now bent, then she rolled her knees on top of my new sneakers to hold me in place.

Only a quarter inch piece of leather separated us from each other. My belly flipped.

"Now, reach up and bring your chest into your knees."

I struggled up and landed within inches of her face. I clamped onto my knees for a few seconds, and held my breath. Down I fell and up again. After ten times, I planted my arms around my knees for strength.

She cradled her hands around my shoulders. "Your flushed cheeks are adorable."

To this I simply smiled, but I could've kissed her. All I had to do was stretch in about five inches and there I'd be on her plump lips. I could barely breathe.

"But, don't think just because you're cute that I'm going to take it easy on you," she said. "I came here to make you sore." She offered her hand to help me up. "Let's get some ten pounders in your hand."

When I placed my hand in hers, my insides turned upside down and jiggled me around like popcorn kernels in hot oil. From the tricep dips, to the squats, to the biceps curls, to the time I landed on the bench press and curled my fingers around the bar, my tummy continued to party. And when Paula came up from behind me and clasped her hand around mine to reposition them in the right place, the party transformed into an all out rave, tickling every nerve in my body. "Push out ten for me," she said, temporarily sweeping my reverie under the foam mat.

"Eight." I bargained, my arms burning still from the dips.

"Eight, if you tell me right now you're coming with us to D.C."

She had no idea I had already dug out my luggage from the attic the night before. "Eight it is, then." I lunged into my first press, and even had the strength to look up at her smiling face.

* *

I walked into Wal-Mart on a mission – get in and get out as quickly as possible so I could run home and surprise Owen with our new dumbbells.

I scanned the large signs hanging over each department. Of course my aisle would be located at the furthest point from the store's entrance. I backtracked to get a cart and wheeled down the aisles like a stuntwoman, weaving around small children and other carts with reckless abandon.

Pillows, curtains, cleaners, frozen foods, all whizzed by in a blur. When I passed the book section, one jumped out at me, placing everything else around it in a haze. As though God himself shined a beaming light from the sky down on it, its yellow cover glowed in a halo and begged to be picked up from its front and center rack. I rolled closer to it like it possessed the answers to all my most important questions – *How to Live Life with No Fear - Hope for Anxiety-Ridden People.*

I yanked it off its book rest and read the back cover.

> *Do you suffer from panic attacks? Are you envious of everyone else around you who can live normal lives without fear of passing out, having a heart attack, or dying in front of others? If so, I challenge you to read what I've got to say and see for yourself that you, too, can live a fear-free life.*

I buried it under my pocketbook on the cart's seat and shoved off to gather my weights.

Pink, purple, black, white, metal, plastic, even foamy barbells were my choices. Posters of fit men and women curling up their biceps stared down at me as if saying, 'Don't even think about it. Go buy yourself a new pair of shoes and call it a day'.

I reached for the pink set, but walked my fingers down two rows to the metal ones knowing Owen would be outraged with anything different. I filled my cart with three different weight sizes. I'd be rock hard in no time if I used the damn things.

Now if I could just build some strength in the bravery department of my life, too, I'd be unstoppable. I wished just once I could have the guts to get on an airplane and travel to Vegas or wherever else Paula wanted to go. We could play the slots until the wee hours of the morning, while sipping

Mojitos and feeding our faces with chocolate strawberries. Just once, I'd like to taste paradise. Sink it in between my teeth and savor its juices.

If only I could snap my fingers and be in that world, life would be great.

* *

How could I ever expect to end up with someone as great as Paula when I couldn't even grasp a simple concept in my new book? The book stated anyone could practice the techniques and offered freedom from fear. Like hell. I turned the book over and glanced at the back cover again, perplexed at how this person ever became a published author, writing such nonsense. *Close your eyes and imagine you are soaking your feet in a warm bath. Now imagine the water absorbing your tension as it draws it out from the top of your head throughout your entire body and out of your feet. Let the water do the work. The panic should disappear rather quickly.* Gene Walters, Ph.D. has obviously never had a panic attack.

I sipped my coffee. For the first time in months, I scheduled an hour lunch break and actually kept it free. Nothing would get in the way of my reading time. I was determined to put an end to my fear once and for all. The other fifty times I've attempted this in the past were just trials. This was the real deal.

Just as I was reading my first sentence, Aziza rushed into the break room. I didn't give her a chance to speak, before bitching to her. "This book is a load of crap."

"Not now. I need your help." Aziza stood frozen in front of me with her mouth hanging wide open. "I pasted bleach on Joanie's new growth and her hair is breaking off in clumps."

"How long ago did you apply it?" I asked, reluctant to climb out of the cozy oversized chair Aziza just purchased at IKEA.

Aziza shifted, biting her lip. "Almost an hour ago."

She overbooked herself and squeezed cuts in between complex perm and dye jobs all the time, and like usual I was the one who dove in and offered her a lifeline. If I were boss, she'd be in big trouble.

"You forgot about her?" I pushed her out of the way to get to that poor woman's rescue. Before I even stepped two feet out the barroom style doors, I noticed none other than Tania West sitting with wet hair in Aziza's chair. I spun around. "Are you kidding me?" I pushed right back into the break room. "Tania?"

"How do you know what she looks like?"

"Every lesbian knows what she looks like." I rolled my eyes at her and crowded her against the pantry doors. When I couldn't sleep, I Googled people. Of course Tania blanketed the Internet, picking her guitar in front of thousands of hungry fans. And of course, I spent nearly two hours scrolling through countless images of her, wishing I could have an ounce of her confidence. "Why is she here?"

"I told you that I met her. We chatted and one thing led to another and I offered her a free haircut if she would donate a signed guitar to be auctioned off for the Arts Council."

I seethed.

Aziza grabbed my hand. "We need to help Joanie."

Two minutes more wouldn't help Joanie now. "Why did you bring her here?"

"Don't be so angry. I didn't do it to make you upset."

"Well, I am upset," I said.

"Look, calm down." Aziza put her arm around my shoulder. "I did this for you. I figured if you met the former competition, then maybe you'd be able to overcome your fear a lot faster than reading some stupid book."

"That's your answer? You think I'll take one look at Tania and just like that my anxiety will disappear forever?"

"Let's face it, sweetie, you're going to get hurt again if you don't change your ways. You need to see what kind of person Paula's into so you don't go screwing this one up."

If she didn't soften her eyes just then, and rub the back of her hand down my face like a mother tending to her feverish child, I would've snapped her fingers in half.

She lowered her voice to a whisper. "Tania is really a sweetie. She gave me the rundown on her relationship with Paula. They were hot at one time, but they've obviously cooled down now."

I've never fully understood why I tended to get jealous over things that happened way before I even existed in someone's mind. For some reason, I felt like I just got stabbed in the gut. All I could picture was Paula making love to her famous girlfriend, devouring her like a piece of creamy cake, not leaving any of her behind. "I hope you're up to date on your insurance payment," I said before whipping around and charging towards Aziza's latest screw up.

Joanie sat tall at the color station, reading a *Vogue* magazine with her lips curled up into a neat smile. Her hair stuck up in the air like a paint brush smothered in dried up Kilz. I eased up to her.

"Hi, Joanie." I tried to sound as professional as possible as I starting poking her roots with my fingertip. Small flakes of bleach powdered down to her cape. Aziza broke the cardinal rule of on-the-scalp-bleaching, crossing that line of demarcation between new growth and previously colored hair. "Aziza is behind, so I'm going to shampoo your hair. I'd like to try a new conditioning treatment on you, too."

"I won't argue. This is like a vacation for me," Joanie said.

Enjoy it, I felt like saying, because it's about to turn into the vacation from hell in about two minutes when all your hair barrel-asses down the drain. "Good for you. Just keep on relaxing."

I brought her over to the sink and investigated further, sneaking a peek at Tania who poked at her hair in the mirror. She had to have full, pouty lips, didn't she?

Aziza snuck up behind and lurched over my shoulder like a nervous squirrel afraid the neighborhood cat was going to eat her nuts. I eased the water on and prayed that her hair would survive the light stream. Her hair repelled the water like a freshly waxed car. Droplets of water netted around the pockets of bleach, remaining on top of it instead of washing through like with normal, healthy hair. I shot Aziza a dirty look.

Time to get my hands dirty and find out Joanie's fate. Would she be walking out looking like Pamela Lee or Sinead O'Connor? I slid my finger into a clump of hair and lifted it to let the water sink it.

Globs of hair washed out of my fingers and into the sink.

Aziza poked me so hard I winced.

"Everything okay?" Joanie asked.

I kicked Aziza's shin. "Everything's just fine. I banged my leg on the pipe, that's all."

Joanie relaxed, oblivious to her new porcupine style.

A smart hairstylist never admitted errors. If a perm didn't take or, in this case, a bleach job disintegrated every other strand of hair, some stylists might take the tactic of blaming it on the product itself. A good stylist would never let on a problem occurred.

"Aziza and I just got back from the New York show and we learned so many great styles for the fall. The new 'in' is a very short, sort of a spiky and textured Sharon Stone *Basic Instinct* look. You have the perfect hair and face to carry it off."

Then a good stylist holds her breath and hopes her reputation at being great at what she does will serve her well so the client latches on to her creative ingenious.

"I would never be able to pull off short hair," Joanie said.

Yeah, well, you have no choice, bleachie. Time for the brutal honesty approach. "Your long, bleach-blonde hair is very dated. You'll take ten years off your face if you wear the new style."

Joanie frowned.

The pressure of the water carved her new style right there in the sink. Aziza would owe me big time if I could figure out a way to persuade Joanie to go for the new do. I went in for the straight shot. "If you let me make you over with this new style, you'll not only have your service completely done for free today, but I'll even throw in four complimentary massages, too."

"Really?" Joanie asked. "What's the catch?"

"When I see the perfect face for a style, I will do anything to convince. We need a new makeover story for our Wall of Fame."

"Ten years, huh?"

"Maybe even fifteen," I said.

"My husband will kill me."

"Your husband will take one look at you and fall in love all over again." I massaged conditioning shampoo into her fragile two inch roots. Loose strands tangled around my fingers like vines.

"What will Aziza think? I thought she liked my long hair," Joanie said.

I looked over my shoulder at Aziza who had plunged back into flirting with Tania, completely disinterested in the mess she created. Of course. At least she had faith in one aspect of my life.

"Aziza is the one who begged me to talk you into it. She said she's been trying to find a way for years to tell you that your style needs updating."

"Is my hairstyle really that bad?" Joanie asked.

"It's just not as good as it could be. People get too attached to their long hair. Free yourself, Joanie. Go for it!"

"I can't be outdated with my line of work. Will it be sexy?"

"Trust me. I'll make you sexy," I said, fully convinced now that I actually would.

"I can't believe I'm about to agree to this. I get this whole thing done for free?"

"For free." I shut off the water and wrapped her hair in a towel. "We'll condition after the cut." No way would I grant Joanie a second more to contemplate. With fragile seconds ticking away, I had to pretend to chop a chunk of her hair off right away so there was no turning back.

"Stay here for a second." I ran to my station and grabbed my scissors. On my jaunt back, I snuck a look at Tania's reflection and my stomach turned. She was even more gorgeous and perfect up close.

Just as I skipped back to Joanie, my cell phone vibrated. Owen never called when I was drinking a cup of coffee or cleaning up my station. No, he always managed to call when I was in the middle of a really important hairstyling moment.

"Owen, I can't talk. Just tell me if you made it home okay," I said, sprinting back over to Joanie's side just in time to block her hand from touching her hair. I couldn't let Joanie feel her two inch spikes just yet.

"It's Paula," she said with a chuckle.

I slid my hand off Joanie's. The blood rushed from my face and down to the hollows of my toes. "Hey," I managed. "It's my personal trainer!" I couldn't hide the excitement, and quite frankly, I didn't want to either.

"How you feeling from your workout yesterday?"

How could I tell her that every muscle besides the ones in my pinky fingers felt like they were bound by a rubber band five inches in width and not come across as being a total wuss? "I feel great."

"Good. Then, what are you up to tonight?"

Okay, if this involved sweat and barbells and smelly men, I'd have to be busy tending to her grandmother's dying wishes of having her three yards of gray hair corn-rowed. "Just working and then going home to make sure Owen is behaving."

"Any chance you can meet me out tonight? A few of my friends are meeting up a Rusty's in a bit."

My heart did a little jump kick. I fluttered away from Joanie like a butterfly in a field of wild flowers, roaming from one spot to another without rhyme or reason. I floated past Aziza and Tania, and then past Angie as she waxed someone's upper lip, and past the miles of hair magazines piled up on the coffee table up front. "Rusty's, huh?"

"Come on, it'll be fun."

Oh, believe me, I had no intention of not going. I steadied myself against the spindled cape rack, jumping head first into the euphoric waves like a carefree dolphin madly in love with the life going on around me. "I can't promise you anything at this point because I'm not sure what's going on with Owen, yet. But, I'll definitely think about it."

"If you don't show up, I'll make you do one hundred push-ups next time we workout together," she said.

Next time? There would be a next time? I jumped in place behind the bunches of capes. Seriously, even if an asteroid pounded planet earth that night, I'd go to Rusty's. "Well, if you can convince me to come with a reward, rather than a threat, then I'll think about it."

Paula exhaled deeply into the phone. I obviously caught her off guard.

"Well, I think I can—" Paula started to say.

All of a sudden someone screamed from the back of the salon.

"What the fuck?!" The voice roared through the salon.

I peeked out from behind a cape and saw Joanie yanking at her hair in the mirror.

"What the fuck happened to my fucking hair?!" she screamed so loud even Tania jumped up and backed away towards the front of the shop along with everyone else, including Aziza.

"Oh, God. Major crisis. I have to go, Paula."

"Better be there," she said playfully.

Even in all of the commotion, and with Paula's ex-girlfriend standing within feet of me, I couldn't help but giggle. "We'll see!"

I flung my cell phone on the reception area chair and ran towards Joanie. I grabbed Aziza by her new sundress and pulled her along to face her fate. She resisted like any two-year-old pitching a fit in the toy aisle as her mommy drags her away from the Barbie dolls. "This is your mess, and you're cleaning it up."

I pushed Aziza in front of me as we approached Joanie. She looked right at me and with a tone high enough to grate a boulder into sand, she said, "Is this what you meant by a hip, new style?"

Joanie could have poured the left over bleach in my eyes at that moment, and I would've still been unable to hide my smile.

I just stood there in front of a borderline bald customer and smiled inwardly, not caring if even ten asteroids slammed into the planet. I was going on a date with Paula.

* *

Once I swept up the last piece of hair on the floor, I bolted up to the front desk. "Who broke up with whom?" I asked Aziza.

She counted the pile of twenties in the register. "Six-hundred, forty, sixty, eighty, seven hundred." She placed the pile back in its slot and huffed. "I don't feel like talking about it right now. Do you realize how screwed I am? She's calling her lawyer."

So maybe that wasn't the best time to tell her about my date with Paula. But I needed a babysitter. "It'll all work out. What you need is to forget all about today."

"How do you suppose I do that?"

"You could babysit Owen while I go on a date with Paula."

"Get the hell out of here. You got a date?"

All of a sudden, she climbed out of her pity hole and resurfaced with a smile as bright as a full moon.

"I got a date!" I jumped up and down like I'd just learned I won the lottery. "I know Owen is old enough to manage on his own, but I just hate leaving him like that. I'd feel better if you were with him."

"You got it. Go get ready."

I kissed her forehead before darting out the front door. "Everything's going to be fine with baldy. You'll see."

Everything was going to be just fine. What could possibly go wrong now?

Chapter Five

Rusty's Bar and Grill was the hot spot in Providence for chicken wings. I'd spent many nights perched on a barstool chugging beer and wiping the hot sauce from my chin. When I entered through the outside patio entrance just after ten o'clock, I prayed Paula would still be there. As usual, I was running late. This was just the sort of thing that happened when you were a single mother trying to raise a decent kid.

The stars were shining like diamonds in the clear, summer sky, and the music blared over the enormous speakers set up undisguised in each corner of the deck. Empty beer pitchers sat like centerpieces on most every table along with piles of chicken bones shed clean of their hot-winged meat. I turned the corner and walked inside to the bar, and what I saw immediately stopped my stiletto heels from moving another inch across the sticky floor.

Paula stood on a chair in a mini-skirt and heels singing "It's Raining Men", swinging her hips in a seductive beat. A guy with dreadlocks yelled out above the hooting "Go, hottie! Show us your wild side."

Paula flipped her hair playfully and blew Mr. Dreadlocks a kiss. He feigned overload. She danced around the stage, each wave of her hip more fluid than the one before it. When the song ended, she looked my way and chuckled. Paula had to be the prettiest girl in the entire room. Her face shimmied under the stage lights, her smile lit up her face.

"You came," she said, curtseying before me like some proper Englishwomen.

"A soccer coach, teacher, personal trainer, and now performer. What next?"

"Well, if I keep losing bets, God only knows. Maybe I'll start riding a unicycle."

"You lost a bet?"

She blinked heavily. "I came in last in a fat loss competition."

The only plump cells that belonged to this woman were hanging out nicely in her boobs. "Are you insane?"

"Five of us competed on how much fat we could lose in one month. The loser had to prance around stage in heels and a mini. I gained half a percent instead of losing. I tried to win. Honestly. I did everything a good competitor would do. I drank prune juice, I ate bran cereal, I even did some weird liver flushing concoction where I had to drink half a bottle of olive oil and a powder mix. I think that's where I went wrong."

"You think?" I poked her abs, and in my best soap opera attempt, faked pain from the pressure.

She grabbed my finger, then brushed her lips with it. "Better?"

An electrical surge coursed through me. If I didn't shift gears to break the heat that crackled between us, I would've exploded right there. "Does Owen realize his coach is a nut?"

"No." She wriggled her waist like a belly dancer. "And none of my players must ever know. I don't want a bunch of hormone-driven boys focusing on my moves instead of my commands." She bopped her tummy to the side with one last dramatic wiggle. "Now, come on," she said taking my hand, "help me get out of these clothes and into something a little less slutty."

A nervous chuckle chased my shock.

She lowered her head and looked up at me like a coy child. "I just want you to be my lookout when I change in my truck." She eased back and showered me with a smile.

"They have bathrooms for moments like this, you know."

"Have you taken a look at the stalls in this place?"

No, I had not. So, two minutes later, while standing outside her truck, I tried my best not to look like a criminal waiting for the right moment to heist a vehicle or buy drugs.

People walked by my and glanced at me as though I was wearing a face mask and holstering a gun. When a car full of cop look-a-likes drove past us, I flipped my phone and pretended to text.

Finally, Paula emerged dressed in boot cut jeans and a fitted t-shirt. She offered me a smile. God she was sexy.

Right then, I knew, I'd end up kissing this woman before the end of the night.

* *

Once we got back inside the bar, Paula searched for her friends. New people sat with menus at our table. "Maybe they went around the corner to the backside of the deck." I followed Paula as she circled around the trail of tables and peeked around the corner. Just a few more packed tables, but no sight of them. "I guess they left," she said.

I stretched on my toes to get a better view of the place. Not even the bar had an empty stool. "Want to wait for a table?"

"I have a better idea," she said. "How about we just grab a smoothie next door and take a walk around the neighborhood?"

I shrugged, acting as though my insides weren't flipping upside down. "Sure, why not." I took her arm and followed her towards the door. "I'm not a big wing person anyway."

She chuckled, and we walked out of Rusty's door and into the mild summer night. It felt like a warm velvety blanket. I could snuggle up to it all night long.

We stopped in front of the smoothie shop. A closed sign hung in the door. I didn't really feel like feeding my face with anything cold anyway. I tugged at her belt loop. "Let's just walk." Our night couldn't end in the smoothie shop parking lot.

We walked for a few blocks past Waterplace Park where, during special nights in the summer, Providence hosted their famous Waterfire celebration. I couldn't imagine strolling next to three-hundred and fifty thousand people to catch a glimpse of the smoky wood dancing on water. Owen had come home from it a few times smelling like he just stepped out of a campsite, and told me all about how the fires leapt on water. He'd get so excited that his breathing always ran ahead of his voice, so he'd end up pulling himself back to his words so I didn't miss a beat. He briefed me after his first time: *One-hundred bonfires, Mom! They were blazing on fire sculptures, right in the water! And there was this kind of eerie music playing all around us.* I didn't doubt the beauty of the fires, but I'd much rather burrow deep under my fluffy comforter than be ushered along with hundreds of other people along the side of a river, much less a river on fire.

The closer we got to Brown University, the hillier our trek became. Old houses with historical face plates on them hugged the street. Their charm welcomed people's stares past the tiled window panes. One house in particular drew me in with its soft candlelight glow and library of books. I imagined a century earlier, friends would come and sit together and gossip about neighbors and fellow church-goers, a hundred years away from televisions, computers and cell phones.

Once past the houses, we rounded the corner to Thayer Street, which housed book shops, clothing stores, cafes, ice cream parlors, and restaurants. "I love this restaurant," Paula said coming to a halt in front of the bar and grill. "This is where I'd hang out with my friends when I was in school. We'd leave the library and head here for Greek salads and beers."

"Me, too," I said.

"Really? You've been there?"

"Yeah, a few times." Only every other night when I was in high school. Everyone knew that Basta's served anyone with an ID, real or not. I always used my cousin's license back then. It didn't even matter that my cousin was a guy named John.

We walked past the Brown library and to a quieter section of town. "Right in here is the Brown main quad area of the campus where I threw a lot of Frisbees and dribbled a lot of soccer balls on the grass," she told me.

"So, you were a Brown Bear?"

"Yup. Played soccer for them and got a degree at the same time. Sweet deal, huh?"

I nodded as we walked through the archway of the quad. I looked around mesmerized by the beautiful architecture of the multistory buildings lining the pathways. The quad opened up to a big grassy field, edged with manicured bushes and park benches. All of those times I walked down Thayer Street, how had I stopped short of this area? Who knew all this existed? "Very sweet deal."

She stopped under the arch and looked out to the small collegiate village inside. "Just as I remember it."

A few people scattered along the grass here and there, adding to the typical safe feel of the University.

"I always wanted to attend a prestigious university," I said. I didn't have the foggiest idea why on earth I would've just opened up that can of worms.

"Which one did you end up attending?"

"I didn't. I went to hairdressing school."

Even in the dark, I could sense when the unease popped on Paula's face, knowing that if possible, she would've picked up the remote control and hit the rewind button. "College is overrated anyway."

"I highly doubt you feel that way," I said.

"It's not the only way to get ahead. I think hairdressing school is underrated—"

"Relax." I squeezed in closer to her. "The truth is I probably would've been a good student. I started to take some classes at the community college, but with Owen being a baby at the time, I needed something not as demanding."

"So you went into hair?" She asked like I chose rocket science over basket weaving. I wanted to kiss her right then. I laughed instead.

"I ended my one and only semester with a 4.0, but was bored to tears with math and science. I just wanted to be creative and do something fun with my life."

"You're a natural with hair. I loved watching you that day. You're an artist."

Cutting hair was like walking. I found a groove and paced ahead. "I still regret that I didn't get a degree."

"Why, so you can go sit behind a desk all day and pretend to look important?"

Because one day I wanted to be able to stand on my own two feet instead of lean against Aziza for the rest of my life. "Just makes smart business sense to have an education."

Her eyes lit up. "So you want to open your own salon?"

"Someday."

"One class at a time is all it takes," she said.

"Maybe someday."

Her eyes narrowed as she shook her head up and down. I could see the wheels cranking.

"Let's make a bet and if you lose it, you have to agree to take one class this coming fall semester."

"You're not very good at bets, remember?"

She nodded and looked down at my stilettos. "Let's race."

"Right now?"

"I'll make it fair. We'll both take off our shoes and run on the grass from one end of the quad to the other."

"A race against you? Miss former Brown Bear soccer athlete?"

She stood up and extended her hand out to me. She could've put a live wire in my wet hand and it wouldn't have had as much power as her bare skin did. I inched closer to her.

She whispered to me. "It's a worthy proposition, isn't it?"

"What do I get if I finish first?" I followed her gaze down to my lips. My heart pounded below my new Victoria Secret's camisole. We stood hand in hand, in the dark, inches away from each other, staring at each other's lips.

"If you finish first, you can choose to punish me anyway you'd like," she said.

I cocked my head. "I like the idea of punishing you."

She moved in closer. "But, if I finish first, I not only get a reward, but I get to see you enroll in a marketing class this fall."

Her breath, as refreshing as spring, fanned my face.

I eased back a step, then stretched my arms over my head and bent to the each side. "Whatever. You might want to warm up a little. I have a little bit in me." I did run cross country after all.

"I'm not afraid," she said.

"You should be. I used to run in high school." Of course I wouldn't let on that I spent half my practices in Maura Setter's living room eating pizza and swigging sodas instead of running the required three miles. I only joined the team because most of the runners were adorable.

She smiled and bent forward to touch her toes. "If you're anything like your son, I probably should stretch."

I twisted side to side, not taking my eye off her as I spoke. "Can't wait to see what your punishment's going to be?"

"What do you have up your sleeve?"

I continued to look at her with a playful glance, with no idea at all what I'd do to her. I recognized the look on her face, and it wasn't saying *I'll take a milkshake for my reward, please.* No, her eyes told a different story, more like *I really like you and would like to pull you into those bushes and show you just how much.*

"According to you, it shouldn't matter because you're going to win anyway," I said.

"I'm willing to take my chances."

"Shall we get started then?" I asked.

"Let's do it."

We walked to the archway. I kicked off my heels and set them on top of a bench alongside her sneakers. See, I could be just as adventurous.

We both bent forward at the hips in running position. "On the count of three, we go," she said, flexing her long, muscular legs as though she were bracing for her chance at Gold.

"I'm ready," I said.

"Three!" Paula screamed and darted ahead.

We both flew out of starting position with a fierce power. I propelled forward and passed her like I had a jet engine strapped to my back. But, she widened her stride and floated forward with an agility of a mountain lion. It didn't take long before I lagged behind in her dust.

She flew, guided by the light breeze, right towards the finish line with enough time to double back and do it again if she wanted to. Huffing to the edge of the quad, I bent over to catch my breath and calm the sudden upset of the pizza I'd eaten before dashing out of the house. When confident that I could stand tall without upchucking, I looked up at her. Thankfully she was heaving in and out, too.

"I guess I'm the one who has to work on my betting strategy," I said.

She cleared her throat and stood up. "Well done, though, miss track star."

"I'm ready to face my punishment. One marketing class it is." I matched her noble stance. "What's your reward going to be?"

She circled around me like a ring leader. "Hmm. My reward?"

"Be easy on me. I ate a lot of dust back there."

"Be easy, you say?" She closed in on me, peering into my eyes with mocking vengeance.

"My reward. Your punishment. Should I have you dress up in football gear and have you run around the track with my team watching?"

"You wouldn't."

She thrashed an imaginary whip at me. "Or perhaps I should have you stand in front of my team and yodel?" She narrowed her eyes at me and laughed in a wicked shrill. She lifted her knee up to her waist with each exaggerated step she took closer to me. She placed her hand on my shoulder and pushed me backwards towards the tree line.

"No one has to get hurt, here," I said backing up without a fight, eager, on one hand to be cast into the darkness with her, guilty on the other because hooking up with Owen's coach was wrong on so many levels.

"Are you afraid?" she asked.

"Should I be?"

The tree stopped us and forced her closer. At that point I could only see her silhouette in front of me.

"Don't worry, I'll take it easy on you," she whispered into my ear. "Now, close your eyes."

I closed them on command, unwilling to fight the vibes brewing. "Be easy," I said.

"Good girl," her voice lowered.

I heard a crinkling next to my ear. "What are you doing?"

"Now open your mouth."

I parted my lips slightly.

Her finger touched my lower lip and nudged it downwards even more. "I have something for you."

"I love surprises," I said breathless, unable to feel my feet on the ground anymore.

"Keep your eyes closed." She placed her finger on my lips again.

Suddenly, I smelled chocolate and felt its smooth and creamy texture tickle my lips. I opened them and welcomed the sweetness into my mouth. It melted and coated my tongue in bliss. I nibbled a little and circled my tongue around its delicate, sinful beauty. When she drew away, I blinked my eyes open like in one of those old Hollywood love stories. "That was the most delicious kiss I've ever tasted."

"I thought you'd like it."

"Hershey kisses are my favorite," I told her, dropping the hint for future purposes. "Do you have any more?"

She reached into her pocket. "Maybe one or two more."

She pulled out another shiny, silver Hershey's kiss and unwrapped it with her teeth.

I watched it disappear in her mouth. I couldn't help myself. I dove in after it. My lips landed like a feather on hers and I sought out the irresistible kiss with great hunger and desire.

Even once the chocolate melted, I continued on my adventure. This time I led her back towards the tree. I leaned against her and devoured her sweet breath right there under the leaves of the maple tree. Hungry, I sought out her tongue and led the dance this time. Smooth, velvety, and moist, her mouth softened on mine, welcoming me into its warm embrace. I all but melted at her feet.

Finally coming up for air, I looked deep into her eyes. "I've wanted to do the first day I saw you."

She sought my mouth out for more. "Don't stop then."

Her lips fit perfectly against mine. I could spend a lifetime kissing them and always find myself breathless. They felt so right against mine. Everything about Paula felt so right. Well, everything except the fact that she was Owen's coach, and the fact that she had no clue underneath this sultry act of mine, I was nothing more than an anxious mess, afraid of thrill, adventure and anything she would most likely consider fun and necessary.

* *

At midnight, I unwrapped from Paula's arm and sat up straight under the maple tree. "I should get going. Aziza's probably pacing in front of my window."

"So, she's your boss, best friend and babysitter? Quite a trio for you."

"She owes me."

We rose together, then she wrapped her arms around my waist, pulling me in close for another long, romantic kiss. When she pulled away, she stared deep into my eyes as if searching for an answer to a perplexing question. "Why are you coming into my life now?"

Her words snapped me out of my fabulous dreamy state. "Hmm?"

"Why couldn't you've showed up sooner than this?"

I rolled my eyes, playing along to her rhetorical question. Only, she didn't react with a smile. Her remorseful eyes tugged at me, then nudged me away like a dog surrendering her bone in exchange for a good long pat on the head.

"Are you okay?" I asked her.

She remained quiet for a few seconds longer than I would've wanted. She reached out and laced her fingers through my hair before smiling again. "I told myself, don't get attached. Just go out. Have fun. Make a new friend. Go home. But how can I do that with you? It's like your lips were perfectly sculpted to fit mine." She kissed me again, then pulled away.

I yanked her back and pressed on, inhaling her breath as my own, refusing to let go of what would go down in my history books as the most romantic night of my life.

"Lauren," she mumbled, freeing herself. "There's something I have to tell you."

In those few quiet seconds that she took to compose her next set of words, I promised myself that if she wasn't married, or a criminal on the run, or a long lost sister that I didn't know about, then nothing she could tell me would stop me from pinning her against the tree and giving her the ride of a lifetime right there in the shadows of her Alma Mater.

"I'd love to just take you away with me," she whispered. "Just book us both on a flight and see where this adventure takes us."

Flight. Adventure. No two words used in that context could've extinguished my fire faster. "What do you mean by take me away with you, exactly?"

Paula placed her finger on her lips. "I don't want to ruin this night."

"How could you ruin it?"

"It's complicated," she said. "I just want enjoy being with you while I can."

Why was she talking like she was going off to war? I panicked. "I don't understand."

She once again leaned in to kiss me, but I backed away to avoid her lips this time. "What's complicated?" I asked, surprised how strong my voice projected itself despite the dread that lurked behind it.

She stared at me the way someone did when they were about to tell you something really devastating. "I told myself I wouldn't get involved with you, but then I couldn't resist. I had to see you again. So, I got my haircut. Then, I told myself that would be it. Then you shampooed my hair and I couldn't resist again. So, here we are. And now it's too late. I'm —"

"Too late for what?" I didn't blink, didn't breath, didn't swallow.

"Too late to pretend I don't have feelings for you."

"Why is that a bad thing?" I asked.

"Because," she said, pausing for a few seconds longer than natural. "I'm interviewing right now for a new job."

"Okay, so why is that a problem? Are you becoming a spy for the CIA?"

A smile crept on her face. "Nothing as exciting as the CIA. Well, at least not to people who don't live, breath and sleep sports. I'm interviewing for a position as an athletic director of a high school in need of some innovative leadership. It's a very challenging position, and one that I've dreamt of pretty much since high school."

"Why is this complicated?"

"The position is in California."

Her words hit me square in the gut and knocked the wind right out of me. I saw my chance with her float away like a feather in the wind. It swayed in front of me for a few seconds before being swept off in a gust, getting farther away from me until I could no longer reach out and pull it back to me. My voice, barely a whisper echoed against the empty quad, "California?"

"It's an incredible offer. Once in a lifetime."

Well this sucked big time. This hurt far worse than when Aziza accidentally ran my foot over with her brand new Cavalier the first day she drove it off the lot. In fact, it hurt even more than when my appendix burst.

Don't act like a fool, I pleaded with myself.

"Once in a lifetime, huh?" I punched her arm and plastered the most believable smile I could muster on my face. "We'll have to celebrate when you get that offer."

She hugged me close and kissed me again. "I might just have to stow you away if I get this."

I chuckled and pretended to be happy, meanwhile my heart caved into a hollow abscess. I could've earned an academy award, I performed so good. All the way back to our cars I bubbled over with joy as she went on and on about the possibilities. Year-long summers, endless trails to hike, new coastlines to explore, snorkeling and diving every weekend. Life just couldn't get any better. For Paula.

Someone like Paula would never get someone like me. She'd stare at me with that same puzzled look most people did when they realized how pathetically irrational I was. Paula would have better luck jumping out of a plane without a parachute and surviving without a scratch than ever getting me on an airplane. A fact is a fact no matter how outlandish it was.

Not until I turned right and she turned left on Hope Street, did I burst into tears. I sobbed like a blubbering baby all the way home.

Life just wasn't fair.

* *

When I got home, Aziza ran right up to me and hugged me. "Oh, sweetie. What happened? Your eyes look like you just got beat up."

I melted into her arms and sobbed. Without saying anything, I let go finally and headed for the bathroom.

I turned on the water and splashed my now black face, no thanks to the cheap mascara I used that morning. Aziza stood behind me, staring into the mirror at me with her sympathetic, brownie eyes.

"She's moving to California," I told her.

"Huh? What's in California?"

"Certainly not me," I said softly before dunking my head back into my wet hands.

"Wow, baby doll, that sucks," she said. "But, it's not like you two were a couple or anything. I mean at least you didn't get attached."

I shut the water off and dropped my head in the white, fluffy towel by the sink. I clung to it hoping she would just walk away and leave me to feel sorry for myself. But she never walked away from drama.

She wrapped the soft towel around my shoulders like a child's blanket. "Baby, I think this is a blessing in disguise. From the sound of it, you two were opposite anyway. You never would've been able to deal with an adventure-seeker. This is definitely, definitely for the best."

"I suppose you're right, Azi. You're always right about these things."

Chapter Six

On Saturday mornings, I usually woke up at eight o'clock, jumped in the shower, ate breakfast, sent Owen off to our neighbors' to hang in their pool and then sailed to Bella's to face a grueling nine-hour day on my feet. This particular Saturday morning, I slept through the alarm and woke at eight thirty-two. I had exactly eight minutes to get my act together. My coffee wouldn't even have time to brew.

"Owen, get up!" I yelled at him from the bathroom door. "We're running late. Can you throw a bagel in the toaster for me, please? Oh, and spread some of that almond butter on it that Auntie Azi brought over the other night."

He giggled from his room and then whispered something inaudible.

"Owen!" I called out louder, standing in the hall now wrapped in a towel. "Did you hear me?"

"Yeah, Mom." He rushed out of his room with the receiver pressed to his ear. "It's Coach. She invited us over to go swimming today. Can we go, please?"

"I can't," I whispered.

He stretched his face, pleading, mouthing please to me.

I could easily drop him off on my way to the salon. And, if I was lucky, I'd get to see her, even if for just a second. Big deal, so I'd be twenty minutes late for work. My first client would understand. She had maybe one hundred strands of hair anyway. I could cut and style her in ten minutes and still have time to spare before my next appointment.

I grabbed the phone from him. "Hey, there," I said to Paula. "So another one of your big pool parties?"

"Hey," her voice cooed out to me. "No big party. I was hoping for just a quiet time with you and Owen. It's going to be ninety degrees, no clouds. It couldn't get any more perfect for a day by the pool. I even have a little surprise for you both. Can you swing by around eleven?"

I loved surprises more than I loved Jimmy Choo shoes. I stared down at my freshly painted coral toenails, volleying thoughts around my head. What a shame if Paula couldn't see how adorable my feet looked all decked out with baby rhinestones on each big toe. It wasn't like I called out sick all the time. I could easily reschedule everyone for Tuesday. She had a surprise for me for Christ's sake. How would I ever be able to concentrate on hair? In fact, I'd be doing my clients a major disservice if I worked on them that day. I'd jeopardize their hair, endangering it from falling out mid-shaft, burning at the end of my flat iron, or being chopped up in weed-whacker fashion. I owed it to my clients to stay far away from them with scissors, bleach and anything that could oxidize and cause irreparable damage.

Paula could possibly be moving across the country.

I was fragile, a menace, a force that needed to be stopped in my tracks by something powerful and almighty—like the sun and a kidney-shaped body of water.

"Eleven you say?"

"Is that good?" she asked. "Oh wait, isn't Saturday your busiest day?"

I was already committed. I already planned my outfit and hairstyle – orange bikini and a twist. "I happened to have this huge cancellation to my day. I had a whole bridal party cancel on me. My day just disappeared into one big empty column."

A little white lie couldn't hurt any. Screw the salon for one day. "What can we bring?"

"Bring your suits."

Ah. A day of basking in the sun watching Owen toss himself in and out of the pool like a dolphin and staring at Paula sport around in a swimsuit. "Are you sure I can't bring anything else?"

"Honestly," her voice lowered, "I just can't wait to see you again."

I now stood waist deep in a pool of joy. Definitely screw the dry land for the day.

* *

When Owen and I arrived at Paula's, Chuck greeted us at the front door in bare feet, wearing nothing but a bathing suit. A person could learn a lot about someone's character by looking at his feet. Aside from one pointed edge on his big toe, Chuck seemed to live up to his well-groomed look.

"Come on back," he said waving us in. "Paula should be firing up the grill by now."

As we walked through her living room, I stole a quick glance around. A plush, textured, upholstered sofa with matching eyelet-covered burnt orange and cream pillows sat in front of the bay window. All I could imagine was Paula chilling out in front of a fire on it, sipping Merlot. The room had an air of poise and sophistication to it. A painting of a sunset at the beach hung above an antique desk. A coffee table with books stacked five high tied the cozy scene together. A built-in bookshelf housed artful vases, picture frames, and classic books bound in leather. She had even arranged a vase full of pansies on the table by the window. The small bouquet of smiling flowers lit up the room. What couldn't this woman do?

We continued on through the archway into the kitchen, but not before I tossed a curious glance down the side hall where her bedroom must have been. A massive, colorful, folded paper fan hung on the hallway wall, but Chuck ushered us by too fast for me to get a full view of it. *Later.*

When he walked us through the kitchen and onto the patio, I had to pick up my jaw when I saw Paula floating on an inner tube in the middle of the pool. She looked like a bronzed statue, all sleek and shiny.

"Hey, sis, they're here."

She flew up from the tube and dove towards the pool's ladder. When she surfaced, tiny beads of water formed all over her tanned skin. She looked absolutely delicious.

"Jump in. The water's eighty-degrees."

Owen wasted no time. He slid his feet out of his sandals, tore off his t-shirt and flung himself high above the pool, splashing water all over my beach bag.

"Come on in," she said to me again. "You're not chicken are you?"

Jump in with my lace-trimmed tank on? "Can I use your bathroom to change?" I asked.

"Sure, it's right through the kitchen, down the hall, and on the right." She wasted no time to turn and splash Chuck when he mounted the diving board.

So off I went to trample unsupervised through Paula's personal space. First, I helped myself to a hearty eyeful of her kitchen. No grime. No smears. Just gleaming granite, shiny enough to see my freckles in. The room smelled like a garden of sliced cucumbers. A plate of chocolate chip cookies called out to me. I snuck my finger under the Saran wrap and pulled one out, then wiped the counter clean of crumbs.

I walked towards the hallway chewing on my cookie when I noticed a miniature totem pole hanging on the wall near a key rack. Colorful ceremonial type masks sat on top of each other, staring at me as if asking me, *why are you being so nosy?*

I brushed on by and rounded the corner to the hall. A skylight ushered in the warm, natural light, drenching the hallway and offering me a clear view of the decorative fan perched on the wall. In its folds was an old man smoking a pipe with streams of smoke billowing up and into the small, straw cabana behind him. Tiny red flowers surrounded the scene. In the bottom corner, the artist brushed in calligraphy style strokes, *Live the Dream in California.*

I touched the fan. Its chalky texture gave me the chills. I slid my fingers down to the bamboo base and lifted it slightly to see if it was hollow. Just then, I heard a rip and before I could react, the fan dropped to my feet and the thumbtack that leveraged it against the wall landed right smack in the crook of my big toe. One of the red flowers now had a big slit running through it.

Oh gosh! I shoveled the fan into my arms and rose to my feet. Right where the fan used to be was a poster board with "The Dreams I Will Accomplish" written across its top. Torn, glossy magazine pages were taped to it – an ad of the same exact truck Paula owned with a checkmark by its side, a picture of Brown University with another checkmark. I counted ten checkmarks next to snapshots. Her over-sized sofa, a woman running a marathon, her pool, a four-poster bed, a mountain bike, a brochure of Europe, an ad for a soccer coach, a set of expensive-looking pans, a postcard of Costa Rica, and the Rocky Mountains. Images still waiting for checkmarks blanketed every spec of white space. In the dead center: a picture of California's coastline. Of course. Its title, "Welcome Home."

If any morsel of hope existed that Paula would stay in Rhode Island, then I had better march right into that bathroom, slide into that slinky suit Aziza talked me into buying during the spring sale at Water World, and pray for a miracle.

But first, I needed to figure out how the hell I was going to get that fan back on the wall in one piece, and repair the gaping hole I created in it. I dug in my tote bag for my clear nail polish. I twisted the top of it off and hoped it would do the trick. But, two miracles in one day was an awful lot to ask for.

Please, life owed me.

* *

By the time I pranced onto the patio the three of them were hanging their heads at the edge of the pool, tuckered out already.

"You cheated on that last stretch," Chuck said to Paula, heaving in and out.

"Don't be a sore loser." She lifted herself up on the edge and struggled out of the water. "Let's eat. I'm hungry."

She halted as soon as she laid her eyes on me in my sequined bikini. She bit down on her lower lip and winked.

I loved fashion.

I smiled from ear to ear as I catwalked towards her. I wished Chuck and Owen weren't staring at us so I could wrap my arms around her and make out with her right there under the sizzling sun. "Are we eating outside?"

She nodded, not taking her eyes off me. "Could you *be* any more gorgeous?" She mouthed.

"Me?" I wrinkled up my nose. Ah, the power of a bikini.

"Oh, come on," Chuck rushed by us, pulling Owen by his arm. "Let's eat."

I smiled. "We better join them."

"Do we have to?" she asked. Then, she whispered, "Maybe they'll think we're just swimming."

I melted like gum in the hot sun. I gave Paula a let's-pickup-where-this-left-off look before turning to lead her inside.

But she pulled me back and swept me off to the little cabana. I didn't even wait for the door to shut behind us before pressing my lips against hers. God, she tasted sinful. Her sweet breath swam around my mouth. Then, she pulled back slightly, just far enough so I could gaze into her eyes. She leaned in again and kissed the corners of my mouth before grazing my lips with her petal soft touch. She kissed me softly and slowly while caressing my face. Then, she gently slid her tongue between my lips, brushing against the tip of my tongue then teasing me by pulling away.

I wanted more. I needed more. I couldn't stand not to have more. Ravenous with desire, I kissed her harder and more passionately. I couldn't get enough of her. I tangled my tongue around hers, lassoing it to mine. Tingles spread throughout my body, sending shivers up and down my spine. I felt the sparks forming in between my legs, lighting me on fire. Her heart beat like a boom box against my chest, as my fingertips pressed into her back. I wanted one thing, and one thing only. To make love to Paula McKenna and never stop.

"Mom?" Owen yelled outside.

I jumped a good five feet backwards when I heard his innocent little voice. Breathless and wet, I struggled to straighten myself before opening the door. Paula ran her fingers through her wet hair and braced herself against a table. I couldn't feel my legs.

"In here, sweetie. We're just looking for some...for some, um..."

"For some beer," she answered for me. She reached behind her and opened the fridge for the beer. She shrugged, and I gave her a thumbs up before we walked out together and into her house. I struggled to catch my breath. Chuck just laughed.

Off to the side of the kitchen was a breakfast nook that I missed entirely on my cookie-snatching adventure. A powder-coated aluminum table with four matching chairs centered the screened-in room. A simple cream vase with a few sprigs of evergreen brought a Zen-quality to the blissful breezy room. Who needed California?

The food danced in my mouth. Where did the baby back ribs and herbed slaw come from anyway? Did she have a secret room where she hid Emeril? And then the strawberry cream pie surfaced and suddenly her house smelled like a strawberry patch.

The hell with frozen patches of green beans and gooey cranberries crammed into little inch-by-inch compartments; I had to convince Paula to stick around if for no other reason than to teach me how to cook a decent meal. Even Owen all but licked his plate clean.

Once we finished devouring our food like a pack of wolves, I stood up and began gathering the plates, while Owen snatched up the dirty forks and spoons.

"No, we'll take care of these later," Paula said, shooing us away. "Let's go back to the pool."

Before I could argue, the three of them were already running through the kitchen. So, what did I do? I grabbed another cookie on my way out and shoved the whole damn thing in my mouth. By the time I got to the edge of the pool and dangled my toes in the water, all trace of the sweet, chocolate decadence vanished.

Good thing because Chuck yanked at my ankle and tossed me into the crystal water. I swallowed a mouthful of chlorine and it instantly burned my nose. My eyes were like faucets spilling water out of them. I closed them for refuge, but they only stung more.

What an ass!

I leveraged my hands against the water and pushed gallons of water at him. He splashed it right back at me. Fully engulfed in water war, I cornered him in rapid fire. Soon, Paula and Owen cheered me on, encouraging me to go in for the victory. I pounded him until he dove under in surrender. When he rose up from the crystal blue depths, he shook his head like a wet dog and sunk into treading position, balancing on a noodle.

"I need a beer," he said.

I liked Chuck. He reminded me of my cousin. All my friends had crushes on him and begged to be set up on dates with him. They viewed my cousin like a god, but I never got it. I only saw the same goofy kid he was at five-years-old.

I wondered, as I floated on by Chuck, if girls probably befriended Paula just to get closer to him. The straight ones were probably too mesmerized by his good looks to see the goofball in him. His golden hair and tanned skin could've earned him a cover spot on Men's Health.

Owen tossed a beach ball at him and Chuck volleyed it right back. Owen didn't even include his adored coach in the ball toss.

In a flash, I saw my ideal future. The four of us bonded into a family unit where barbeques, pool days, and horsing around filled our days.

Paula swam to the steps and scaled them to get to the inner tube. Her butt looked so yummy in her orange one-piece.

"Hey Paula, can you grab us a few beers while you're out?" Chuck asked.

"Yeah, one for me!" Owen shouted.

She shot Owen the kind of warning look most kids would run from. He quickly altered his request. "Or maybe a soda?"

She dropped the inner tube and circled into the cabana. She came back out armed with a cooler. Chuck wasted no time swimming to the steps. I trailed right behind him, just as thirsty for an ice-cold beer.

Paula tossed Chuck a can, and then passed a soda to Owen. But, she waited for me to get closer and opened my can and handed it to me. "Here you go, babe."

She just called me 'babe'! I'd give up my collection of handbags to hear it again. I forced myself to calm a notch or two so I wouldn't appear to be a total geek spilling my giddiness around like a loose fireman's hose. "Thanks," I decided on saying.

I sat at the edge of the pool and dangled my feet in the water. She sat right beside me. Our thighs touched. The chemistry reigned in tight, unparalleled to anything.

Chuck downed his beer and tossed the empty can on the patio.

"Ah, nothing like a cold beer on a hot day, huh? Sis, can I get one more?"

"Uh, you still have to be sober in a couple of hours?" she said to him. "I promised these two a little surprise, remember?"

"Come on," he said. "I'm not going to be drunk on two beers."

Paula draped her arm around my leg. "I'm comfortable now. I think you should get the beer yourself if you want it."

"So are you ready to soar around the great Rhode Island skies today?" Chuck asked me walking up the pool steps.

My mouth flew open. "Huh?"

"That's my surprise for you two!" Paula squeezed my leg. "Chuck has his own Cesna at North Central and wants to fly you to Block Island today."

I gulped.

"Wow." Owen's eyes flew open wide. "Yes!" He wound his hand up like he was about to start a lawn mower's engine. "This is so awesome!"

My heart dropped and my throat immediately dried up.

"You alright? You look like you're ready to throw up," Paula said to me.

"My mom's scared of flying."

I splashed Owen.

"Scared of flying?" Chuck asked. "Then, what the hell are you doing hanging out with my sister? She's got wings growing off her back."

"I'm fine with flying," I insisted, pointing my eyes at Owen so hard I think I could've pinned him to a wall and hung him there for a while in silence.

"Owen, you're not chicken are you?" Paula asked.

He tore away from my power grip. "Nah. I've been up in one before."

I stared at Owen in shock. "When did you fly in one?"

"On my ninth birthday, remember, when Tim's dad took us camping in New Hampshire?"

Pitching a tent in a state-insured campground that erected slides and teeter-totters and hosted teen-night at its rec center was a little different than flying five-thousand feet above the earth. What kind of a mother didn't know about her son flying in an airplane? "Oh, yeah, I forgot about that," I said, stirring the water with my leg now.

"I'm taking one last dip, then we can go," Chuck said, lunging into the water with the perfect arch and hardly breaking a splash.

Like hell. I'd whack my arm off in the sliding door this time if that's what it took to stay grounded.

* *

Of course I had to attract myself to someone with a brother who flew airplanes for a living. Of all professions, couldn't Chuck be a police officer, a lawyer, a waiter? I could just see it now, Chuck and Paula planning Christmas dinners on some deserted piece of land that only accepted visitors via those planes that land on water. How would I ever fit in? They'd be packing up the presents and the turkey dinner, and I'd be buried under my blankets faking a migraine?

Chuck not only worked for American Airlines as a pilot, but he also owned a Cesna. Perfect. No wonder they flew all over the world together like a couple of cowboys saddled up on Mavericks exploring wide open spaces. Life was one big adventure for the McKennas. Free airfare, first class upgrades, they droned on and on about the perks the whole ride over to the airport.

By the time we reached the gates to North Central Airport, Chuck had managed to describe to Owen every detail of how a plane's wings worked. Owen stared at him widely, not even taking his eyes off him when they parked. Chuck, the new super hero in his life; the guy who could've told him he needed a cavity filled and Owen would've opened his mouth to let him start drilling.

I still had no idea how I'd get out of taking off in that airplane. I'd bet every piece of cashmere in my closet that I'd find a way, however.

I lingered behind their laughs and high-fives as we crossed the roped area to the runway and hiked out to the last plane on the Tarmac. A beige and white plane about the size of my shoe closet waited for some hotshot, brave soul to fire up her engine and take her up in the air to surf on the clouds. Wasn't catching sunrays, or even playing a round of golf, a better way to spend a Saturday afternoon?

My stomach sunk. Even if by some morsel of hope I got Paula to stay in Rhode Island, airplanes, Tarmacs, all this shit would become my life.

As Chuck and Paula tinkered with the propeller, pouring oil into it like they were lubing up the Tin Man himself, I wandered around the backside of the plane. I inspected every line, every curve as though I knew what the hell it all meant. I scraped off a piece of chipped paint from the window's edge. Not even the paint could withstand the pressure of the wind.

Owen followed Chuck and Paula around like a well-trained bloodhound on the hunt for drugs on board a 747. He stuck his head right between them when they examined the tires and nodded right along with them as though he understood exactly what they meant when they confirmed the tires had plenty of pressure. What did he know about tire pressure? He didn't even know how to operate a vacuum cleaner.

My cue to stage my classic getaway came when Paula fitted Owen with his headset.

"Um, Paula," I snuck up next to her. "Is there a bathroom I can use?"

"Yeah, I think there is. But, it's a short flight. It should only take us thirty minutes or so. Can you wait 'til we land there?"

She spoke about the flight as though we were taking a simple drive in her pickup truck to the beach. Quite honestly, I'd rather tell her I had the runs, than confess my need to keep two feet on the ground at all times. "Actually, I don't think the strawberries are sitting right in my stomach. I think I should go now."

"Okay, then, just go through the double doors there and check in the pilots' lounge area. Should be in there."

"I'll be right back." I started to walk, then decided a little squirt of believability needed to be pumped into my little acting stint. I called out of my shoulder, "Don't leave without me."

"We're not going anywhere without you." She tossed me a wink.

So, what did I do? I did what any reasonable woman afraid of losing her dignity would do. I frolicked towards the building like I was enjoying a beautiful walk on the rolling hills of England. Once I got inside, I clocked myself. Ten minutes ought to do the trick.

I found the bathroom and checked my hair. What a mess. I dug in my bag and pulled out a tube of hair polish, then scrunched the silicone into my curls until my ends formed smoother waves. I might have to fake being sick, but that didn't mean I had to look like a drowned rat in the process. I hoped my hair wouldn't turn green from the chlorine. Well, nothing a little clarifying shampoo couldn't dissolve.

By the time I trekked back out to the plane, Owen was stuffed into the backseat already.

"Mom, this is so cool!" he said, hitting the top of his headset like an overjoyed Orangutan who just scored a banana from a zookeeper. Chuck monitored the controls and spoke codes into his microphone. Paula stood outside the door with an extra headset in hand.

"You're going to need this to hear us talking. It gets kind of loud up there."

Here it came, time for my acting debut with her. I tapped my belly and scrunched my face up to look like I just ate a spoonful of Captain Crunch cereal doused in orange juice.

"Can I take a rain check? I just got sick in the bathroom."

She dangled the headset in her hands and just sort of looked at me blankly.

"Okay, but we're all ready to go. Owen, I mean look at him." She laughed as if trying to convince me that the world was round and they couldn't possibly travel around it any other way. "He's excited."

"Oh, I didn't mean to cancel the trip. I'll be inside waiting. I've got a book in here." I tapped my tote.

"Sure you'll be okay?" she asked, a wave of relief washing over her face.

"Yes, I'll just go sit on the couch in the lounge area." I pushed her towards her seat. "I'll be fine. Just take care of Owen. Make sure he doesn't pull at anything he's not supposed to up there."

"We'll have plenty of chances to get you back here." She climbed into the seat. "We should be back in an hour and a half tops."

I backed away from the plane, being sure to keep my hand on my belly.

I watched them taxi off towards the runway, all three of them waving their hands at me like those people you see right before a cruise ship takes off. When I could no longer see Owen, I turned and sprinted back to the safety of the building feeling very much like I imagined a lottery winner did once realizing she was holding the winning ticket. Free, at least for the moment.

* *

I paced the lounge keeping a vigilant eye out for them. I must've checked my cell ten times already, praying they'd text me and tell me where the hell they were. I wanted Owen to enjoy himself, but Paula promised she'd have him back in an hour and a half. Three hours was definitely too long. Something bad had to have happened.

I looked over at the manager's office again. His big feet still hung over the edge of his desk. If their plane had crashed and burned, would he really be lounging? But if they crashed on Block Island, what could he do from North Central?

I couldn't stand not knowing a second longer. I skirted around the row of attached seats and marched into his office.

The skinny, bald man looked up from his notebook.

"Hi!" he said to me as if no plane in history had ever crashed. Couldn't he see I'd been treading around there all afternoon, making a hole in the Berber carpet next to the window?

"Have you heard from Chuck McKenna's plane at all?"

"I don't think so. Saturdays we get a lot of pilots in and out of here." He dropped his legs to the floor and popped his head up like a weasel.

I stared at the issue of *Airplane Digest* he tossed on the desk. It wasn't like he managed the radio tower at TF Green Airport. How could he not remember?

"It's just that it's been a while and I was starting to get a little worried."

The man stood and peered out the window.

"Well, no need to be. Isn't that him coming towards the building?" He pointed to the three of them skipping across the tarred lot.

The last time a wave of relief this big washed over me, Owen had been running up to me after getting lost in Wal-Mart when he was six. I turned for one second to get a box of tampons and when I reached down for his little hand, he was gone. I stood alone amidst a sea of maxi pads and adult diapers, frantic that someone had snatched my little boy. I had screamed his name out loud and ran like a rabid dog through the aisles, tossing bins as I tripped over them. Crying and hysterical, a store manager grabbed me by the shoulders and shook me until I chilled out long enough to cough up Owen's name and description. In a flash, the doors locked and a Code Adam notice blared out of the loud speakers. And just as fast, as the army of Wal-Mart workers snapped into search and recovery mode, Owen crawled out from under a rack of men's t-shirts red and ashamed, with his pants soaked through. I never ran up to him so fast before in all of my life. I threw my arms around his little body and vowed never to make him wait again if he asked me to go to the bathroom in a store.

This time, his face left no room for tears. His smile lit up the room like a thousand-watt chandelier. He ran up to me and hugged me tight. Was it normal for his heart to beat that fast?

"Mom, you *have* to come next time. We saw our house. I took a picture of it. And then we saw the Newport Bridge!"

He swelled with joy retelling every detail.

I smiled and urged him to continue, slowly deflating to a blob of guilt. I knew full well his newfound freedom was about to be struck head on and squashed like a squirrel on the road. If he could hang with Chuck and Paula like this, he could probably grow up and be a pilot just like Chuck, or even better, a fighter pilot in the US Armed Forces who'd end up saving a small town of innocent villagers from enemy attack. Yeah, he had a better shot at being the Queen of England than flying next to his mom in Uncle Chuck's Cesna for weekend flights to Martha's Vineyard or Block Island or even to the end of the taxi runway. I couldn't run off and hide in a bathroom stall every time Uncle Chuck decided he wanted to take us flying.

"How's your stomach?" He turned his bright eyes up to me.

"I don't feel like talking about me right now." I kissed the top of his matted head. "I want to hear all about your trip. Did we look like little ants down here?"

He giggled. "The cars on the highway looked like Matchbox cars. Didn't they, Coach?"

"Your mother will have to come up and find out for herself." She tossed her arms around each of our shoulders and walked us towards the exit. "Maybe we can arrange to fly down to Baltimore and see the Red Sox beat the O's next time."

I realized in that short walk to the car that I'd just arrived at the turnoff that would lead to the end of our road. I hoped it was a long road at least.

Chapter Seven

I had only missed one day at the salon, and before I could even flip on my curling iron switch, Meredith, a yippy stylist who reminded me of an annoying little terrier biting my ankles, spilled some news to me.

"You should have seen Aziza's face. She turned beet red — almost purple—when the flowers delivered. I thought I was going to have to squirt her down with the hose to cool her down. I think she's in love this time."

Flowers? Love? What?! Aziza never even kept a new tank top purchase from me, never mind something like this.

"Where is she?" I asked.

"She's out back straightening the color tubes."

I dropped my keys and pocketbook on my station and bolted to the backroom. Aziza was stuffed headfirst in the closet tossing empty color boxes on the floor behind her.

"Why didn't you call me?" I asked.

She jumped and hit her head on a shelf. "Shit!" She bent over and rubbed it.

"You didn't think to call me and tell me you got flowers?"

She rolled her eyes and sat down in the plushy chair. "You were sick. I didn't want to bother you."

Bullshit. If I had as much as a toothache, she'd scoot her schedule aside to spoon feed me chicken soup and wrap me in warm blankets. "Who sent them?"

"No one important." She avoided my eyes. "Just some girl I met when I was out."

"How come you didn't tell me about her?"

"Because she's not a big deal."

"What kind of flowers were they?" I needed details. I needed to be a part of this somehow.

"Why does it matter to you? Flowers are flowers." She stood up and walked out towards the front desk.

"Were they roses?" I yelled out to her. Everyone in the salon now lifted their eyes up at us.

"What if they were? So, what? It doesn't matter anyway."

"So, they were roses," I said matter-of-factly, slightly scarred already from being left out. I'd never seen Aziza turn beet red before.

"Yes. They were roses. Really, no big deal."

"Were they red?" I closed in on her this time.

"Can we talk about this later? I've got a client waiting." She brushed a chunk of her black mane over her shoulder. A patch of red blotches dotted the sides of her face.

"You're blushing. They were red. Who were they from?"

"Why do you have to be so freaking nosy?" she asked.

"Why are you making me dig like this?" I lowered my voice now because this was verging on way too personal for the rest of Bella to know. "You're supposed to offer this information up to me before I hear it from someone who doesn't even know your home phone number."

"Fine, I'll tell you. But you have to promise not to get mad at me."

"Well, unless they're from Paula I can't see why I'd—" Wait. I knew exactly who sent them. I had slapped the counter shocking even the very hard-of-hearing Mrs. Williams to attention. "They're from Tania aren't they? You went out with her, didn't you?"

"Well, only once. I know how this looks," she said. "But, she's really cool."

I narrowed my eyes at her feeling very much like an abused puppy with no one to turn to help lick my wounds but myself. "Let's just get to work and talk about this later."

* *

The rest of the day flowed as smoothly as it could. I avoided Aziza as much as possible. When I needed to mix a color at the same time as her, I'd send a junior stylist to prep it for me. When she asked if anyone wanted take-out for lunch, I was the only one who declined ordering, even though the only thing I had to eat at the salon was a bag of crushed pretzels I found stuffed at the bottom of my pocketbook. Eventually skinny Maggie, the nail goddess at Bella, offered me half of an egg salad sandwich and a dill pickle. I hated dill pickles.

At the end of the day, I cleaned up my station as efficiently as possible, sticking my combs in the sanitizer, wiping my blades down with oil and unplugging my flat iron and curling wands. I was responsible. Aziza on the other hand didn't have a freaking responsible cell in her body, obviously. Who dates the ex–girlfriend, wait—the celebrity ex-girlfriend that is—of her best friend's new girlfriend?

I decided to duck out while Aziza washed down the sinks, grateful to be free at last to stomp my feet like a spoiled brat right there by my car. I even punched the dashboard before speeding off to home.

This lesbian community was way too small. I wished I could just escape and start over someplace where I knew no one.

How could Aziza be okay with this? How did she answer the phone that day and say yes to Tania knowing full well I'd be pissed at her? Did she even care about me anymore? Was she that selfish?

Watch them become this big couple. Aziza–the new Paula, traveling on Tania's arm from one tour stop to another, offering her standing ovations, and handing her CDs to sign as crowds gathered to get her autograph.

Aziza would run into work each day and shovel all this nonsense at me, and all I'd be able to do is close my mouth and pray that none of it sunk in.

What about the holidays? Would I have to invite both of them over for gift exchanges and eggnog by the tree? Maybe me and Tania could even swap sex-stories about Paula. Gee, wouldn't that be right in line with the Christmas spirit? And I'd have to go shopping to buy Paula's ex-lover a present. What would I get her? A framed picture of me and Paula? And what would the gift tag say? Merry Christmas, Love Your Ex and Her New Girlfriend. I'd rather eat Chinese takeout out of the box in front of a tire fire in a back alley somewhere than hold hands and sing Christmas carols with this new power couple.

By the time I got home, Aziza had called my cell phone twice without leaving a message.

I yelled down the hallway to Owen. "If Auntie Azi calls, tell her I'm taking a shower or something."

"She already called and said she's bringing pizza." He skated around the kitchen in roller blades, raiding the cabinets for licorice, then rolling past me to grab a Coke out of the fridge.

I needed a drink.

I poured myself a glass of Merlot, spilling it over the edge of the glass. "Well, when she gets here, tell her I went to bed."

Owen inched closer. "Why are you mad at her?"

"Because sometimes she acts like a selfish you-know-what," I said, "We'll be fine. I just need some time to myself."

He grabbed hold of the counter and edged himself even closer to me. "What did she do?"

"That's none of your business."

He shoved off towards his room. "Whatever."

I wiped the butcher block countertop, which Owen left stained with fruit punch. What did he expect me to do for the rest of my life? Be his maid? Was everyone out to get me that day?

And, just who did Aziza think she was barking out her upcoming entrance like she was already a celebrity's girlfriend? *Aziza was bringing pizza. Oh, stop the world people, the Great Aziza would be gracing the pitiful folks of condo C-3 with her presence.*

I piled the dirty breakfast plates from that morning into the dishwasher. I never should've told her about Paula. Leave it to Aziza, the praying mantis herself, to get all involved and then tangled up in the web. I'd bet my life that if she hadn't met Paula before meeting Tania, she would've kept on hating Tania's music every bit as much as she did the day we saw her at the Newport Folk Festival a year ago. Aziza's exact words after Tania played her first set – *I wish I were deaf.*

Ugh.

Owen adored his Aunti Azi and would trade just about anything to make sure she stood by his side as much as possible. He hated when we fought. So, when he emerged from his bedroom, holding his stomach like a bad actor feigning an appendix eruption, I just rolled my eyes. I knew what he was up to.

Dressed in his soccer ball pajamas, he hunched over and held his belly, clinging to the wall as he walked toward me. "It really hurts, mom. Can you call Auntie and ask her to bring some of that pink stuff?"

Ten minutes ago he had been gliding around the floor like a champion hockey player. "Give me a break."

He bent over and groaned. "I think I'm going to puke."

I reached under the sink for a bucket. It smelled like lemons and ammonia. "Use this."

Owen inhaled the stench and threw the bucket down on the ceramic tile. He straightened. "Are you trying to kill me?"

"You know damn well you don't have a stomach ache."

"I do." He buckled over again.

"Good. Then, get in the car." I walked towards the front door.

Owen trailed behind me. "Where are we going?"

I grabbed my keys off the nail and opened the door, ushering him past me. "To the hospital."

He made it as far as the door and stopped. "I really just think I need some crackers and pink stuff."

"I don't think so." I pointed my finger towards the parking lot. "Go."

He miraculously stood up tall. "Why are you always mad at her?"

I stared at his big watery eyes for a few seconds before moving past him back into the condo. I flung my keys on the coffee table. He was so sensitive. "Everything's fine, Owen."

"I just hate it when you're mad at each other."

There I went again putting my son in the middle of one of our fights. What did he know about the rules of dating amongst best friends? I couldn't bear to look into his sad eyes for another second. "Is she bringing pepperoni?" I asked him.

He nodded and a smile lit up his face. "And Feta."

I wrapped my arm around him. "That's my favorite."

"That's why she's bringing it."

Who needed couple's counseling when we had Owen to keep the peace?

* *

I opened the front door and took the pizza from Aziza's hands. I noticed fresh tears pooling in her eyes and before I could open my mouth, she dropped into my arms like a child who had just been returned to her mommy after being kidnapped. She buried her head in my shoulder.

"I hate when you're mad at me," she said, her words pitchy and scratchy. "I should've called you and told you about it. I just didn't know how to handle it, sweetie. I'm so, so sorry."

And just like that, I forgave her. "Let's just put it behind us," I said, closing the door with my foot.

"Thank God." She unwrapped herself from me. "I bought some beer, too." She slid the twelve-pack of my favorite, Sam Adams Summer Ale, on the counter. "Figured we could use some tonight."

How could I stay mad at my best friend? Adorable as she was and all. I needed one more hug to make sure we were okay. It gave me strength because then I added, "I want to hear all about it."

"Really?"

"Yeah." Not really. But, wasn't that what best friends were supposed to do?

The three of us sat around the breakfast bar and shoveled slice after slice into our mouths and talked about the upcoming trip to D.C. that weekend.

"I'll come over tomorrow and help you guys pack," Aziza said, a pepperoni fell to the plate in front of her. "I've got something you can bring with you." She winked at me.

107

She had no clue that a school trip didn't mean I could put the kids to bed and go color the town with Paula late at night. I could only imagine that Aziza's mystery travel item had less to do with practicality and more to do with red lace.

On that note, I stood up and started to clean up our mess.

A few minutes later, Owen went to bed and we went out onto my deck with our cooler of beer. We stared out at the lake in silence. The oversized deck provided a panoramic view. The sun had just about set, and a half-moon rose over the northeast side of the lake. A few straggling kayakers floated in the distance. The early summer night air snuggled against us like a fuzzy blanket.

I smelled burgers.

It didn't take long for Aziza to explode with details about her date with Tania.

"She took me to this piano bar and we sat next to each other on this secluded leather couch. Next thing I know, the waitress is handing us a couple of shots of Agua Dente. I lost count how many we had. But I'd say by the third was when I was feeling really good. She just started making out with me in the candlelit nook with "Songbird" playing in the background. Seriously, the most romantic night of my life."

I sucked my bottle of beer dry and reached for a fourth. "Go on."

"The only kind of bad thing was that when I got back from the bathroom, she was smoking a cigarette."

"Oh," I said, projecting my most convincing sympathy possible, which proved difficult considering I had to press myself against the wicker chair to avoid breaking out into a series of cartwheels. Suddenly, Tania West wasn't so perfect anymore.

"A smoker. Yuck, huh? I would never guess Paula would be into a smoker."

"She said it helps keep the raspy quality of her voice," Aziza defended.

"So, it's a career thing?" I couldn't help interjecting some sarcasm on that one.

"Look, at first, I was kind of grossed out. But then, the longer I sat there with her, the less it bothered me. Aziza scrunched her face to the side. "I actually smoked a few myself."

"You didn't? Really?"

"Yeah. So there we were puffing away and who walks in?" I stared at her. "Who?"

"Do you remember that really hot girl that I took to the New York show a few years back?"

"Bend-Over-Backwards-Lizzy?" Aziza had described this girl as being more limber than Gumby.

"Yes! So, she came over and started flirting, even with Tania draping her arm around me. Can you believe it?"

"Well, she was into the whole threesome idea, so yeah, I can see her trying to pry herself into you both." I sat up a little taller. I loved drama.

"Well, I think Tania got a little jealous of all the attention, so we left and went back to her place. She has the best view of the city. She's on the eleventh floor overlooking the bay. It's incredible."

"Did you have sex?"

"We did." Aziza giggled. "I've never had sex like this before. It lasted hours. I couldn't get enough of her."

I gulped back another long swig of beer. My head spun, making the moon light hip hop dance on the water. Padded by alcohol helped me to hear Aziza through. "Hence the roses, huh?"

"Don't be mad at me for what I'm about to do." Aziza stuck her hand in her pocketbook and pulled out a pack of cigarettes. "I'm just really craving one right now. The drinking, the talk about sex, it's just all too much for my senses right now."

She stuck the cigarette in her mouth and let it dangle there while she found her lighter.

"You don't smoke." I snatched the unlit cigarette before she could light it.

"Lighten up. This is the same pack I bought that night. I just feel bad throwing them in the trash after paying six bucks for them." She plucked another cigarette from the pack and lit that one, leaving the unlit one dangling from my fingers.

I was too numb to fight. So, I let my best friend puff away. Tiny plumes of smoke billowed out the side of her mouth.

"This whole sex thing with Tania won't change anything with any of us, right?" she asked me.

"How can it not, though. I mean, it's not like we're going to be able to go on a double date now. That'd be a bit awkward, don't you think?"

Aziza reclined back a bit, and then inhaled a long drag. "We'll work it out like we always do."

By her second cigarette, it actually enticed me. I didn't even mind when her smoke billowed in front of my face. In fact, I breathed it in deeply when it did.

"I have to pee," she said, standing up and leaving the newly lit cigarette on the edge of the table.

I swallowed more beer. The smoke floated by my face, calling out to me. The last time I smoked was right before I got pregnant with Owen, which was also the last time I'd been this drunk, too. Fuck it. I picked up the cigarette and took a good long drag. I closed my eyes and savored its light-headed effect.

When Aziza returned, she caught me inhaling another drag and laughed. "Alcohol. It always brings out the smokers in us."

I took yet another drag and ended up smoking the entire cigarette as I relaxed and listened to my friend drone on about her new fling. In thinking it through, I had nothing to be concerned about. If Paula really wanted Tania still, then Aziza wouldn't have had the chance to spend hours devouring her.

* *

"Make sure you pack enough underwear to last the weekend," I yelled out to Owen the next day. I tucked my blow dryer in between my bathrobe and windbreaker. Washington D.C. had experienced their worst drought in years, and figured, now that I was packing up to visit, the weatherman pointed to a string of storm clouds on the television screen.

"Are they going to have a pool there?" Owen ducked his head in my room.

I had studied their website the night before, investigating every nook and cranny of the deluxe room I reserved, the lounge, and the pool. "Yes. I already told you to make sure you pack your swimsuit." The boy never listened to me anymore.

"I'm so glad you're coming." He hugged me.

I savored his grip. Soon, he'd be too old to show such emotion.

He let go and tossed himself on my bed. "Do you think Coach is really going to move to California?"

"Did she tell you she's moving?"

"It's just a rumor. Someone overheard her talking to some lady about it at practice the other week."

My stomach dropped. "Who knows, sweetie. Just try to enjoy her while she's here."

He twirled one of my ponytail elastics in his fingers. "I don't want her to move. She's the best coach ever. And she's cool to hang out with. What about you? Isn't she your girlfriend now?"

A surge went through my body. My *girlfriend.* I loved the sound of that.

"What would make you ask that?" It wasn't like we showed affection in front of him.

"I'm twelve. I know what it means when you lock yourselves in her cabana."

I panicked. Could there've been a crack in the cabana and maybe the poor kid saw his mother making out with his coach? "We were looking for beer."

"Mom has a girlfriend! Mom has a girlfriend," Owen chanted, jumping on my bed.

I blushed and tossed a pillow at him.

"I love Coach, Mom. I think you make the best couple!"

"We're not a couple, so don't go spreading rumors about it." I picked up my now packed suitcase and dropping it on the floor. The hinges were practically popping off. I couldn't help overstuffing it. What if it didn't rain? Mid-Atlantic was just as unpredictable as New England. I'd need a whole different a wardrobe for sunny weather.

"I think coach really likes you."

Correction. Coach really liked the parts of the woman I had presented to her. She knew only the façade – the trendy clothes, the manicured nails, the perfect makeup, the feigned confidence, the thin veneer that camouflaged the terrified, reticent girl beneath, all keeping me safe and hidden. The scared child in me would repel Paula like two same magnetic ends.

"Let's just get you packed."

We walked into Owen's room and I tossed a few shorts, socks, and t-shirts in a smaller suitcase. I reached across his bed to pick up his bathing suit from his headboard bookcase, which he haphazardly hung over the top of the football Tom Brady had given to him at the Patriots' summer camp the year before. Next to his blue swim trunks sat a framed picture of him, Paula and Chuck in front of the plane.

I picked it up. "How come I didn't see this?"

"I don't know." Owen slipped into his bathroom and grabbed his deodorant. "Chuck framed it and gave it to Coach to give to me at practice."

"That was nice of Chuck."

Owen shrugged. "I wish you could see more of the plane in the picture."

I looked more closely at the picture. All of them smiled like they were on set in a toothpaste commercial, arms slung around each other and looking like a happy-go-lucky, adventurous family.

Chapter Eight

I thumbed through my latest issue of *Vogue* as our bus rolled down I-95 en route to the nation's capitol. I reread the same sentence over and over again and I still couldn't comprehend a damn thing. I had to pee something awful. Paula warned us all before closing the bus door, *if you have to pee, do it now or hold it.* This was the worst thing she could've done. I squirmed in my seat, scrunching up my face tight. All anyone ever had to do was mention the word bathroom and I had to go. It's a psychological thing that started a few years earlier when I stupidly drank a pot of coffee prior to walking into a three hour funeral. I had to pee so bad that day, I seriously believe I bruised my kidneys holding it in. Well, ever since, all I had to do was drink a drop of water and needed to go like I had gulped gallons.

So, when Owen slid up behind me and whispered that he had to go, too, I jumped in to rescue him. I leaned in close to Paula and whispered, "I think we should get off at the next exit." Her musky perfume revved up my heart.

"Why?" she asked.

"I have to pee."

She looked down at her watch. "We're making such good time. You can't hold it?"

I shook my head and pouted.

She groaned. "You're not going to do this to me, are you?"

I ran my finger up and down her forearm. "Please. For me."

She breathed heavier, then turned her big brown eyes to me. "It's a good thing you're cute." She stood up and braced against the seat. "Hey, Mattie," she yelled up to the driver. "We need to make a bathroom stop."

Suddenly the entire bus erupted in a thunderous cheer.

Owen leaned over the seat and whispered to me. "Wow, she must really like you."

I was pretty sure Paula would have driven thirty miles out of her way to find me a bathroom if necessary. At that point, I still leveraged plenty of power over her. All I had to do was bat my eyelashes at her and she caved. I planned to enjoy the honeymoon stage as long as possible.

Soon enough she'd discover all my phobic faults and bail faster than she could free-fall out of her brother's plane.

* *

The whole ride, all we did was talk about Paula's teaching and coaching and my hair career. Turned out she had enrolled at Brown University wanting to be an astrophysicist. But, then she volunteered her first semester to be an assistant coach for a local school's soccer team and her path forked. Yeah, well, I wanted to be a cartoonist. Instead I took funny-looking people and turned them into real life beauties. Good thing destiny intervened. I couldn't imagine how we would have hooked up otherwise.

Aside from a two-mile backup on the George Washington Bridge and a small detour on the Jersey Turnpike, we arrived at our hotel just shy of Paula's eight hour goal, coming in at eight hours, twenty-two minutes. Not bad for a Friday in the early summer. I didn't care if it took eight days to get there. I loved sitting alongside her with our legs pinned up against each other.

* *

116

Once in the lobby of the hotel, Paula rounded up the gang of ten kids and lectured them on the weekend rules. "I have two more chaperones coming, so that makes five adults you have to listen to. Understood?"

A series of hushed yeses buzzed out of the kids.

Two kids. I could handle that. Of course then all the kids started laying down their claims.

"I'm rooming with Owen." Jake called out. "They've got the couch and the big screen TV."

"Me, too." The other star player folded his arms over his chest.

"Everyone can't room with Owen and Ms. Woods," Paula said.

Ms. Woods? Since when did I have a gray bun sticking out the back of my head? I wouldn't last an entire weekend being called what my friends used to call my grandma. That would make me feel about as sexy as walking around Newport in flannel pajamas. "Please, don't call me that," I said to the group of riled up kids. "Call me Lauren."

"How about Ms. Lauren?" Paula asked me.

I turned to her and smirked. "Is that really necessary?"

"It's a respect thing."

"Hey, Coach," a lanky, freckle-faced kid said. "Can't we just call her coach's girlfriend?" He rounded his arms up to gather the laughter that fired from each kid's mouth.

To my horror, Paula's face reddened. I wanted to dig myself into the dirt of the planter near the Concierge's desk. Suddenly, I was thirteen-years-old again caught sucking face with Ricky at the school dance by all the 'cool kids' who whistled and clapped like I just scored them a touchdown at homecoming, and having Ricky run away like he just kissed a pile of garbage.

All eyes pinned against us like a firing squad. I narrowed my eyes at Owen. He didn't dare look up at me. He just dribbled an invisible soccer ball between his feet. The kids' jeers just seemed to multiply like Morning Glory weeds in a tomato garden, choking the breath right out of Paula. Her face went from a first to third degree burn in seconds, obviously pained at the thought that she would be associated as my girlfriend.

She shot them a no-nonsense look and clenched her teeth. "Ms. Lauren and I are friends, just like Mrs. Swanson and I." She motioned towards Billy's grandmother, who had about 30 years and 150 pounds on me. "So, cut the horsing around and let's get checked in."

A manic storm knocked at my temples as I watched Paula noncommittally gather her gym bag and haul it over her shoulder not even giving me a second glance.

She was embarrassed of me. I felt like an idiot.

I tried to shake this feeling off of me like a boxer would right after a blow to the head. Since when did I need a girlfriend to make me feel whole? This was her loss, not mine. Let her move to California and try to find someone better. I certainly wasn't planning to change my life around just to please her. Girlfriends might do that, but not casual friends.

I was a little smarter than that. I lifted the handle on my suitcase and rolled right on past my casual friend, Paula, to the head of the check-in line.

* *

"I would have been hurt, too," Aziza said to me over the phone.

I shoved my suitcase in the closet and slid the door shut. I checked myself out in the full-length mirror and decided that maybe I should've worn the capris instead of the shorts with those sandals. I examined my face. More freckles had popped up during the ride, and I forgot to pack my sun block. Great. I'd look just like the stargazer chart hanging in Owen's bedroom before the weekend ended.

"I didn't say I was hurt. I said pissed. There's a huge difference."

"Not with you, there's not," Aziza said.

"Hey Mom, can we rent a video game from the TV menu?" Owen stood in bare feet in front of a screen bigger than him.

"Put your socks on," I said to him. "Dirty feet have touched that, too." Disgusting. "I'll let you know how it goes," I said to her.

As soon as I hung up, I pulled a bottle of disinfectant out of my bag and went to town squirting everything not upholstered. I saw too many of those investigative specials where they uncovered massive amounts of bacteria lurking on the remote control, the ice-bucket, even the room service menu. Gross.

By the time Jake and Owen had played a round of virtual golf, I had sanitized the entire suite, down to placing my own linens on the pillows. A few minutes later, someone knocked on the door. I opened it to Paula standing in the hotel hallway, barefoot. I couldn't help but chuckle to myself. I tossed the bottle of Lysol into the bathroom before she could see it. She bolted into the room like a kid overloaded on sugar, bounced on the bed, and grabbed the remote from Owen. "Let me show you how this is done."

She swung her body in full motion and the golf ball sailed to within inches of the hole. The boys cheered and smacked her hands and they all broke into a strange chicken dance. With his hands glued to his lower back, flapping away, Owen asked Paula, "How did you do that?"

"I'll show you later. We're all getting hungry. What do you say we go for a walk and find some burgers?"

The boys straightened and ran through the door, leaving me and Paula in their dust. The door shut behind us. I grabbed my pocketbook on the desk. "Ready?"

"Wait." She grabbed hold of my hands and brought me in close to her. "You look beautiful."

I brushed away the family of butterflies that rushed my tummy. Now she wanted to get all sentimental and loving, when no one else could see. "Thanks." I forced a smile. "We should go. We don't need more rumors spreading."

"Everything okay?" She pulled me back and hugged me.

"Yeah. Of course." I pulled away and headed for the door. "Are you going to go hold Mrs. Swanson after this, too?"

She laughed. "Yup, I just bought her some lacy lingerie from the store in the lobby. Not sure it will work with her sagging double-dees, but we'll see."

I didn't laugh. In fact, I think steam burned its way through my body and straight out of my ears. "I wasn't joking."

She slipped her hands around the small of my back and pulled me in close. "I don't care what they say as long as you don't care." Our bodies touched, electricity and heat surged. I wanted to stay mad. I wanted to distance myself. I wanted to be the one in control.

I rocked gently back and forth with her. The whole room spun along with my heart. I closed my eyes and embraced the tender moment instead of fighting it. I could stand in her arms all night long. My brain yelled for me to back away from her to a safe distance where I wouldn't melt into a puddle of lusty goop. But, I couldn't resist her beating heart and faint breaths on my neck. So, what did I do? I inched my face up and kissed her, settling back on that familiar comfort of her touch.

How could I be upset with her? How could I think Paula didn't care for me a little more than as a friend? Do friends sneak kisses like this?

What we had going on veered way beyond any friendship I'd ever experienced.

Besides, labels were overrated.

* *

I sat next to Paula in front of a really sad and unappetizing display of desserts. First of all, who put lumpy brown icing on a cake and called it a scrumptious slice of heaven? And the person who baked up the idea to squirt a whole can of whip cream on top of a crowd of lady fingers and leave it in the eighty or so degree restaurant had to be insane. Melt away perfectly good sweetness? As I lobbed my head to the side to get a better look at the banana cream catastrophe, Paula's mystery chaperones finally walked in – Chuck and his flame-headed fiancé.

Chuck dropped a kiss on top of his sister's head and flicked her hat off.

"Chuck!" Owen squealed like he was five again. He ran towards his new, favorite buddy and Chuck wrapped him in his arms and twisted him like a pretzel. Owen yelled out *uncle*, and Chuck uncoiled him and straightened his hat in one steady move.

I smiled at his fiancé who returned the smile and forced forward to shake her hand. "Lauren, right?" Her teeth were whiter than chalk.

"Yes, that's right. And, I'm sorry, I never caught your name that day at the party."

"Amber," she said before turning away and snuggling up to Chuck like a playful kitty.

I wondered if Amber was born with that red hair or if her parents were just really intuitive?

"I didn't think you guys were ever going to show," Paula said.

"We had to take off on a later flight," Chuck said.

"What happened? Couldn't get first class seats on the 4:10 flight?" Paula asked.

"We took a detour to Pennsylvania first to get some of those crunchy pretzels."

Chuck slid in the seat next to Paula. "Figured it was on the way so why not?" He dunked a tortilla chip in the salsa and shoved it in his mouth.

Yeah. Why not just detour to Georgia, too, and pick up some peaches? Who hopped on planes like they were local buses?

For the next hour, the kids talked over each other, Paula debated with Chuck about whether the Patriots would win the next football season, and Mrs. Swanson and Amber discussed a recipe for apple pie. Meanwhile, I squirmed in my seat with nothing interesting to say, overstuffed on fries, and trying to appear more appealing than that dripping slice of cheesecake in the dessert case.

* *

By the time we had wrapped up dinner and walked from the Jefferson Memorial to the Washington Memorial, I had some real concern that my feet wouldn't be able to carry me the few more steps from the bathroom to my bed. Jake and Owen were equally exhausted and already snoring in the time it took me to wash my face and brush my teeth.

When the alarm buzzed in the morning, the three of us jumped like spring-loaded toys. Suddenly, being first in line for the White House Tour didn't seem like such a brilliant idea anymore. I didn't even like politics. Why on earth did I insist we absolutely must be number one in line to see Lincoln's study? Because Paula wanted to? Since when did I become one of those girlfriends?

Just like Aziza with the whole smoking fiasco. Aziza complained whenever a smoker lit up within twenty feet of her. Now look at her keeping the cigarette companies in business for yet another week just because her new sex partner smoked. This was so not Aziza. I was hoping by the time I got back from my trip, Aziza would tell me that Tania lit one up while they were having breakfast and she flipped out on her, told her to quit or else, and then poof, no more recaps of Aziza and Tania sex. She'd go back to being repulsed by smelly smokers and the world would be right again.

Maybe I could convince the gang to dump the whole White House idea and settle on a nice breakfast in that cute garden restaurant I saw down the street from the hotel. I could blame it on Owen—that he had a mad craving for waffles. Paula would totally back him up on that one. Let's see would Paula choose staring at an antique desk that Truman's wife wrote letters at eons ago or swallowing buttery cinnamon rolls, smoked bacon, and all the chocolate chip waffles she could fit in her belly?

Just as I guessed, Owen gladly took the fall for me. Not even an hour later, syrup dripped down his chin as he frantically stuffed a forkful of pancakes into his mouth. I hadn't even finished buttering my wheat toast when he slammed his fork onto the table claiming winner of the race that no one else seemed to be competing in. Jake played with a sausage link. Michael cut his waffle into squares. Amber stirred Splenda into her first cup of coffee, and Grandma Swanson mumbled something about her cold tea.

Owen couldn't wait to see the IMAX movie. When we all darted out of the restaurant and started walking towards the museums, he almost ran me over right there on the sidewalk. I grabbed him by the arm and pulled him aside. "Seriously? Is this how you're going to act all day?"

He sulked and wriggled.

"You need to last all day. We're going to be doing a lot of walking and I'm not going to ask Coach to carry your butt back to the hotel because you used up all your energy in the first half hour."

He craned his neck to see around me. "They're getting way ahead of us."

I looked behind me and they were a good fifty yards away already. But, not Paula. She stood a short distance from us scanning the restaurant's menu, the one she already studied in great detail while ordering. Ah, what a lady.

"Fine just go," I told him. Why lecture? He wouldn't listen anyway. When we got home, I'd cut all sugar from his diet. Period.

"Honestly," I said to Paula as he whizzed by me. "Since he turned twelve, he lost all ability to listen to a word I say."

"He'll turn out just fine. He's an active kid not wanting one single morsel of life to pass him by. Be thankful. The majority of the kids I teach are fat and lazy. It's a miracle they actually get up out of their seats when the bell rings."

"I guess I'd rather him be a firecracker than a dud. He's always been a bundle of energy. He used to drive me nuts when I'd take him to the park as a toddler. He was the only three-year-old who could climb the twenty steps to the big kid ladder and self-propel down it. He'd fly down on his behind so fast that he'd knock me down on my butt every time. The kid has no fear."

"Fear is boring and useless," she said.

* *

I stood in line for the IMAX movie. The kids bubbled with joy. In exactly eleven minutes they would stick their 3-D glasses on their faces and watch sea monsters come to life. The ticket agents promised lots of colorful fish and danger. I just wanted off my achy feet. But I didn't want to fall asleep, just yet. *Sea Monsters, 3-D?* Really? I'd much rather go see that jellyfish exhibit. They mate instead of just spread their eggs around like chicken feed. They have sex. I read it that morning on the Internet. How fascinating. Paula taught a science class. She'd get a kick out of that for sure.

I scanned our group. Chuck and Amber stood off to the side holding hands. How hard could it be for them to watch mine and Paula's group? I tapped Paula's arm and pulled her away from the kids. "Want to sneak out of this and go watch jellyfish make babies?"

The way her mouth curled up like the Joker in Batman one would've thought I asked her to go have sex in the tank. "Really?"

I leaned into her. "Go ask your brother if he can watch the kids for us."

"It's *Sea Monsters*, though!" she said as if Jimmy Choo was giving away free shoes.

I lowered my eyes. "Please."

"Jellyfish, huh?"

I pushed her forward. "Go ask him."

Paula halted. "Are we really going to watch jellyfish?"

I slid my fingers down her arm and smiled innocently. "Maybe."

She winked and strutted over to her brother. Twenty seconds later she jumped back by my side and led me towards the staircase. "Let's go hang upstairs and people watch."

For a moment I thought to run back and tell Owen I'd wait outside the theater for him. But, he'd be more surprised to actually see me sitting in the theater. So, I just scaled the steps two at a time alongside Paula hoping we could find some deep, dark nook somewhere on the top level where we could act like a couple of horny jellyfish. Gosh, I was a terrible mom.

By the time we reached the third floor, I could barely breathe. We stood and looked out over the enormous foyer below us. People billowed in and out of the front entrance like ants lined up for a bread crumb picnic. I looked around. The reptiles and amphibian exhibits lined the walls behind us. "Let's go check out some frogs."

I was in control now.

We walked towards the entrance to the exhibit and passed a half-opened door. "I bet that's where they catalog all this stuff." Paula stopped and stuck her head through. "Just a dark hallway with a couple of stacked boxes."

We waltzed over to the display of skeletal frogs, which were labeled with great detail. "Pretty much leaves nothing to the imagination, huh?"

She looked about as excited with the frogs as a kid would be with reading an encyclopedia on summer vacation.

She managed to swallow a yawn discretely.

"Museums do that to me, too," I said. "I don't know what it is. As soon as I enter, I start yawning. I think maybe it's the stale air."

"I always thought museums should be more interactive. You know, like have these frogs leaping all around this display."

"Actually, they have the insect zoo around the bend," I said. "You'll see lots of live things hopping and crawling around." I read all about it that morning. I picked up her hand. "They let you pick up a tarantula and hold it in the palm of your hand." I circled my finger around her palm, looking down at it, studying her calloused hand. "Wanna try?"

She just stared at me. She traveled her gaze down to my lips and back up again. "I have a better idea."

She led me back towards the cracked door. "Wait!" I skidded to a stop. "We could get arrested going in there."

"We're not going to get arrested. Trust me." She pressed us closer to the door.

"Paula, seriously, if we get caught…"

"Who's going to catch us?"

"There's security everywhere. They've probably got a camera on us right now." I scanned the corners of the room. I hated that everything had to be an adventure for her. What would we do? Travel down the halls and look in boxes to see unmarked skeletal systems?

She nuzzled up to my ear. "I need some alone time with you."

I liquefied right there in front of the life-sized poster of the warty frog. Suddenly, an afternoon in jail didn't seem all that bad a consequence. I trailed her into the dark hall and closed the door behind us.

Circled in black air, I shuddered when Paula's lips landed softly on my neck. She lowered me to the floor, propping me against some stacked boxes. Her lips caressed my skin as they traveled down the side of my neck and onto my collarbone. I tilted my head back and invited her to explore down further.

"Now isn't this worth it?" she asked.

I'd risk a whole year in jail for five minutes alone with this woman.

She leaned into me and grazed through the opening of my v-neck, stopping just shy of my breast's curve. She moaned and traced my breast with breath so hot, it seriously could've melted the polar ice caps.

I ignited, glowing like red, hot coals. She continued to descend towards my nipple. When her mouth wrapped around it, my whole body pulsed. I steadied my head against the boxes and rode out each ripple bracing for the orgasm.

Her moaning intensified.

I was so close, right there teetering on the edge of pleasure. I reached out for it. It teased me, lying right there within my grasp. There I went, full force ahead running for that euphoric cascade of delight.

But, then, her tongue stopped mid-flick.

"Oh God, please don't stop," I mumbled, reaching desperately for my orgasmic fix.

She slapped the floor behind my butt and then shot up on her knees, squealing like a cornered pig in a pen being chased by fifty hungry men. "There's a snake crawling behind you." She scrambled over my legs and tore the door open, still squealing.

A mother, father and their two kids stared down at us with open-mouths. I kicked the door shut.

"I'm sure it's not a snake." I wrestled to keep her from opening the door again.

"I've got to get out of here." She broke through my arms and ran out, leaving me standing in the dark with one boob resting on the edge of my v-neck. I shoved it back in my bra and steadied my shaking as best I could.

So this was what the ole' blue ball syndrome felt like to a guy? I seriously contemplated closing the door and finishing the job myself. I needed the release in a bad way.

I searched the wall for the light switch. I flicked it on and looked at the ground. A cable. A stupid cable.

Paula was still grappling for air by the salamander case when I brought out the piece of cable. "Here's your snake."

She smiled weakly at me and bowed her head. "I just assumed," she stammered. "We were in amphibian and reptile territory, in the dark. Just seemed logical under the circumstances."

I didn't care that the family stared at us from a distance like we were a couple of hoodlums from the streets. I hugged her right out there in the open, enjoying the rare moment when someone was actually more afraid of something than me.

Okay, now she was even more adorable than I'd ever thought possible.

Chapter Nine

Paula and I weren't the only ones having fun in Washington. We met the gang on the top floor of the rotunda at the exit to the IMAX. Owen bounced towards me claiming that he now wanted to be an Oceanographer. Last week he already had his admissions essay worked out in his brain for the Naval Academy because he was sure he was supposed to be the first man on Mars.

"Who wants to go to the Air and Space Museum?" Chuck asked the gang.

"But we didn't get to see the insect zoo," Owen said.

"We can come back here tomorrow," Chuck said. "You're going to love the Air and Space. They have a flight simulator ride."

"Let's do it, then." Paula led the group forward and everyone followed like a herd of sheep. Chuck quickly caught up to her and took over the lead.

My feet began to throb. According to my map, the Air and Space was at least a ten minute walk. I wanted to punch Chuck.

He just strutted forward like he owned the nation's capitol. We walked dutifully behind him like idiots marching behind our leader. Didn't anyone else feel like dropping to their feet and plopping in the plush carpeted lawn? The smell of hotdogs and pretzels begged me to stop and indulge. By then, even Amber lagged behind him limping ever so slightly on her right foot, because her left ankle was bleeding.

If me and Paula went to Massachusetts and got married, she'd be family.

Too bad at the start of life we didn't get a catalog to take along with us. It would be like the Sear's Wish Book I used to browse to tell Santa what I wanted for Christmas. Instead of circling dolls with growing hair or tea sets with pretty pink cups and saucers, I'd choose a sunny, fall day on the coast of P-Town where Owen walked me down an aisle lined with my smiling friends and family right into the arms of Paula. I'd be wearing a gorgeous, fitted wedding gown and my hair would cascade down my open back in loose tendrils adorned with Baby's Breath and miniature roses. I'd turn the page of this catalog and then circle a Cape Cod house with a bay window where my four boxer dogs would wait for me or Owen or Paula to come home. Oh yeah, and I'd circle the most important thing of all—a lifetime with the woman who adored me for who I was. She wouldn't try to change me. She'd take care of me and understand when I wanted to sit out, and not be repulsed that certain things freaked me out a little.

Amber's baby voice snapped me out of my blissful reverie. "My feet are killing me."

"Well, we could just stop and rest on a bench if you want and catch up with them in a few minutes."

Relief brightened Amber's pained face. She cupped her hands to her mouth and yelled up to Chuck. "We'll meet you in there."

Chuck just waved back at her and marched onwards. Paula scooped her head back and I waved her forward, too.

We parked ourselves on a bench overlooking miles of grass that extended from the capitol building to the Jefferson Memorial. A group of college students flung a Frisbee back and forth with great precision. Then a beagle sniffed at us as he walked by with his owner, wagging his tail like the propeller on Chuck's plane.

"I love dogs," I said to Amber.

"Me, too. We want to get two of them when we get married. I want a small lap dog, and Chuck wants a Rottie. The only thing is trying to figure out a way to have two dogs with all the traveling we plan to do. We take off quite a bit. And now, with Paula maybe moving to California, we're never going be home. We'll have paradise calling us. We'll probably move there if she takes the job. I can't imagine Chuck without Paula. That'd be like Joey without Chandler. There's a reason that Joey spin-off show never worked out. Now if they had cast Chandler on it, too, I bet they'd still have jobs."

I lagged a few sentences behind imagining Paula standing under a palm tree holding a glass of beer in one hand and a gorgeous Californian beauty in the other. "Did she say if she's seriously considering packing up and moving there?"

"Well, of course. I mean, who wouldn't jump at the chance? It's California."

"Paula hasn't mentioned anything more about it," I said.

"How do you feel about her moving there?"

"I haven't thought about it too much." I fidgeted, my lie tripping out of my mouth.

"It's a great opportunity for her. It's triple in salary what she makes now."

"Triple?" How could I compete?

"Six figures." Amber cocked her head to the side to drive home the winning point.

"Paula doesn't strike me as someone motivated by money," I said. "I mean she'd be so far away from everyone she knows. She can't just pick up the phone at ten o'clock at night and catch up with Chuck, you know? It'd be like what? One o'clock in the morning here?"

Amber stared straight ahead, unwilling to make eye contact. "Chuck wants this for her. She's dreamed of California her entire life. She sees her life there. Athletic director, gosh, it doesn't get any clearer that this is the right decision for her. She's born for that role. What she does here with some of those troubled middle school kids is admirable, but hardly a good enough reason to stay."

What about budding love for a reason to stay? People couldn't go around placing price tags around the neck of love. What good was money without having someone to share it with? That'd be like wearing a diamond necklace with a t-shirt from a 5-K road race.

"That'd be really hard on the kids," I said, in a way that almost accused Amber of being unreasonable and downright mean.

"Hard on *you*, you mean?"

No one had ever bitch-slapped me across the face before, but I was pretty sure that Amber just did. "Why would you say that?"

Amber continued to stare ahead, like the Frisbee game was more exciting than Tiger Woods shooting the last hole of the U.S. Open. "We're just looking out for Paula's best interest."

Was I not in Paula's best interest? "I think Paula's a grown woman who can make reasonable choices on her own." I stood up. I didn't like Amber anymore. She was burying her red claws into my life, my business, and I wasn't about to let her mess it up.

"Are you willing to pack up and move to California?" Amber asked.

Was this girl crazy? Heck no. "Maybe."

* *

I strolled up to the group. "Where's Amber?" Chuck asked.

"She's still out there on the bench."

Chuck studied my face. "She said something to you, didn't she?"

"We talked, yeah."

"What did she say?" Chuck's face softened. He placed his hand on my shoulder. I always wanted a big brother like him. I wanted to cry suddenly and warn him his fiancé was the devil with flamethrowers for eyes. I wanted to warn him that he was about to marry a psycho who would probably stomp on an injured bird just for kicks.

"I don't want to talk about it right now." I circled my head around the foyer. "Where's the bathroom?"

He pointed straight ahead. "We'll wait here for you."

What a nice guy. Amber didn't deserve him. "I'll catch up with you all. Where are you going to be?"

"We're going to ride the simulator!" Owen leapt forward at me barely missing my toes.

Great.

* *

I splashed some cool water on my face in the bathroom. No amount would erase the fact that I was a big liar. I was a walking nerve bomb afraid of those very things that thrilled Paula most. I don't think we could've been any more opposite.

* *

A few minutes later, I found the group huddled in front of the ropes to the simulator entrance. Amber hung onto Chuck's arm like he was a mink coat she was showing off. She snubbed my smile, looking out over my shoulder at the wall behind me.

I decided I could never like her.

"Ride with me?" Paula asked.

I examined the series of simulators lined up against the wall. Suddenly Owen pulled me down to his level and whispered, "Jake said if you close your eyes you won't feel like you're flying."

I craned my neck out to swallow more freely. I smiled weakly at Paula ready to tell her that unless she had a little magic pill in her pocket that would knock me unconscious, she'd be flying solo. But before I could dig up my voice, Paula ran off to the ticket counter to buy our tickets. Chuck followed.

Amber stood there looking like a broken teacup.

"You're going to really get on it, Mom?"

"Hell no. You can go in my place," I said to him.

A mocking smile crept on Amber's face. "You're afraid to fly, aren't you?"

"No," I said. "I just don't feel like it."

Paula came back before I could answer.

"Ready to ride?" Paula asked me.

A playful flicker sparked in Amber's eyes. "I think she's too scared."

"Scared?" Paula asked me.

"Of course not," I said, flicking Amber anything but a playful spark. I'd just close my eyes through the whole ride. My feet would only be twelve inches off the ground. How bad could it be? "I'm ready when you are."

* *

Some people craved alcohol, others pasta and bread. I never in my wildest dreams thought I'd wind up craving a woman who craved thrills. But, yep, there I was kicking my pace into high gear to keep up with her as we headed up to this simulator thingy that would soon toss me backwards forwards, sideways, and from the looks of the one all the way to the far corner, upside down.

My stomach dropped, and I hadn't even stepped foot onto the ride's platform.

Paula stepped up the stairs first to have a look around our new home for the next five minutes of my tortured life. Anything for love right?

I hated this.

I looked back at Owen before reaching up for Paula's hand and he shrugged and pointed his mouth into a funny lopsided wave. He squeezed his eyes shut and opened them fast and nodded at me. That was his last piece of advice to me before the simulator door shut and swallowed me up whole.

I had spent years trying to avoid this very, vulnerable state I now so easily, and stupidly, put myself in. I'd flown only a couple of times and became the first person in the history of the planet to ever nearly drive my nails through the arms of an airplane seat. The first time, my trip to Disney World with my favorite Aunt Lou and cousin Vinny, didn't go so well. Vinny tried his best to prepare me. But, he left out the all important part about when the landing gear receded back inside the belly of the plane. There we were, a few thousand feet hovering mysteriously above Providence and this loud, grumbling noise shook the floor below me like an angry tummy churning out some bad beans. My first attack was born literally out of thin air.

My friend Lilly from fourth grade tried to explain what it felt like to have the air sucked out of my lungs and to feel like I was about to die, but until my world turned upside down that day thirty-thousand feet in the air, Lilly might as well have been telling me a fairytale. My first attack was much more gruesome, sort of like *The Shining* on steroids.

137

We took the train back from Florida.

Two more times after that nightmare, I somehow ended up back in the air. My grandmother insisted I mount that bird one more time to ruffle up the feathers of fear and shake them for good. Yeah, right. That didn't go so well. The plane hit what Gran had called "a pocket of air" and I immediately hit the bathroom and locked myself in there for the remainder of the three-hour flight to Fort Myers. Clinging to the miniature sink, and under fire from the pounding of fists against the door from the flight crew, I braced for death and screamed with every "pocket of air" they bumped into that very bad day.

I had warned my Gran.

I rode a bus home that time.

Then, finally, when I was ten, my parents tricked me into flying again. On the morning of the family trip to Bar Harbor, my mom gave me one of the little blue pills that she took every morning with her coffee along with another mysterious pill. They told me we were driving to Maine and that the pills would help me sleep on the ride.

Well, they lied.

I woke up strapped to an airplane seat and floating by a group of clouds.

"See, it's no big deal, sweetheart," my mom said to me with a smile more fake than Joan Rivers plastic face.

Yeah, "no big deal" if I was hanging out poolside showing off my new bikini, not suspended in mid-air gasping for my last breath. The flight attendant actually had to radio the captain to tell him a passenger needed immediate emergency assistance. To the dismay of the two-hundred other passengers that day on route to fill up on fresh Maine lobsters, the captain turned the plane around and landed back in Providence to dump me off on the gurney waiting curbside for me.

To that day, I had no idea how a camera crew from Channel Twelve Eyewitness News got wind of the breaking story. One would have thought Elvis came back to life with the sea of microphones huddling around my mouth like an NFL football team at the start of Super Bowl Sunday.

I landed on the television screens of millions that night as the girl who ruined flight 626 because of a panic attack.

Scarred.

For life.

Now, staring at the control panel of this simulator ride, I prayed for mercy. I looked over at Paula whose big grin stretched across her face. "This is going to be so cool." She wriggled in her seat like a restless kid in church on Easter Sunday waiting for Mass to just end so she could go pluck Easter eggs from the grass outside.

"Ready for some thrills?" she asked.

I wanted to throw up.

Fucking Amber.

* *

The ride hadn't even started rocking and my head whirled. I smiled weakly at Paula. As the ride warmed up, a runway burst onto the screen in front of us. The scene felt so real. Even in my peripheral vision, I could see a fake building to my right and planes parked alongside the runway waiting their turn to take off into the all-too-real blue sky. A breeze blew at us and suddenly, the seat bolted backwards and vibrated. We were racing down the runway full force, heading towards a group of trees. Just moments before we reached the end of the runway, the plane took off, and the ride titled backwards, spilling the blood out of my head in an instant.

I squeezed my eyes shut, but still felt like I was suspended mid-air. The ride rolled side to side as the plane shot up. The growling tummy of the undercarriage, the shimmying, the pockets of air were all there to capture the reality.

My head spun out of control. I opened my eyes and looked down at the control panel. I couldn't see. Everything blurred like I was sitting in a bowl of water looking out at the world. I tried to grasp onto something, anything, for balance, but my hands were soaked in sweat and slipping from the plastic.

My heart pounded too. The air thinned. I couldn't get any of it in my lungs, just small little squirts. I gulped, pressing my eyes shut again and concentrating on taking in small, deep breaths. But, I was overloaded like a badly wired circuit. I shook violently and could only manage shallow gasps.

Suddenly, Paula hooted and flipped the machine over in a mid-air somersault.

I hurled out a blood-curling scream. "Stop! Get me out of here!"

She continued flipping over and over again, laughing like the evil Wizard.

I clawed at the door handle, yanking at it, willing it to pop open, still screaming as loud as my vocal chords would allow. My life depended on it. I was going to die.

I broke out into hysterical, convulsive cries for mercy. "Please stop! I'm not kidding. Get me out." Then, finally, I screamed, "Stop the fucking machine!"

And just like that, she dropped her hands from the controls and held them up like a suspected criminal in a raid. "You okay?"

I held my throat and wrestled to breath. "Not feeling well."

After that, everything went black and fuzzy. The next thing I knew, a group of strangers stared down at me, one slapped a wet cloth across my forehead. Someone lifted my head and forced me to drink water, which of course, spilled down the front of my white shirt.

Paula leaned in and kissed my forehead. "What happened to you?"

I propped up on my elbows and bit my lip trying to find the right way to break into the truth of who I was really. "I don't think I'll ever be getting back on one of those again."

She didn't say anything. She just stared at me confused like I just told her I was from Mars.

* *

We walked back to the hotel room in silence. Even Amber managed to keep her trap closed and eyes pointed straight ahead. Paula marched ahead of me kicking rocks. She had no clue what I was going through on that ride. We'd never be happy together. I'd just hold her back. I would never be that adventurous partner always in search for the next adrenaline high. I was done pretending. I was who I was, just as clearly as she was who she was. I'd put the truth out there for her and let her choose.

If she wanted to get her fix riding in a simulator ride every day for the rest of her life that was her choice. It would never be mine. If she wanted to toss herself off a cliff with a parachute attached to her back, then so be it. It didn't make any difference to me or change my view of her in the least bit. I couldn't imagine she'd feel the same.

If I understood Paula, I'd bet she'd try to fix me. I hated when people thought they could. From the height she was giving those rocks, I could tell she was combing her mind for ideas on how she could do just that.

"Hey, what the hell happened back there?" Chuck snuck up from behind me, hushing his voice to a whisper.

I was so tired of pretending to be this super brave woman afraid of nothing. So what if I was afraid to fly? Paula was afraid of a silly snake. That didn't make her any less of a woman to me. "I don't like rides." There I said it.

"Amber told me you're afraid to fly."

I wanted to chop off all of Amber's hair and flush it down the toilet where it belonged. I wanted to hurt her, not in a twenty-years-to-life type way. I just wanted to have a little fun at her expense. Make her whimper like she stubbed her toe really hard on the edge of her bureau. "She's a smart one." I couldn't hold back on the sarcasm.

"So, she's right?"

I hated her.

"Yes. Okay. I am deathly afraid to fly and have tried all the techniques out there to get over it. I've read books. Tried hypnosis. Talked to people. Watched a special on Oprah. None of it works."

"Lots of people are afraid to fly. Amber was, too, until I coaxed her up in my plane."

"Well, good for Amber."

"I can help you."

"Absolutely not."

"You'll come around." Chuck swung an arm around my shoulder and picked up our pace. "You can't hang with the McKennas and not fly."

My stomach dove deep. "I'm not going up in the air."

"Wanna bet?" In one motion, Chuck swept me into the air and up over his shoulder and started running.

I couldn't breathe I was laughing so hard. "I'm serious. I'm not!" I punched his back and kicked my feet. He just kept running with me and all I kept thinking was how much I'd miss him if he wasn't around.

* *

Okay, so maybe Amber wasn't too terrible of a bitch after all. When Chuck begged Paula to have a drink at the bar with him, Amber stepped up and offered to not only watch their kids, but also to watch Owen and Jake while I took a bath. My legs throbbed and the only salvation was hot water and an aspirin.

I believed my panic attack scared the life out of her. Owen confessed that she told him she thought I was dead when I was lying there on the floor at the foot of the simulator. Death can have that effect on people. I'd seen it turn a stone-cold man into a gentle one when I was in hairdressing school. My instructor, Mr. Arnold, was the meanest instructor in the school. We swore he was the devil himself. He'd whack my knuckles with a comb when I wound my roller sets wrong. And once, he made Aziza bleed when he was demonstrating how not to cut someone's cuticles. Even when Aziza screamed in horror at her bloody finger, he showed no emotion. But, the day he received a phone call that his beloved sister died in a car accident, he softened like a stick of butter in a pile of warm mashed potatoes. After that, he spoke with a soft breeze and a delicate smile pursed on his face. He even tossed compliments around the clinic floor.

So, I was a firm believer that the near thought of death could change a person.

As I relaxed into the pool of suds, I immediately laid my head back against my bath pillow and forgot all about the day's fiasco. I thought of Paula and how great her legs looked in her shorts. I loved the way her calves curved when she walked and the way her ass bobbed back and forth in perfect rhythm with each step she took. I wondered how she would taste and how soft the skin between her legs would feel against my lips.

I grabbed a handful of bubbles. They smelled like lilacs and felt like silk on my fingertips. I could've really gone for a glass of wine, and oddly enough a cigarette, at that point.

I feathered another helping of bubbles in front of me.

If I could just make love to her, bring her over that edge of ecstasy, maybe she'd never leave. Maybe she'd accept me as I was with all my wacky fears. We'd turn into horny sex addicts towards each other, spending our mornings and nights tangled up together riding out the waves of euphoria.

Chapter Ten

Challenges of the human spirit always intrigued me. The more someone resisted, the more I couldn't help but to dig further. That didn't always work to my advantage. Like the time Pat Swift stormed through the front door at Bella and demanded someone fix her ruby-red roots or else suffer a curse. Now, most logical people would laugh at such a threat, chalking it up to some mental disorder, but the girls at Bella were a little more gullible. Pat told the girls that she was a witch, and everyone, including me, believed this to be true. In fact, I sensed Pat was fully armed and ready to toss her evil darts if someone didn't throw her down in a chair that second and plop some serious ash brown on those flame-throwing roots that the salon around the corner gave her.

Everyone, including Deogie scoured off into the break room, leaving me fending for a life free of Pat's curses all on my own. After all, Pat was suspected to be the one who destroyed the wax machine after Dolly, an esthetician, tore off one of her eyebrows by accident. An hour after Pat left, huddling her hand over her eye like a frantic pirate, the wax machine mysteriously boiled over, dribbling hot, molten wax all over the cart and tile floor below. The huge mess cost Aziza nine hundred bucks to clean up. Aziza should've been the one shaking up at the front desk, repelling Pat's negative force. Instead, she was the first one to plow through the back room doors to safety.

Thankfully, I managed to massage the lady's ego into submission. Pat left smiling and praising the ground I graced.

From that day forth, she proclaimed me to be safe under the sun for the rest of my life.

Maybe this proclamation was what lifted me off my seat on the bus ride home and head straight to the source of my angst. We were a quarter into the drive home, when I scooted up to where Chuck and Amber sat. "Hey, mind if I sit for a minute," I asked Chuck, cocking my head over to the empty seat next to Paula so he'd get the hint and move out of the way.

Thankfully he squeezed out of the seat. "Be nice," he whispered to me on his way past.

My whole goal was to be as nice as possible. To be the bigger person. To be Paula's first girlfriend to ever climb to the Mount Everest of winning Madam Amber's approval. But, befriending her would no doubt be harder than anything.

I'd swallow my pride and curse words and rise to the challenge. I'd break through the ice and plunge naked into her frigid world if that's what it took. Okay, maybe not naked, but I'd at least attempt to be sincere in my efforts nonetheless.

I slid into the seat beside Amber and smiled. "Thanks for watching the boys last night."

"I only did it because Chuck promised me a massage later on."

"Still, thank you."

"I talked to Chuck last night and he told me he's going to help you get over your fear of flying. I think that's great that you're going to try."

Oh boy. Amber attempted to connect to me in a natural, unforced and nice way. She actually looked pretty in that moment. Our connection was as fragile as a cotton ball on the edge of a windy rooftop ledge, nevertheless a connection.

Keeping the air as still as possible between us, I simply did the bigger thing and forced my mouth into a smile.

"I know we kind of got off to a rough start yesterday. Can we start over again?" I asked.

Amber took a deep breath and looked down. "Look, don't take this the wrong way, but I'm not sure we could ever be good friends. We're too different. Let's just keep it casual and I think we'll be good."

I laughed. I couldn't possibly tell her to go fuck herself the way I really wanted. So, I settled on making the first fake move. "Sure thing. It was great talking to you."

My teeth were still grinding together by the time I kicked Chuck back to his spot near his ungodly, inhumane, beast of a girlfriend. "She's all yours. Nice and warmed up for you, just the way you probably like her."

Chuck rolled his eyes. "She'll come around." He got up and went back to his seat. Paula just smiled, laughing to herself.

"I don't think she likes me." My teeth pressed into each other so hard, I swore my fillings would pop.

"You are even cuter when you're angry." Paula weaved her fingers around mine. "When do I get to be alone with you again after this?"

I quivered. I couldn't remember ever wanting someone as much as Paula. I just sat there for a few moments staring into her eyes, drinking her up, when her cell rang.

She smirked before reaching into her pocketbook to grab it. "It's from California."

In an instant, my throat dried up like a prune, making it very hard for me to swallow. She looked ready to sprint out a few cartwheels down the aisle.

"Hi, this is Paula McKenna... Yes... Absolutely I can make myself available." She looked up at me, her eyes nearly popping out of their sockets. "Sure, Friday, noon sounds great. Okay, great. I'm looking forward to it, too. Thanks for calling. I'll talk to you Friday."

All of a sudden, she sprang to her feet, hitting her head on the roof, and not even flinching. "Chuck, Friday! I've got a phone interview with the vice president. I made it to the finals."

Chuck popped up like a thermometer on turkey breast. "Awesome, sis." He reached out to high-five her.

A smile rested on the corners of her lips. She finally pulled me in tight, clinging to me.

"Wow. The finals?! That's great!" I lifted my voice high enough to keep it from shaking under the sudden explosion of sadness that threatened to swallow it whole. "This could become a reality, huh?"

Paula beamed as if plugged into an electrical outlet. She could have quite literally lit up the city of Providence with the voltage coursing through her. "Wow. I'm dumbfounded. I honestly didn't think this was possible. My last phone interview was well over a month ago. Then nothing. I just assumed I was out of the running." She bent forward and exhaled, assuming the position of a crash landing. "I don't know what to do with all this excitement right now. I feel like hanging my head out the window and screaming out to the world how awesome a day it is. Imagine, southern California? Palm trees, flowers, sunshine, ocean, year round. Walk out the front door into seventy-degree weather every day."

"Huh, yeah, imagine that," I said, stupefied that no one else seemed concerned that California was about to soak up Paula McKenna for good. The kids just kept on playing with their handheld video games, ears plugged with white iPod earbuds, and Chuck and Amber bounced in their seats probably planning their first reunion trip.

* *

"I'll have a grilled cheese with a tomato, please," I said to the waitress, not taking my eyes from the happy couple in front of me. How could Aziza really think it was okay to invite Tania? Especially when I called her crying.

"And I'll take a Reuben on rye, please," Tania said. "Hold the fries. Instead could I have a side of carrots?"

The waitress nodded.

What a dichotomy. Eating carrots with one hand and smoking a cigarette with the other. Disgusting. I thought my stomach couldn't turn anymore until Aziza lit a cigarette, too. "Still?" I asked her.

Aziza took a long drag and shook her head. As disgusting as smoking was, for some reason, pretty girls like Aziza looked damn sexy with a cigarette between their lips. How was that possible? And how was it that the longer I smelled it, the more I wanted to join in the smoke fest? Seemed everyone sitting at the sidewalk tables in front of Hal's lit up that morning, except for me.

I dunked my spoon in my coffee and twirled the Splenda around. I sipped it slowly, savoring the fresh aroma of coffee beans under my nose.

"Tania's leaving for Chicago tomorrow and wanted to meet you before she left. She's touring the midwest coast for three weeks before coming back to record her next album. Isn't that exciting?"

Through the smoke and haze, I could see a real smile on my best friend's face. They truly looked infatuated with each other. Tania caressed her face before kissing her lips. "I'm going to miss you so much," She said to Aziza.

I didn't hate Tania nearly as much as I thought I would. It helped that Aziza glowed next to her.

"I was even thinking of going out to her show next weekend. Think you could handle the salon for that Saturday?" Aziza asked me.

A pang of jealousy lopped me in the gut. Aziza found love and would get to keep it. I would soon turn into the third wheel. "Of course."

"Aziza tells me you have quite an adorable son," Tania said.

I couldn't help what came out. Call it impulse. Call it anger. Call it fear on some level. "Did she also tell you who his soccer coach is?"

"Of course. He's in great hands."

Great hands? Is that how she felt about Paula still? "Did she also tell you I'm in great hands with her, too?"

Talented, smoking-hot Tania's mouth gaped open.

Aziza kicked me under the table, causing me to double over in pain. I hung my head on the table and rubbed my shin, fully accepting the punishment for the cheap shot. The cheap shot clearly needed to be taken, though.

"It's okay, honey," Tania said to Aziza. "It's understandable." Tania placed her hand on my shoulder. "I'm in love with Aziza, not Paula. I hope that this isn't going to be weird between us."

Her sweetness sneaked in and derailed me.

What could I say to this? She loved Aziza. My best friend deserved this for once. I peeled my eyes up towards Tania. "I'm sorry. That was really rotten of me."

"I totally understand." Tania stole her hand back from my shoulder and extended her hand. "Hi, I'm Tania, and I'm crazy about your best friend."

I laughed and shook her hand. "It's nice to meet you, and also nice to see my best friend happy for a change."

The waitress came back over to refill my coffee. "The sandwiches will be out in a few minutes," the waitress said. "The cook didn't see my slip with the order."

"No problem," Tania said to her. "Can I get a coffee, too?"

The waitress slipped away and Aziza got up to go to the bathroom. "Got to use the little girl's room. Sure you two can handle each other on your own?"

I rolled my eyes. "Just go."

Instinctively, I reached out for the pack of cigarettes. "If you can't beat 'em, join 'em, right?" I lit the cigarette. "Aziza's going to kill me one way or another. May as well be of something I can get a little buzz from."

"You shouldn't start. It's impossible to quit." Tania flicked ashes in the ashtray.

"I've always just been a social smoker. I can walk away from them no problem. Every once in a while I take a minute or two off my life. Big deal." I inhaled and questioned how true my statement really was. I found myself craving them more and more.

"I was hooked by my second one," Tania said. "I was fifteen."

"Did Paula smoke, too?"

"Paula?" she laughed. "Listen. If you're really serious about making it work with her, don't ever let her see you smoke."

I sucked another drag and let it linger deep in my lungs. This would be my last cigarette I decided right then and there.

I didn't need any more obstacles fencing us off from each other. I crushed out the cigarette and wiped my hands clean signifying the end of a nasty indulgence.

* *

Later that day, when Paula called and said she had some great news she needed to share, I assumed the worst. And the fact that Owen stole Paula to play a game of Guitar Hero the moment she walked through the door, only agitated my fragile state to the point I contemplated dropping to my knees and begging her to just tell me the freaking great news already. I looked over at Aziza who continued her Sudoku game.

With the guitar strapped over her shoulder, Paula hit every note on the expert level. She was so damn brilliant at the game that she even managed to look over at me a few times and wink and still win.

I couldn't hit three notes in a row on the easy level.

Before long, Aziza settled her Sudoku book down on the sofa and began humming the melody to *Stairway to Heaven*.

"So want to hear the great news?" Paula asked us mid-way through the chorus.

I nodded coolly trying my best to not snatch her by the shoulders and shake the news right out of her.

"I went to Seven Eleven today to buy a caramel latte and came out a thousand dollars richer on a scratch off ticket."

"Wow!" Owen screamed out, jumping up and down with his guitar in hand. Paula laughed and joined him in a high-pitched cheer. I couldn't control the urge to jump either. The three of us suddenly used the carpeted floor as a trampoline. We totally clinched the essence of a happy family unit. Meanwhile, Aziza went back to crunching numbers into a row.

"What're you going to do with it?" I asked, breathlessly.

"Spoil my two favorite people in the world." Paula landed in squat position and looked up at Owen. I felt warm inside suddenly.

"First, tonight, I'm going to spoil your mom by taking her out for some fun. Then I was thinking maybe you and I can go buy you a new bike sometime this week."

"Are you serious?" Owen danced around in a circle flinging his arms overhead like he was doing the wave.

"Where are you taking Lauren tonight?" Aziza asked, looking up at Paula over the rims of her glasses.

"Wherever she wants."

I scanned Paula's bootlegged jeans and fitted tee and decided to indulge in McCormick and Schmick's another night. "I feel like playing pool."

"Pool?" Aziza asked.

"Pool it is." She dropped her guitar on the couch.

I reached for the keys, not giving Aziza a second to destroy a great suggestion.

I kissed the top of Owen's head and hugged Aziza before grapping my jacket and heading towards the door. "Be good," I told Owen.

"Have fun ladies," Aziza called out after us.

Oh, we would.

She opened the passenger door for me. "Want to go to Hannigan's down by the beach?"

"Sure, I haven't been there in years."

I sunk into the convertible's leather seat and swung my legs inside. She bent down and kissed me with fresh minty breath. "You look gorgeous as usual."

Oh, sweet, God, I prayed this would be *our* night.

We rode down the interstate towards Narragansett. Paula hit the gas with some force, weaving in and out of traffic. Adrenaline pumped through me—a brand new, wonderful feeling. Paula maintained control with the agility of a race car driver, and with only one hand on the wheel. She smelled like woodsy cologne and looked extremely sexy. Her hair fell messy around her face. She wore a simple pair of trendy, dark-wash blue jeans and a crisp, white button down shirt that showed off just enough of her bosom to spark my body into overdrive.

Once we arrived at the restaurant, we headed straight for the bar. "Want to just eat here and take in the sights?" she asked.

I nodded and climbed up on the stool.

"Want to do a shot?" she asked.

"I don't know. I'm not—"

Paula scoffed and waved the bartender over. "In honor of successful gambling feats!"

"Alright, but just one."

When our shots arrived, I gulped it down, then bit into the lemon wedge. I buzzed instantly, floating in a peaceful trance with a drunken grin on my face. I laced my hand around her and stared into her eyes. "Is this what you had in mind for some alone time?"

She massaged her fingers into my palm then lifted them, entwined, up to her mouth. "We're getting warm." Her lips brushed them, then she nibbled just enough to send a series of shivers up and down my spine.

The bartender arrived back with our burgers, two frosty mugs and a frothy pitcher of beer.

Paula poured us each a glass.

Too numb to appreciate the burger, I took three bites and pushed the plate aside. Next thing I knew, I needed a refill, but first I had to pee.

"I'm gonna head to the little girls' room."

I slid off my stool and the rush of alcohol flowed straight to my head. I latched onto the stool. When I took a few steps, the room began to spin again. I slid my fingers along each available railing until the hallway wall was within reach. I had to pee badly. Even if I had to crawl on the floor, I'd get there.

Next thing I knew, I arrived back at the stool and she was pulling me towards a pool table in the far corner of the room. "Looks like we have the whole corner to ourselves."

I cradled my beer mug between my hands and watched as she racked the balls. I walked over to her and hugged her, breathing in her tantalizing scent. She handed me the white ball. "Show me what you've got."

I clasped onto my stick and plucked the ball from Paula's hand. "What are we playing for?"

"Whoever wins gets to dare the other person to do something."

"You say that like you've already thought this through."

She held the glass up to my lips. "Just take another sip."

I licked the foam from my lips, before spinning off to the table. My first shot barely broke the rack. The balls dispersed as small clusters only two inches from their starting position.

She placed her beer down. "That striped ball in the corner pocket."

I swallowed more beer and watched her sink four more balls.

"Better catch up," she said when it was my turn.

I played pathetically, while Paula showed off.

155

When I finally sunk a solid ball, she picked me up and swung me around. We giggled and fell to the floor. I had to grab hold of the pool table leg to get up. And when I finally rose, I realized she had already walked back over to our table and began capping off my beer again.

I swallowed a mouthful. "I don't see you drinking as much beer." I moved closer to her. "In fact, I think you're trying to make me drunk."

She shot me a half smile, then lined up her stick for the final shot of the eight ball. She leaned over the table to get in real close. I drank in the beautiful sight of her two plump boobs, which were nicely cradled into a cream bra.

She took her sweet time, wiggling this way and that way, teasing me until she finally caved and took the shot. She tapped the stick to the ball and watched as her eight ball glided towards the open pocket.

I leaned against my stick and closed my eyes, feigning disappointment, but very interested in hearing the dare.

She hugged me from behind, and whispered "I won." Her breath sent chills down my neck.

I faced her. "What do you dare me to do?"

She moved in closer. "You can start with kissing me."

I kissed her softly and when I moved back she pulled me back and kissed me with hunger, coming up for air only to say, "Let's get out of here."

Once outside, we stumbled onto the beach and trudged through the sand, giggling and clinging to each other. The light from the houses along the beachfront swayed and the dried up seaweed tangled at my feet, pricking my sandaled foot like tiny needles. Normally, I'd be inspecting every inch of sand before stepping in it. That night I could've been walking in seagull droppings and cigarette butts and wouldn't have skipped a beat.

I stopped in front of a lifeguard chair and pressed her against one of its stilted legs, kissing her with intensity. I wanted her right then.

"What do you dare me to do?" I asked her.

She pushed me up. "I want you to make love to me."

I caught my breath. "I thought you'd never ask."

"Let's go someplace a little more private," she said.

I leaned on her as she guided me towards the dunes. My heart raced. Further away from the water, I tripped over a mound of soft sea grass and landed face down in the sand. She climbed on top of me and rolled me over until we were face to face.

I closed my eyes and enjoyed each warm, moist lap of her tongue on my skin. My body pulsed under her touch. She slid her hands up my back and removed my tank top. Her fingers moved slowly around my waist and undid the top button of my jeans. I pulsated as she slid them off of me.

I reached up and buried my hands in her hair, enjoying her hot breath on my chest. I moaned with each lick, each nibble.

She tempted me like a forbidden fruit, dangling in front of me just begging to be plucked and gobbled up in a mad frenzy. I rolled her over and straddled her. I pulled off her shirt, not caring whether I broke any buttons as I slipped off her bra with my teeth. "My turn to feast."

I wrapped my lips around her hard nipple and sucked, grazing my tongue along it as I brought it deeper into my mouth. I traveled back and forth between her breasts, unable to satisfy my hunger. I wanted more. I propped up on my knees, lifting her up to me. Our tongues tangoed once again. I shook, grinding my body up against hers, crying out for more.

She teased me by backing away. I latched onto her and pulled her closer. I wanted her in a savagery way. I pulled her close until I could feel her wild heart beat and hot breath on my face.

She lifted me on top of her naked lap, facing her. With our breasts touching, she gently slid her fingers deep inside me and watched my body rise and fall under the moonlight.

I never, ever felt anything like this.

Still craving more, I pinned her against the grass again. My lips traveled down her until they landed in the moist, succulence between her legs. We fit together like a jigsaw puzzle, each serving up pleasure to the other in one mind-blowing wave after another. The more she moaned, the more I feasted, devouring her inch by ravenous inch.

The thrill ride edged far into the night, unadulterated, remote from the rest of mankind.

* *

As the sun started to rise above the water's edge, Paula rolled over and showered me with soft kisses. We were still naked. And I didn't care. She hugged me close and whispered, "That was the most amazing night of my life."

I moaned softly. "Mine, too."

We kissed again, and suddenly I straddled her once more, leading her hand into my wetness, wanting one more taste of ecstasy before going back to reality.

The moment was like I'd always dreamed right down to the dreamy eyed stares we shared. Everything was perfect.

"Just promise me one thing," I said.

"What's that?"

"Promise me you'll stay here in Rhode Island with me and Owen."

Her eyes popped open, the stilts of reality carrying their weight. "That's tempting, but a little unrealistic."

"It was worth a shot." I giggled to camouflage my unease.

She stood up and put her crumpled-up clothes back on. "You can always come with me."

Chapter Eleven

A ray of sunshine poked at my eye the next morning, rudely waking me from my three hours of sleep. I climbed out of bed and dragged myself to the bathroom, dousing my face in cold water.

Once dressed, I sat on the edge of my bed and decided I'd indulge in a Dunkin Donuts coffee.

So, off I went to get my liquid rush, and once I downed several sips I began to wake up. I stared straight ahead over my dashboard at a group of bikers sipping coffee and devouring donuts alongside their chrome hogs. They laughed and nodded their bandana heads around. Not a care in the world. Obviously not tormented by bittersweet love like me. The only thing that got in their way was winter when they'd have to hibernate their noisy mufflers and ride out the five months on four wheels.

I sipped my coffee again. What was I going to do if she took that job? I wasn't going. I couldn't. If she wanted to be with me, she'd have to stay. I couldn't just uproot Owen. He had school, his friends, and sports. And of course, I also had indispensable things like a clientele that could easily fill the lingerie department of Sak's Fifth Avenue if lined up shoulder to shoulder with each other.

I'd never get on an airplane. Never. I could drive. But, then what about Aziza? We needed each other. Bad enough a flight took six hours. Driving would take days. I'd fall apart without her.

161

I drove, sipping my coffee. I passed Mel's Gardening and the Outer Limits Bowling Alley and turned onto the highway going north. I sped up past an old Mustang that sputtered oil and a smelly city bus. Sipping again, I glanced into my rearview mirror and watched the Providence Place Mall disappear as I traveled onto Interstate 146 towards Lincoln.

I should stop this before it went any further. Wasn't the job of lover to bring out the best in each other? I'd just destroy her life with my pathetic fears. And, she'd destroy mine with her need for adventure and change.

I kept driving and saw the sign for the airport and took the exit. Maybe if I watched enough planes taking off, my fear would blow away along with the white vapor in the sky.

I pulled in and parked my car, then walked around the main building to the runway. I dropped to the ground and sat against the building.

Maybe I should take Chuck up on his offer.

A plane barreled down the runway and shot up into the air, smooth and balanced like a model with strings attached. How could anyone enjoy that feeling of suspension? I'd rather face each day wearing clothes from a thrift shop than trust a hunk of metal to keep me up in the sky.

If I ever wanted to fit into Paula's world, I'd have to take Charlie up on his offer. Even if someone clubbed me over the head and knocked me out for the six hour flight, I'd have to do it again and again if I ever wanted to come back and visit Rhode Island, my home forever, if I ever wanted to be Paula's true partner.

Just then, a plane lowered to the ground and skidded, spewing black smoke and dust behind it. I gasped and jumped up not sure if I should run off or stay and watch the plane explode into oblivion. It didn't take but a few seconds for the plane to stop. I backed away from the building and the runway and ran off to my car.

I'd never fit into this world.

* *

In the day-and-a-half since our night of making love on the beach, me and Paula had talked to each other on the phone at least half a dozen times. Each time she started to make a reference to the California statement, I deftly sidestepped answering. Without fail, Owen would magically appear by my side asking for juice or help to a homework question. Just one of the perks of having kids.

But now that I sat face-to-face with her at a booth in Backdoor Diner, I couldn't hide behind my mothering..

"So, how did the interview go?" I finally asked unable to calm my nerves from an all out stake-out on my heart.

She scanned the menu, casting her eyes up at me and offering a wink. She looked back at the menu and studied it like it was the Holy Grail itself. "It's mine."

"Huh?" My head buzzed. I was pretty sure my heart stopped beating and all of my other vital organs demanded a full shut down of operations. "They offered it to you already?"

Paula chuckled. She shook her head from behind her menu. "Not exactly, but does having a really good feeling that the job is mine count?"

The waitress interrupted us, which was great because I needed a few seconds to stop my erratic heartbeat from running wild.

The lady's hair was wrapped into an unforgiving bun and her eyes sunk into her bruised sockets like a couple of rotten eggplants. "Can I take your order?"

"I'll just take two blueberry pancakes with a side of bacon," I said, then decided to add, "please."

163

"And, I'll have a mushroom and cheese omelet with extra Jalepeño peppers and a side of hash browns." Paula picked up our menus and handed them to the waitress.

"Do you want anything else?" She stuck her pen behind her ear as if to warn us we would've crossed the line if we requested more.

We both shook our heads and watched her stagger away.

"So, you were saying?" I asked her.

"I think they're going to offer it to me." She sat there with a gigantic grin beaming on her face, looking out of the window without a care in the freaking world, obviously in dreamland. Had she really thought this through enough? Palm trees and sunshine were nice, but what happened when Christmas came around and she was stuck sipping juice from a coconut all by herself?

"You really want this, don't you?" I asked, braving all to open the dialogue and hopefully knock some sense into her before she hopped a plane and left for good.

She lifted her hands out like two scales. "Let's take the two jobs. Here we have Sheffield Middle School in Rhode Island." She lowered her left hand. "Great school. Great kids. Great boss. I teach, coach, get summers off. Everything is pretty much in order." Then, she lowered her right hand. "And here we have the job offer in California. This school had a graduating class of fifty-four seniors this past year. This class started out with over seven hundred freshman."

"Not really making a case for yourself." I swallowed my shit-eating grin. "What happened to them all?"

"They dropped out," she said. "California may seem perfect to people like us who trudge through snow and ice five months out of the year, but it's got the same problems. They do drugs, they don't keep up with their schoolwork, they're in gangs, and they are facing the same issues as kids in any major city in the United States are."

"And you want to go teach and coach there?"

"Absolutely."

Okay, a simple yes would have made the point. I did my best to remain calm as I continued to listen to her insane reasoning.

"These kids need someone on their side. They start out with all this potential and then there's no one there to keep them rolling towards it. They need a leader."

"And you feel you're that leader?"

"Don't you?" she asked me.

"Well, yeah, but I mean..."

"I know it sounds rough, but I'm up for it. The former athletic director let their sports program slide so far out of control, they barely have enough players to make up a team. They need someone to go in there and take control and stir up excitement and rally for the kids."

Screw being supportive. I needed to squirt a dose of reality into her idealistic bubble. "You think sports is the solution? That six-hundred-plus kids will start attending school again because there's a soccer team now?"

"I'm not concerned with the big numbers," she said defensively, moving out of the way so the waitress could place her mushroom and cheese omelet in front of her. "I'm thinking about the ten kids that might start up drugs next year because they didn't have someone in their lives they could trust."

I followed her hands as she dropped and folded them neatly in front of her. I thought of Owen and how he could have gone either way with his choice of friends. Owen always acted accountable for his actions, due greatly in part to Paula. She expected great things from him and the other players, and not one of them wanted to let her down. She was like that silver lining for struggling single parents.

"What about the kids at Sheffield?"

"I think these other kids need me more."

Why couldn't she just be valiant by hammering a few floor boards into a Habitat house in Providence or guiding some troubled kids on an Outward Bound trip? She spoke like she already decided she'd move there without a solid offer in hand. Without considering me. "Are you going to have the resources to make the kind of changes that need making at this new school?"

"They've got the money; they just don't have the leadership. It's not a pretty picture I'll be walking into. But, that's the fun part of it for me. I'm bored. I need a challenge. I need more of a purpose."

"So toss a soccer ball in between a group of trigger happy teenagers?" I tried really hard to be open-minded. But, come on?

"You don't get it," she said, her voice hinging on anger, frustration.

"There's not a hell of a lot to 'get' here." My voice cracked. The tears started to well. "If you're going to give up a possible great future between us to go help a few misguided kids, then, you know what? Go save the fucking world, Paula."

I had about thirty seconds before the geyser of emotion would explode from me. That was just enough time for me to stand up from the table and walk out of the building. I collapsed in a blubbering heap on the side of the diner.

She followed me out and sat next to me. She grabbed my hand and gently tilted my chin up so that our eyes met.

"Lauren, I have to tell you something," she said, taking a deep breath. "When I was thirteen, my mom and dad divorced and fought over who would raise us. We'd spend two weeks at our dad's, then he'd drop us off on our mom's front lawn with our baggage, then no sooner would we make friends in school, and our mom would start back up on her coke. Then, it was back to dad's. I went to twelve different high schools. I had gang members holding me at knife point because they hated gays. I could have just as easily slipped into my mom's drug habit life to escape."

I stared at her in shock.

"Coach Davis saved our lives. He took us in like two of his own. We shared a dinner table with eight kids. It was great. He fed us, disciplined us, educated us. He taught us what a family was all about."

"No wonder you're such a great role model."

"This job is really important to me. I feel this need to give back everything Coach did for me. I can't sleep at night unless I know I'm making a difference in the lives of kids in need."

She proved that good things happen to good people. "How did you find out about this job?" I asked.

"A headhunter called me."

"Just out of thin air like that?" I sat up straighter.

"Poof, just like that." She snapped her fingers. "I just got done grading Teddy Scaglia's test, and still had ten more to go, when she called me."

"You even remember whose paper?"

"Are you kidding?" She placed her hands on top of mine. "It was the one of the most important calls of my life." Her eyes sprang open wide. "I don't want to lose you over this. I know it's a lot to ask for you to move there with me. But, I'm serious. I really want you to come with me."

I looked down. "You know I can't go. My life is here."

167

"People start over all the time. They pack up the U-Haul and off they go to a new life. People in California get their hair cut. There are schools for kids, better ones than the one I'm going to."

Oh God, how I wished I could be that person. I'd love to sit under a palm tree sipping from the same coconut with the love of my life.

"I wish I could just up and go."

She pulled my hands up and kissed them. "Do you realize how crazy I am about you?"

I smiled and stared into her eyes. "I feel the same way."

"I'm in love with you."

"You're in love with me?" Tears stung my eyes.

"Madly in love."

Okay, so maybe the dirt lot on the side of the diner wasn't the most idealistic place to profess our love for each other, but we could've been swimming in the middle of a shark tank, and it wouldn't have made a bit of difference. I knelt and rose up to kiss her. "I love you, too."

Her eyes twinkled under the orange light of the setting sun. "Then, please come."

I backed away. "I really can't."

"What are you afraid of?"

"It's a huge step."

Her chin quivered. She looked off in the distance and bit her lower lip. "Wow. I really thought this would be easier. I thought you'd be excited. I thought we'd start a life together. I know we haven't been together long, but I knew the night at Brown that I loved you."

I prayed endlessly for a moment like this to happen to me. "This has got nothing to do with how I feel about you."

"What else is so important, then? Aziza would be able to keep the salon under control. Owen is young and friendly, and he even asked if I could sneak him into my suitcase if I go. So what's the problem?"

"Everything I know is here. This is home."

She exhaled and shook her head. "That's not enough of a reason."

She stared at a crack in the sidewalk. I lifted her chin. She shook my hand away. The last thing I wanted was to make her feel like I didn't want to be with her. The excuse floated above us like some frivolous pollen ball. "I'm afraid to fly."

She snapped her eyes up to mine. "So, if you weren't afraid to fly, you'd come with me?"

"I'm not like you. I can't pretend that I'd ever enjoy flying around the world with you on your endless adventures. So, even if I get there by car, then what?"

"Look, I have to level with you," she said, "I'll always be there to support you through anything. But, I'll never nurture fear."

"I don't want your pity." My parents threw pity at me forever, which is why I didn't relocate to Maryland with them when my dad took a job with Andrews Air Force Base. They always dotted over me, afraid to break me, to rattle my nerves. No wonder I turned out to be such a freak.

"Please don't let your fear get in the way."

Snapping into defensive mode, I lashed out. "Yeah, well, you said yourself that you're afraid of snakes. I wouldn't expect you to pick one up and sling it around your neck."

"But, it's not like our relationship's future depends on me wearing a snake."

"Well, isn't it great that you're not the problem with us then?" I shook my head and watched as a couple with a young son walked by us, giving us a strange look as they walked in. "I'm sorry I'm a freak, Paula. But I've been like this my whole life, and I'm probably never going to change."

She darted her eyes back down to that crack again.

I wished I had a rewind button so we could've backed up to when we ordered blueberry pancakes and omelets again and just forget about all this serious stuff. My last statement sounded too final. It couldn't be final. I reached out to mess with her hair, lighten the load. "You need another haircut."

"Well, I'm not getting another one until you get on an airplane."

I laughed out loud. "You with unruly hair?"

"Nah," she said, "I have complete faith that you're too good of a stylist to let it get messy."

"You're serious aren't you?"

"Yup."

She rose and extended her hand to help me up. She dusted the back of my jeans and led me back inside the door. The hag of a waitress looked relieved that we hadn't chewed and screwed on her.

As we sat back down, I whispered and nodded towards the waitress. "You'll have hair like hers."

She laughed, caught up in the moment. We smiled at each other over our coffee mugs. Two women falling in love. Just like a scene right out of a Norman Rockwell painting. Add in the underlying tension that threatened our existence as a couple and suddenly we'd be Michelangelo's *David*, broken.

I was going to lose this woman.

* *

"How about this one?" Aziza pointed to the computer screen. "They say they can cure you in ten sessions, money back guaranteed."

"Yeah, but it's group therapy. I don't want to sit in front of a bunch of strangers and have to tell them about the time I accidentally flushed my Gran's roller down the toilet, and how that eventually screwed up my childhood because Gran had some weird attachment to that roller. Then, they're going to want me to talk about the day I started my period and how that made me feel. And worse, then they'll move to more perverse analysis by asking what made me gay. Then it'll come out that my mother reprimanded me for undressing in front of my friend when we were eleven and how she blames that harmless little bathing suit swap for making me gay. I'm not interested in group analysis or psycho analysis."

She rolled her eyes. "You're insane." She clicked onto Amazon's site.

"I'm not buying another book." I stood and walked away towards my station. "That last one was a bunch of psycho babble. It just made me hyperventilate."

I opened my drawer and dug out a brush and started to brush my hair straight. I reached for the blow dryer and shot the hot air onto my hair, blowing away the frizz. "And another thing," I said, hoisting the blow dryer in the air, "I'm not taking any magic pills. All they do is make me gain weight. The last thing I need is to prance around the white sandy beaches of California with a two inch slab of fat hanging over my bikini bottom because of my daily dose of happy pills."

"You're not just insane. You're ridiculous. Do I look like I carry a spare tire around my belly?"

I shut off the blow dryer. "No. But why would you? You don't take anti-anxiety pills."

She licked her upper lip. She did this whenever she was stressed. "Well, I mean, I… Oh, what's the freaking use? I take an anti-depressant. There. Now you know."

I placed the blow dryer in its holder. "For how long?"

"Since last year when Heather broke up with me and I went to see that psychiatrist."

"I knew you were sad about Heather, but a psychiatrist? And pills? You told me you were jogging to help you get over her. That's exactly what you told me."

"You're right. I told Ashley, I think. I needed her to pick up my prescription one day before the pharmacy closed." She traced her eyes around the ceiling as though plucking memories from the tiles above like fruit on a farmer's market stand. "Actually, no, I asked Kimber, the old receptionist."

"You told Kimber?"

"Yeah, Kimber." She chuckled. "She was a real winner, huh? Talk about your classic airhead. Anyway, she was on them, too."

"I don't understand why you didn't tell me."

"I think I was afraid you'd try to talk me out of it. You're not the easiest person to talk to about this stuff. You're a quick judge."

"A quick judge?" I stomped into the back room and locked myself in the bathroom. When Aziza knocked I barked at her like an angry junk yard dog.

"I have a key," she yelled back.

I tore open the door and glared at my friend. "You could have told me."

"How do we always do this? We start out with one problem and gain another?"

"Because after all these years you still haven't learned that I am sensitive and sometimes you can be plain mean." I marched back up to my station and plopped down in my seat. "How am I a quick judge?"

She came up from behind me and placed her hands on my shoulders. She massaged them as I stared her down in the mirror. I steamed like a pot of clams and Aziza confronted me like a worn out potholder.

"I know how you feel about all these kids in America being put on Ritalin. So, I'm pretty sure you feel the same way about people running out and popping a pill when they get the blues. I didn't feel like justifying my prescription to you because it would end up in a fight. Just like this."

I closed my eyes and worked out the anger bubbling over inside of me. A quick judge. Please! Look who was talking.

"Don't be angry with me," she whispered into my ear. "Come on, you know I love you."

She had a way of softening me into a moldable wad of clay. She was right. I would have jumped down her throat and explained she could handle her problems with exercise or diet or meditation instead of a pill. I watched my mother down those suckers like they were Jolly Rancher candies. She used them as crutches; without them she'd fall over and break. I never wanted to be so dependent on anything.

"Do they help you?" I asked her.

She bent over and wrapped her arms around me. We stared at each other and finally surrendered to friendly smiles. "You have to admit that I am less bitchy than I used to be."

"Um, News flash. You're still bitchy."

"I guess that would be more like a miracle pill, huh?" she asked.

"I would salute the inventor of that pill."

"They've helped me."

"I still don't want to take any."

She kissed the top of my head. "Then, let's go find you a good hypnotist."

Chapter Twelve

After the load of high-maintenance clients I dealt with earlier in the day at Bella, I looked forward to my workout session with Paula. Since our initial personal training session, I had surprised myself with how quickly my muscles adapted to my new daily routine of dumbbell lifting. Every morning I stood in front of the mirror, blasted hip hop on my iPod, and supercharged my muscles with power lifts. I couldn't wait to show off to her how much I'd developed my techniques and strength. The last time I could barely lift ten pounds above my shoulders, but now I could manage twenty.

I walked through the gym door and smiled at Hank who was polishing a trophy. He caressed the shiny gold boxer statue like I would a new pair of Lia Sophia earrings. "Hey, Hank."

"Hey, beautiful," he said with a wink. "Paula wasn't good enough, huh?"

"Huh?" I squinted as though that would help decode his grumbled string of words.

"What happened, Paula didn't work you hard enough last time?"

I just smiled at the nice weirdo. "She pushed me just enough."

"Then why'd you fire her?"

I wanted to pull on his ratty hair to make some sense come through the cracks in his yellow teeth. "What are you talking about?"

"Chuck said he's taking over today."

My heart sank. Did I act that pathetic the day before? "Chuck?"

A piercing whistle screamed across the gym. I looked towards the back mirrors where the stair climbers were and saw Chuck dressed in an orange muscle shirt and black nylon mesh shorts. He whistled at me again and waved me over to him.

A series of questions ran through my mind as I tripped over weight benches, barbells and floor mats to get to him. Did Paula go home and think about my selfish outburst and decide she'd rather spend the rest of her life in paradise alone than another second with me? If she didn't plan to ditch me like some moldy sponge, then why didn't she at least call me to warn Chuck would be taking over? More importantly, what was Chuck thinking when he decided to dress like a jack-o-lantern at the gym? Did he not look in the mirror and see that orange was ridiculously wrong for him?

When I reached the halfway point at the lat pull-down machine, I began to sprint towards him. I needed answers.

Just as I hurdled a weight bench some twenty yards in front of him he tossed a small medicine ball at me. If my feet hadn't touched down on the mat just as it struck me, Hank would be calling an ambulance to come scrape me off the floor. "What did you do that for?" I yelled at him before slamming it back at him.

"You're late." He caught the ball with one hand. "And, I've got a bone to pick with you."

"A bone to pick with me? What are you twelve?"

Chuck ignored my dropping the ball on the floor. "Paula couldn't make it," he said picking up two twenty pound plates from a holder and racking them on the chest press machine.

I walked over to the machine. "I hope you don't think I'm going to lift those?"

Chuck pushed me to the seat. "You're going to lift those."

"There's no way I can press a combined forty pounds."

"You have zero confidence in yourself. Very unappealing by the way."

My face flushed and when I exhaled, scalding steam, hotter than what usually comes out of my hair straightening iron, blew out my mouth. "I'm not interested in having you train me." I turned to walk away and looked back over my shoulder before exiting the nautilus area. "You're too mean."

I trotted away from him and he snuck up on me, flinging me over his shoulders and spinning me around in circles until I screamed so loud, Hank actually shut off Bon Jovi's "Livin' on a Prayer".

I punched his back, right between his shoulder blades as I kicked my feet wildly like a panicked swimmer drowning in a riptide. "Put me down." I pinched the back of his neck, twisting his skin between my fingers. He squealed like a girl in pigtails and ribbons, and finally put me down.

"That was meaner." He narrowed his eyes at me as he rubbed his neck.

I stood in front of him with my hands planted on my hips. "I most certainly do have confidence."

"That's not what I heard."

My knees starting to quiver. "What did you hear?"

"You're chicken. Your son said so." He twisted back towards the machine and unloaded the twenty pound plates. "And frankly, I think you are, too."

I wanted to bend down and kiss the ground that Paula wasn't the one who spread word about my spineless back. I watched him replace the twenties with tens. "Stop." I scurried up to him. "I'll try the twenties."

"You get them, then."

He turned his back to me and waited while I put the twenties back. How ridiculous. We acted like an old married couple, bickering over something as trivial as whether we should order the oatmeal or a stack of French toast. I spared no one's ears when I pushed the weights on the poles and let them slam into the base. How dare he accuse me of being chicken?

When I sat down on the bench, I finally looked him in the eye. "Satisfied?"

"Impressed, actually." He curled his lips up into his usual cocky smile. "Glad to see you have some fight in you. Means there's hope for you yet."

"Yeah, yeah, yeah." I rolled my eyes at him. "How come your sister's not here?"

"She's interviewing right now."

"With the school?" I tried to swallow the lump in my throat, but it wouldn't budge.

"Yeah, she's using her Webcam. They called her fifteen minutes before she was ready to head out to meet you here. So, I jumped in instead."

Oh God, this was serious. What if they offered it to her today?

"Do you really think she's going to get it?" My eyes burned from blinking away the first drizzle of tears.

"I'd be willing to bet my Cesna they'll offer it to her."

I just stared at Chuck who stared back at me with surprising warmth and sincerity. He could've been my brother-in-law someday. He could've been Owen's uncle. He could've been mine and Paula's future son or daughter's uncle. What if I never saw this big teddy bear of a guy again? Within seconds, my levee broke and a storm of tears flooded my face and poured down on my pink Lycra top.

"Hey, don't cry." He placed his hand on my shoulder and pulled me into his big arms. He rubbed my head the way I did Owen's when he got upset, which just created a tsunami of tears. The more he comforted me, the more I bawled.

Thankfully, Hank was smart enough to blast the music again. Billy Idol's "Rebel Yell" screamed over the loud speakers and drowned out my pathetic sob story on front and center stage. If I were in Bella right now, everyone would be gathered around me drenching me in sympathetic kisses and knowing stares. Not here. As I backed away and cleared the last of my runaway tears from my cheeks, not one person dared pay a single morsel of attention to the blubbering idiot on the floor, other than Chuck.

I twisted my mouth into a half smile. "Sorry. I don't know what just happened. I just..." my mouth started to quiver like Jello. "I just really like your sister and I don't want to lose her." I sniffed back the tears.

Chuck's eyes lit up. "She loves you."

"She does?" I wanted to hear it again.

He nodded. "Do you love her?"

"Of course I do. I love her so much that it actually hurts."

Chuck opened his mouth to speak, but closed it just as fast.

"What?" I asked.

"If you really love her, then you should want what's best for her."

"I do."

"What's best for her isn't in Rhode Island. This new school needs her. She needs it. If you're really in love with her, then you should know that deep-down, and not stand in her way."

I bit down on my tongue, anything to squelch the real pain from stinging me. "But my life is here. And we belong together."

"That's a selfish thing to say. Don't get me wrong. I don't blame you. I don't want her to go, either. Because my life is here, too. Flying six hours every time I want to hang out will be a little cumbersome."

"At least you have that option," I said.

"You do, too."

"I wouldn't expect you to understand. Not many people do."

"You're right. I don't understand how you can let some silly fear get in the way of living your life."

"If she loved me, she'd understand that, too," I said, as if reasoning with Chuck would really keep Paula grounded.

"You're about to lose someone really special. How are you okay with that?"

"I'm not okay with that," I said.

"Please don't try to convince her to stay here out of your inhibitions."

"But we love each other," I said in a tone that begged him to understand my dilemma.

"You're the only girlfriend of hers I've ever actually liked. But, if you intend to stay here, then the right thing to do is to let her go."

"But, I don't know how."

"You're a smart girl," he said. "Figure it out."

He walked away, straight to the entrance and left without looking back.

I added another pound to each side of the machine and focused all my energy on pushing the weights, convinced that I needed to get my act in gear more than ever now.

* *

I admired Dr. Walters' confidence, but come on? Like hypnosis could really work. If it wasn't for Aziza poking my leg with a sharp pencil and following it up with a stern glare, I would've just completed my rise from the chair and walked right out the door. But Aziza had faith in all this. I discovered Dr. Walters' latest breakthroughs on the Internet, where she detailed successful accounts of her star patients. I had the distinct feeling that the great doctor wouldn't be listing my name anytime soon.

We stared at a poster on the wall claiming all fear could be conquered. Dr. Walters pointed to it and confirmed with utmost certainty that I could get riding on airplanes in no time. The simple drawings reminded me of the ones I'd find pinned to a corkboard at a local library, colored to ill-perfection by wannabe winners of an art contest. Who designed these posters? Ten-year-olds? I had a fear of flying not learning.

I snapped my eyes back to the cuckoo lady who thought she could wave a little necklace in front of my face and make me forget years of phobic trauma.

I peeked over at Aziza, wanting desperately to share a *can-you-believe-this-crack-job* moment, but Aziza focused on the doctor's words like she was being hypnotized.

"I'm sorry," I stood up, despite Aziza's reflex attempt to push me back down. "I can't do this. I don't believe in anything you're saying. How could you possibly relax me enough to get me on a plane? Breathing exercises? I already tried and failed. When I focus too much on my breathing, I break out into a panic attack."

"Please sit," the doctor said. "What do you have to lose? You paid for an hour session already, so why not see what it's all about?'

"But you just said a few minutes ago that it'll take ten sessions to help me. What good is an hour?"

"Each session teaches you something little, and when combined together, all these little things add up to one very big leap of progress. Let's just focus on one session at a time."

I sat back down without blinking. The doctor did possess a gift of putting me at ease. A little anyway. "Fine. Alter my state of consciousness or whatever it is you do."

I ignored the daggering look from Aziza.

The doctor walked over to a leather recliner. "Why don't you have a seat here."

I followed, still biting back the urge to scoff.

The doctor pulled the lever to raise my feet.

"Now, what I'm going to do is help you relax like you would be when watching television or sitting at a red light. The purpose of relaxing is to get you to a point where you are deeply focused so that you will be more responsive to certain ideas and images."

I stared up at Dr. Walters. "So, in other words, you're going to try and control my mind?"

"Quite the contrary," she said, easing a pillow under my head. "All I'm going to try and do is teach you how to master your own state of awareness. By doing this you can affect the way your body functions in response to stimuli."

I couldn't wait to see how that miracle would work. "I'll give it a try."

"Now, I want you to take some deep breaths."

I inhaled deeply and blew it out.

"Good. Now when you breathe in, hold it for a count of five seconds, then release it for ten seconds."

I followed the good doctor's orders. After ten times, I no longer wanted to stuff my silk scarf into her mouth to stop her fake chamomile tone. In fact, her voice actually rocked me to a peaceful state.

"Now as you hold your breath, I want you to tighten every muscle down to the little ones in your fingers and toes. And when you release your breath, imagine your muscles loosening like rising bread dough."

I squeezed and expanded my muscles into fluffy blueberry muffins, drizzled with sweet cream butter and sprinkled with sugar. Bread never did do a damn thing for me except bloat me.

"Now as you inhale, count to ten. Visualize a place that brings you great comfort as you are counting. Hold onto your breath and flex again. Now on the release, imagine enjoying your bread in this safe place."

The shoe department at Nordstrom's. One-two-three-, open-toed sandals in silver and gold and taupe, four-five-, knee-high boots with a two-inch heel, six-seven-eight, oh and huge sale signs, nine-ten. "I'm there," I said, smiling.

"Good, now hold onto your breath and tighten up."

I crinkled my toes up and curled my fingers, squeezing as tight as I could.

Then, on the exhale, I sunk my teeth into a juicy blueberry as the clerk showered me with free shoe samples.

"Lauren," the doctor whispered. "I want you to tell me what your first flight was like. What scared you?"

I was a little girl again. I looked through her eyes at a world that seemed so real. I sat beside my mother and watched the clouds below us. How did the plane stay up in the air? Air was light, the plane was heavy. How was it possible? Why didn't we just drop from the sky? Just as I turned to ask my mother these questions, the plane dropped and my head spun like all the air was being sucked out of it by a shop vac. Suddenly, I landed back in the doctor's office. I gripped the sides of the recliner and tried to speak, only my voice couldn't come out. I tried again and couldn't move my body.

The doctor mumbled gibberish and placed her hands on my shoulders. She massaged me, slowly thawing me out. Her words started to make sense. "Relax, ghj okdsh. You just need fh relcf."

"I can't understand you," I said. "Wait, I can speak." I moved my hands. "I can move."

The doctor continued to massage my shoulders. "Go to your safe place."

I tried to visualize the shoe racks, but a giant hole opened in the floor and sucked them into it like a giant whirlpool. I bolted up and jumped off the chair. "I need to get out of here." I raced over to my pocketbook and didn't even bother to wait for Aziza to follow. I ran down the hallway and out the door into the fresh air. Still buzzing, I climbed into my leather seat and squeezed the steering wheel.

Aziza jumped in beside me. "Are you all right?"

"Don't ever ask me to go back there again. Because I won't. She's a witch. I could tell as soon as we walked in something wasn't right with her. She put me under some weird spell. She freaked me out."

"That's all part of the process. You have to give it a few more sessions. You're not going to walk into her office one minute and walk out an hour later cured."

"I'm not walking into her office, period." I started the engine and punched it into drive. "We'll figure something else out, right?"

I waited for Aziza to agree.

Aziza just shook her head and lit a cigarette.

* *

A day had passed since my disastrous training session with Chuck and trip to the psycho doctor's office, and I still hadn't heard from Paula. I woke a couple of times in the night with an empty pit in my stomach. I felt completely alone and confused.

"Just call her," Aziza said to me when she finally arrived at work half an hour late because Tania locked them out of the house. Or so she said. They probably were tangled up in each other's legs having ravenous morning sex.

Even though I planned to call Paula at some point that morning, Aziza's three little words powered me up and propelled me to the backroom to make the call. Mrs. Tyler could wait five more minutes to get her body wave. I doubted I could last another five seconds for Paula to pick up her cell. It rang twice and my heart rattled waiting for the third one. I bit the inside of my cheek when I heard her groggy voice.

"Did I wake you up?" I asked her.

Paula stretched her voice just as sure as she was raising her arms way up in the air. "That's okay. You could wake me from a dream about winning the World Cup and I wouldn't mind one iota."

And just like that, my frazzled nerves regenerated. If I could physically snap my fingers and arrive in her arms, I would've. I wanted to look in to her eyes and see for myself that we still connected.

I could pawn Mrs. Tyler off on Ashley, and then Aziza could finish her off. Mrs. Tyler always complained about the way I left too much length on her bangs anyway.

I had so much to say to her. Why hadn't she called to apologize for not meeting me at the gym? Why hadn't she told me about the Webcam interview? Did they offer her the job? Was she taking it? Where did this leave us? Did Chuck tell her about my crying fit?

I had a lot of questions, but only one came out.

"Are you hungry?"

"Yeah, I could go for some breakfast."

I ran towards the front of the store, tossing the strap of my Coach bag over my shoulder. "I'll be there in twenty minutes."

I slowed to a crawl right before I stepped out from behind the product stands and approached Mrs. Tyler with ease. I talked to her with my most patient and relaxed voice, asking the sweet lady if she wouldn't mind Ashley starting on her that day. Her broad smile convinced me that maybe Mrs. Tyler preferred Ashley. "Great, can I get you a cup of coffee while you wait?"

"Yes, please. Can I have that with cream and sugar?"

"Yes, dear, you can have whatever you'd like."

I whipped around and sped up to Ashley. She's all yours. I have to run out."

Ashley blinked her fake lashes at me. "But, I'm supposed to help Aziza with Stephanie's color."

I tapped Ashley's shoulder. "You'll figure it out."

I turned to Nancy, the morning receptionist and yelled out to her on my way past. "Coffee, cream and sugar for Mrs. Tyler."

Blank faces blurred as I ran out the door. You'd think that I asked them to solve the world's energy crisis.

* *

When I knocked on Paula's front door, I smelled waffles and maple syrup. Sure enough, Paula greeted me wearing a red and white checkered apron holding a spatula. "Waffles are your favorite, right?"

I eased my hands around her hips and kissed her, not even bothering to lift my pocketbook from the ground where it fell. "You are so sweet. I love waffles."

She snuck away towards the kitchen. "Good, because I just made six of them for us."

Good God, six? I trailed closely behind. "They won't go to waste."

She pulled out a chair for me. "Sit."

I sat on command, admiring the freshly picked daisy sitting in a champagne flute. "You did this all in twenty minutes?"

"It's a special day." She kissed my forehead before retreating to the counter to grab the stack of waffles and warm syrup. "I've got some coffee, too."

She must have taken the job. Why else was the day so special? What better way to warm up to me than with golden brown waffles? "What's the special occasion?"

She sat across from me and folded her hands under her chin. I studied her face with a half smile.

"Chuck must have told you about my Webcam interview, right?"

Well, duh? God, Paula could be such a guy in the head sometimes. Did she not realize how much sleep I lost the night before? I tightened my lip. "Yeah, he mentioned it."

"It went well. That was the final step. Now I just have to wait for the call to come in."

Still stuck on her previous question, I had to say something. "You knew Chuck told me. He met me at the gym."

Her face flushed. She forked through her waffles, smashing them to smithereens. "Can I be honest?"

I braced for what would sure be the worst news of my life. "Of course. It's what I expect."

"I was afraid to tell you how well it went because I know it's going to change things between us." She dropped her fork and reached out for my hands.

Of course things would change. She viewed me as this meek little phobic who had no control over my emotions. "You're just afraid to see me for who I really am."

"I don't think you give yourself enough credit," she said.

If I had any hope of having a life with her, I had to step up right then and there—prove I could tackle this fear and that it wouldn't ever get in our way. I could do this. I could figure out a way. I just needed time. She didn't need to know how pathetic I really was. "That's not true. Just yesterday I went to my first hypnosis appointment and already it's working."

Her eyes brightened. "You're serious, aren't you?"

I hated to lie. But this wasn't a total lie. I did go to my first hypnosis appointment. Screw the not lying. She had to understand how much I wanted her in my life. "If you get the job, I'll be ready."

She lunged forward and showered me with kisses. She admired me and I ate up every morsel of her praise. I could become strong. In fact, if I opened the door and found and airplane parked right there on the street, I'd jump in and demand that Chuck take me up in the sky. The deeper she stared into my eyes, the braver and less rational I became.

She caressed my face with her hand. "I'm so happy to hear you say that."

I released a smile. "I'm happy that you're happy."

She grazed her lips close to mine. "I am falling deeper in love with you by the second."

The moment her words sunk in, I pulled her in close and whispered, "Well, I can top that. I am so deeply in love with you that you're stuck with me."

Her lips parted to speak, but I drowned her words with a kiss. A deep, longing kiss that melted us together in a sea of warm, sweet chocolate. She was first to rise and lead me down the hall and towards her bedroom. I closed the rest of the world out with the simple lowering of the pull cord on the blinds.

When she led me to the bed, I followed her magnetic pull and landed beside her on the edge. Free to explore again, we leaned in close to each other breathing the same air, giving life to a persistent, unyielding force of love only we could understand.

A strong wave of raw emotions toppled over me, circled around inside my head, and flirted with every morsel of my being. A vacuum of heat, sparks, and desire connected us. Like a well-played game of tennis, we moved back and forth, slow then fast, smooth then chaotic, but always in sync and growing in strength.

In the zone, alert to even the faint wind that blew across the room from the spinning arms of an oscillating fan, I was alive. Every sensory nerve in my body stood at attention, unwilling to turn back.

Her light musk fragrance danced around the room in a fine mist and lifted me to whole new heights.

What I felt was so real, so magical, so unbelievably pure. Light and airy, I floated above anyplace I'd ever been before, gliding like a bird who was free of cages, riding the waves of wind one beautiful tilt of the wing at a time.

In the few moments it took us to lay back against the downy comforter, she had filled every single empty pocket of my heart with more light than a cloudless summer day could ever give.

I handed my heart over to her, gift-wrapped in all that was trusting and honest. She cradled it with tender reverence, caressing it with the most gentle of touches. She blanketed me with the soft murmurs of a woman fully embraced in the moment, ready and willing to share every part of her soul.

When she wrapped her arms around and pulled me closer, I let out a long, trembling breath. Our breathing timed perfectly, billowing in and out. We embarked on what I could only consider to be greater than any fashion show, great hair day or combination thereof of any of prized jewel in the history of my lifetime. This was the grand prize. This was what I waited patiently by the sidelines for, watching the great plays of life pass me by, so that I could be standing there in the right time and place to catch that glamorous buzz as it whizzed by.

She rubbed her cheek against mine, which beat desire through me like a tribal song bouncing off the trunks of exotic plants and jungle trees. Feeling my skin against hers sent a pounding through my blood that not even the most talented of heavy rock bands could replicate.

I traced her face with a featherlike touch, stroking her soft skin. I skimmed my gaze down to her breast feasting on the delicious gifts forming in her curves. So delicate and balanced, begging me to indulge.

I retraced my steps slowly, deliberately back to her eyes where I discovered a sparkle that caused a new source of heat to rise in me. When my lips reached hers the new fuel raced through my bloodstream like lightning, sparking fires in every direction. I traveled my lips down her neck, kissing each curve, each bend, each square inch of steamy, succulent skin I could find. I grazed further down, tracing my lips along the smooth line of her breast, stopping only when my tongue landed on her sweet, erect nipple. I circled my tongue around it, feeling it bloom bigger and more delicious.

Her breath hovered on a moan, rocking back and forth with each swirl of my tongue. The more she purred, the more intense the heat grew between my legs.

My hands journeyed down her body even more. Her body was an unexplored terrain of delicate curves, sun-kissed golden skin, and artfully etched muscles. I wanted to climb, crawl, and tangle myself in each cell. Her body sprang up under my caress, bursting with the eternal life of those miracles only seen and touched by someone deeply in love.

I tiptoed my fingers along her hips and then down her long, slender thighs, following the path with my lips. I stopped only to reverse direction and ascend back up following a whole new path. My fever rose as my fingers and mouth did, and spiked even more when I discovered she was just as hot and moist as I was.

When her hands tangled around my hair and begged me to enter her private oasis, I swept in and explored.

Warm and juicy just as I'd imagined, she tasted of everything fresh and alive. My tongue swam up the peaceful channels of the most beautiful garden. There I discovered hot springs that bathed me in sensual freedom, strumming my taste buds with music that brought tears to my eyes. Each stroke resonated with mouthwatering pleasure, and each buck of her hips against my face intensified the journey down a path that I had only dreamed of traveling. Leaving behind the world, we traveled together on this blissful journey.

I cradled my hands around her hips, moving to their palatable rhythm, listening to their song and following their path to a place deep under the sea of tranquility where only pure pleasure lived.

When she cried out in joy, shuddering, I pulled her knees around my head and rocked her back and forth, gently, lovingly until she released the purest of sighs.

I surfaced to meet Paula and wrapped my arms around her, hugging her close, enjoying the beat of her heart against mine. For the first time in my life, I finally understood what it was like to make love to a woman.

Chapter Thirteen

How could I expect to concentrate for the rest of the day? I had Aziza barking out sarcastic remarks about my lack of professionalism on one side of the backroom door and an angry client complaining about the twenty minute delay in getting her hair styled on the other side. I just smiled and wound the client's hair around the curling wand, kissing her miserable butt with all of the compliments I could muster. Aziza walked past me and stuck out her tongue at me.

Later that afternoon, when I ducked to the bathroom, Aziza followed me in and locked the door. "If you're going to leave my stylists with a list of your high-maintenance clients, then you better arrange it ahead of time like everyone else has to do here." Her nostrils flared.

Still basking in the glow of love, I eased her down a couple notches by pulling her into a hug. "I'm sorry. You're right. But, even you're going to agree, I had to run out."

"From now on, even if your house is on fire, I expect you to follow the same rules as everyone else. No more special treatment just because you're my friend. The others see right through us and they're starting to resent you for it."

I hugged her tighter. Every once in a while she needed to sport the boss hat. She could've slapped a pink slip in my hand that day and I would've still been unable to stop buzzing. "Shush! No ruining this moment." I loosened my tight grip when she yelped like Deogie did when someone pulled his stubby tail. "I just had the best sex of my life."

She pushed away from me. "I see." She raised an eyebrow, clearly interested in the latest dish.

"And you can't fault me for being late. I would bet Tania didn't really lock you out of the house, but that you were engaged in a little early morning love-fest."

She flung my head back, grabbed my face with both hands, and planted a huge kiss on my lips. "You know me too well. Let's just hope no one else catches on."

I smiled as I watched her drift back out to the salon. Then, I grabbed the broom and charged ahead to do a good deed. I swept a trail of hair left behind by senior stylist Joe. He always scattered hair with those clunky-ass platform shoes he wore. Next, I eyed-up the small bear rug of a pile forming around Aziza's station. Before I could get to it, Paula called my cell.

"I miss you already," she said.

"When do I get to see you again?" I asked.

"Tonight, if you'll have me?"

Besides the awesome sex, God only knew what this woman saw in me. "Pick me up at seven?"

* *

"Hungry?" Paula asked when I slipped into the driver's seat next to her.

"A little." I buckled in.

She opened her console and pulled out a red foiled candy bar that sprouted a white bow and placed it in my hand. "For you, my darling."

"Sweets for me?" She could've handed me a gift-wrapped avocado and I would've been just as touched.

"I knew you'd be hungry. I figured I'd offer you a little appetizer before the main entrée."

I tore through the foil like a starving hyena. Wedged in between the foil and chocolate was a white card that read "If sweetness is what you crave, go to Campus Bookstore and look up Willy Wonka and the Chocolate Factory."

I punched her arm. "What's this?"

She shrugged. "I guess we have to go to the Campus Bookstore to find out."

She managed to sport a smirk on her face the entire drive over to Thayer Street, even when she parallel parked her truck in a space barely big enough for a scooter. I had dented at least half a dozen fenders attempting the same maneuver over the years. So when she jumped out of her truck and scribbled a note to the owner of the black Toyota corolla she bumped, I stood on the sidewalk and laughed.

What a newbie.

Once inside, I searched for the book. I browsed by author, by title, by genre and nothing. Paula had long since trotted down different aisles, probably towards sports or something boring like that.

Finally, after asking for some help, I mounted the rungs of a wooden ladder and declared victory with a clap when I found it sitting atop an inch of dust with the other "timeless" classics on the tip-top shelf. By the time I climbed down the ladder with my book in hand, Paula had managed to round up three books to purchase, *A Golfer's Dream*, *Coaching Drills*, and *Trekking across America*. Gee, how fitting.

A red ribbon draped from the middle of the book. I opened it and found a red foiled envelope. Inside another clue. "Something's brewing. Go to The Corner Street Bakery and grab an oversized mug to discover a delicious adventure."

I loved scavenger hunts! Once, I won one by finding a needle in a haystack. Literally. Of course, when the organizer handed me two tickets to the cinema matinee for all my efforts, I wanted to stab the organizer in the eye with the needle.

Paying for our books was an adventure unto its own. Paula and the clerk must've exchanged at least a dozen sneaky glances. When we got out onto the sidewalk, I barricaded Paula against the side of the building. "What are you up to?"

Just as I figured, she laughed and bowled me out of the way, heading south towards Angell Street. "You're wasting valuable time."

Ah, how I loved this woman.

The first thing I smelled when I walked into the bakery was iced cookies. Aziza and I ventured there many a time when bloated with our periods and needed to sink our teeth into something sugary and divine. Baked to the size of a Frisbee, indulging in one of them could easily pack on five pounds.

She ordered two of them to go.

Meanwhile, I eyed up the metal racks of mugs by the fireplace. I scanned them carefully. This could take me all night. There had to be at least one hundred of them in every color of the rainbow. Just as I was about to enlist the help of a couple of college kids huddled up beside the crackling logs hugging a couple of hot chocolates to their lips, I saw my mug propped dead center. It stood out like a lighthouse on a foggy night with its cherry red shellac paint and a hand-painted bow wrapped over a white heart. P loves L scrolled along the handle.

Joy bubbled out of me.

I picked it up and stuffed inside sat yet another red foiled envelope. I tore it open. "A sweet melody is waiting in the room where Owen first heard 'Twinkle Twinkle Little Star.'"

Belfast Mansion? My heart skipped. Paula had to do some serious digging to find that out.

I fell in love with Belfast Mansion early on. My family held every special occasion there. It was an historic mansion built in 1738 for a bride by her husband. From as far back as I could remember, I fell in love with its architecture and grandeur, not to mention the little phyla dough peach cobblers they served at Owen's baptism. When I strolled Owen up through the wooded path to the front entrance that day, I felt like I had stepped into a postcard of the most elegant, secluded place on earth. Somehow Northern Rhode Island cherished this eighty-two acre plot of land so much that they declared it a national treasury, blocking out any would-be tree hoarders from ever touching their chain saws to the bark of the grand maples and oaks that sprinkled the gorgeous backdrop in a sea of green.

Paula stayed quiet on the ride up route one-forty six. The suspense killed me. I turned the volume down on the radio. "You actually rented it out for us?"

"Well, not exactly rented. But, it is ours for the night."

"They didn't charge you? How'd you get that deal?"

Paula raised her hand up. "Too many questions. All you need to do is relax and enjoy yourself."

I rested my head against the seat and closed my eyes, steadying for what was sure to be an adventure I'd definitely enjoy.

* *

I tiptoed behind Paula onto the dark porch. "Why's it so dark?"

She stopped and raised her finger to my lips. "Shh, we don't want anyone to hear us."

"I don't understand. Are we going to stand out here all night?" I grazed the dark landscape and shivered. "Actually it's kind of spooky. Can we just go in?"

She crept up to the corner of the porch and lifted a planted pot from the rail. "Ah, still here."

"Does anyone know we're here?"

"What fun would that be?"

I had trespassed only once in my lifetime. During my junior year of high school, the entire varsity cheerleader squad snuck into the boys' locker room while the guys were at basketball practice in the gymnasium. We sprayed every square inch of metal with shaving cream after hosing their gym bags down in the shower stalls. Payback was a bitch. The boys had started it after all. If they hadn't stolen our skirts right before the homecoming rally maybe they wouldn't have had to lug waterlogged bags over their shoulders that night.

"I don't like this." I flew back towards the stairs. I couldn't scale them quick enough to escape Paula's fingers from gripping me and pulling me back towards her. "Come on. Where's your sense of adventure?"

"I'm not going to trespass." I folded my arms across my chest and stood my ground. "This is insane. We can't just walk into Belfast Mansion and claim it for ourselves. There's a three year waiting period."

"For the weekends. No one stays here during the week unless there's a conference."

"And, how do you know guests are going to start arriving for an early morning conference right now? They host company meetings all the time. One of my clients just had his quarterly sales meeting here last month, and some of their national sales guys flew in the night before and stayed overnight."

"Does it look like anyone is staying here tonight?"

I crept my eyes up to the windows. "I don't feel right about this."

She curled her arms around my waist. "Relax. We've got the place to ourselves. Trust me."

If I wanted to go to jail, I'd break into a bank and then buy one of every single pair of Jimmy Choo's shoes ever created. Not this. "Can't we just go back to my place and sip wine in front of my fireplace?"

Paula nibbled on my neck and whispered, "Haven't you ever done anything wild and crazy before?"

I thought her question through carefully. Aside from hitching a ride from some guy in a pickup truck in Plymouth when I miscalculated the distance from one end of the beach to the other, nothing came to mind. "Can't we just sneak into a movie or something crazy like that?"

"Just close your eyes and enjoy the ride," she said, shading my eyes with her hands.

I turned away and peeked over my shoulder at the dark driveway and shook a chill away. "I can't believe I'm going to break into the Belfast Mansion."

She giggled like a four-year-old and headed for the door.

Once inside, I couldn't even see my hand two inches from my face until she flicked on a flashlight.

I looked around. Just as I remembered it. The coat rack made of antlers still hung in the foyer. And, that familiar musty smell still lingered in the air. I trailed my eyes up the winding staircase to the oil painting of Belfast Lake, where I spent many family picnics. I always slept in the guest room at the top of the stairs first door on the left. I used to like the flowery bedspread and curtains. I morphed into a princess in a fairytale when snuggled up in that room. Belfast was a magical place where great art met up with the delightful aroma of Italian cuisine and paired off with the laughter of guests. Every square inch of Belfast boasted a tradition of beauty and exquisite detail unique to its era.

Here I stood unannounced, uninvited, intruding on a property few were privileged to enjoy.

What a surprising rush.

She bounced the flashlight around the ceiling. "This place is incredible. Look at the carvings on that woodwork."

"You've never been here before?" A stroke of panic pulsed through me masking my short-lived bravado. She had no idea what she was doing sneaking in here. If we got caught…Visions of flashing red lights and loud sirens danced in my mind. Do they have hairdressers in prison?

"Ha! Of course I've been here. My friends and I have snuck in here many times."

"Really?" How naughty. Why did this little fact thrill me suddenly?

"It's fun being a little daring, isn't it?"

"What if we get caught?" I asked.

She wrapped her arms around me and laughed. "So what? They'll toss us in a jail cell for the night and we'll have a good laugh over it."

She had lost it. Someone must've whacked her in the head with a soccer ball. "Do you think we'd actually have to spend the night in jail?"

She stared at me with that twinkle in her eye. "You look like a deer in headlights, babe."

I doubted I could keep up with Paula's pace forever, but I could possibly risk severe heart palpations for a romantic night alone with her. "Just promise me you'll protect me if some butch named Big Momma tries to violate me when we're doing time in the slammer."

"You're doing so much better than Aziza gave you credit for."

Huh? "What?"

"You don't think I'd really put you in danger of being butch-raped in jail, right?"

I searched her eyes for answers. "So, we are supposed to be here?"

"When Aziza told me how special this place is to you, I contacted the manager to ask if I could borrow the mansion for the night."

"Borrow the mansion?"

"A friend of a friend of a friend sort of knows the property manager who lives in the house behind the lake," she said.

I brightened and planted a kiss on her lips. "Oh, thank God!"

"I thought you were going to start sprinting down the dirt road for a second there." She laughed.

"So, when did you and Aziza talk about this place?"

"I called her and asked her your most favorite place in the world."

"You called her?"

"Yup," she said more proud than if I'd just handed her the key to her very own estate. She flicked on the light switch. "Seeing the fear in your face was so funny."

"You're going to pay for that." I lunged forward and jumped on her back. Mid spin, I reached down her pants and yanked on her underwear and didn't let go, giving her the wedge of a lifetime. "No mercy!"

She squealed and tickled my side. Her fingers dug in, sending me into a convulsive cackle. She twirled me around faster until we both wound up so dizzy, we fell into a heap on the hardwood floors.

Breathless, we stared up at the ceiling.

"The craftsmanship really is incredible," I said, dancing my fingers around her palm. My eyes leapt from one beautiful carving to the next.

I sat up and glanced around.

She stood and took my hand. "Let's go explore."

We walked through the hallway to the barroom, which housed thousands of books on the walls constructed of shelves. I detected the faint smell of smoldering wood. Next to the barroom was another hall that led to a vault with a foot wide metal door. "This room used to freak me out when I was a kid."

She scooped up my hand and led me to the Great Room. A Victorian flowery couch centered the room and a dainty marble round table anchored it. On it, baby's breath and long sticks of velvety, cattail plants stuck out of a glass vase. I gazed down at the plush, oval rug that hugged at my heels, scanning across the room to admire the luxurious window shams that blanketed the room in elegance. To the right, a white grand piano sat majestic against a wall of windows.

She walked me over to the couch. "Wait here." She walked over to her gym bag, which she tossed to the floor. "I've got a surprise for you."

"There's more?"

She dug into the gym bag and lifted a present out of it. This one wasn't so square and perfect, though still shiny red with a bow. It kind resembled the type of present Owen would wrap for me. It jutted out to one side and dented on the other, and smelled like a kettle of grease. I was pretty certain it wasn't a necklace from Tiffany's.

"Open it."

My heart raced as I tore into my gift. I uncovered a bucket of KFC chicken, biscuits, mashed potatoes and Cole slaw. I busted out laughing. "Well, honey, you've outdone yourself."

Overcome with laughter herself, she grabbed the bucket. "Only the best for you, darling. With all the running around I did to get the mansion, it didn't leave me much time to plan dinner." She reached into the bucket. "Crap. It's cold."

"Leave it to me," I said. I lit the fireplace and we sat on the exquisite rug, cross-legged, holding our drumsticks over the flames.

She dug in and spooned a pile of mashed potatoes in her mouth. "I love you," she said.

How could Paula walk away from all of this?

Chapter Fourteen

I rubbed the top of the rubber airplane just like the book told me to do. "How the hell am I supposed to make it 'my friend'?" I chucked it across the salon and it landed in the shampoo bowl. "These books are a load of crap. All of them tell me to do something ridiculous. They treat me like I'm a stupid monkey."

I plopped into my chair. "It's useless. I may as well get used to being alone forever, because there's no way in hell I'm ever going to be ready to get on an airplane."

Aziza sat on my lap and massaged my shoulders. "Well, there's no saying she's getting the job."

I brushed a wisp of hair away from her cheek. "You and I both know she's getting it. And, I'm going to end up living the rest of my days as a lonely lesbian in Rhode Island."

"Stop feeling sorry for yourself. It makes you look ugly."

I dropped my head onto her chest. "What am I going to do? None of these techniques are working."

"What about Chuck? He's a freaking pilot. He should be able to figure something out, right?"

I considered Chuck after he offered his help, and I dropped that thought right away. "He'll force me to go up in the plane with him."

She lifted her head up and kissed my nose. "That's the point. He's your best shot at this point." She hugged me. "You can do this."

I would never get in Chuck's plane. Never. No one ever survives those small airplane crashes. "Yeah, whatever. I'll think about."

She climbed off me. She massaged my shoulders from behind. "So, did Paula seriously pull KFC out of her bag?"

"Yeah, and she totally forgot to get napkins so she started wiping her mouth on her sleeve when she didn't think I was looking. She is the cutest thing ever."

"Were you spooked in that big mansion?"

"When I walked by that room with the vault—you know the one Uncle Len accidentally locked himself in at Owen's baptism—chills ran up and down my spine."

"There's a website that talks about that room. There's definitely something there." A crooked smile spread across Aziza's face.

"You know I don't like to talk about ghosts." I jumped up and ran to the backroom.

She ran after me. "Okay, okay. I'll stop." She opened the fridge. "Let's get drunk."

"I have to get back to Owen. He's having girlfriend issues."

"Oh?" She poured us each a glass of wine. "At least have one drink so I can hear about his first love."

I reached out for the glass. "Her name is Miranda and apparently she's mad that Owen doesn't text her every five minutes."

She led us outside where she had recently set up a picnic table for the smokers. "Young love. Those were the days when you couldn't see past a pretty girl, huh?" She clunked her glass against mine in good cheer.

"What are you talking about? You still can't."

206

She pulled out her cigarettes and offered one to me. I reached out to grab one and pulled back. "I shouldn't. Paula hates cigarettes."

She lit hers. "One's not going to kill you." She winked. "How's she going to know?"

God, why did it have to smell so damn good? Once upon a time I hated cigarettes, too. "Oh, fuck it. Let me have one."

"Once you get to California, you can concentrate on quitting. I won't be there to influence you."

"That is such a sad thought," I said, inhaling my first drag.

"The cigarettes or me?"

I pouted. "What would we do without each other?"

She stared through our cloud of smoke straight ahead into the woods. She shook her head. "I can't think about it."

"It scares me, too." I took a deep drag, lingering over the terrible conflict.

"I guess I'll have to break down and set up a Facebook account, huh?"

"At least I have Owen to show me how to set it up. I hope Tania knows her way around the Internet."

"She knows her way around lots of stuff." Aziza batted her eyes.

"I don't think I'll be able to live without you," I pressed her hand to my heart.

"Yes you can. And you will. I can't rely on you to keep my business alive forever. Eventually, I'll have to take the driver's seat. We'll get you up and out of this state one way or another."

* *

I shoveled a heap of raspberry ice cream in my mouth so fast that a glob dribbled off and splattered on my ankle. Owen already had devoured half of his sundae. We had taken took two weeks off from our Tuesday night ice cream ritual and he lapped his treat up like a dog afraid that his master would steal his bowl away.

"Take it easy. You're going to get a brain freeze," I said, wiping his chin before bending down to clean my ankle.

He ignored me and slurped up more.

Aside from his bad table manners, I wondered how I ever raised such a mature, young man by myself. He depended on me alone and somehow he turned out fabulous. I walked, he learned to walk. I spoke, he learned to speak. I ate food, he ate food. I read books, he read books. I smoked, and gosh, he would eventually smoke.

I really needed to act more responsibly. The next day, I would turn the smoker's circle at Bella into a lunch patio. I'd remove all ashtrays and condemn smoking. I'd force Aziza to quit, too. No more. Both of us would return to being the smoke haters we once were in the pre-Tania days.

Poor kid.

If I moved, he had to move. He'd have to leave all his friends, girlfriends, teammates, everything—just because of me. I affected him in every sense.

Mid-lick it dawned on me. What a terrible, selfish mother I was. How could I even think about uprooting my son at such a vulnerable age? He had set himself up with a great group of friends who voted him most popular just a few weeks earlier. And what about his new girlfriend? I couldn't break his little heart by ending their puppy-love.

My mind whirled around. I wished I could just shut it off for even a few minutes. It just kept spinning around and around, out of control like the carousel in front of us. I needed a good night's sleep, needed to stop the thoughts from piling up in the back of my mind cluttering my clarity. One minute I floated, the next I sank. I just needed it to idle for a little while.

If California didn't work, it'd be someplace else eventually. Could be worse. She would probably move to a third world country if given the chance. We'd have to live in mud huts, sleep on straw mats, and eat rice from our hands.

Why couldn't Paula just be happy in Rhode Island?

I watched him stare at some kids chasing the carousel. He'd giggle when they did. He loved life. Somehow this little kid I created could see the good in life, even with a clueless mother raising him.

Maybe I should just let him choose. Take the pressure off myself. He could decide our future and free me from spending the rest of my life wondering what-if.

"Owen, sweetie, do you like it here?"

"At the mall? Yeah, I love it."

"Not just the mall, honey. What about Rhode Island?"

"What are you talking about, Mom? Of course I like it."

How could I in good conscience pull him away from his home? There I had it. He loved Rhode Island. Paula would never hurt Owen. She'd have to stay with us if she wanted to be with me as much as she said she did. I wanted to kiss him and spin him around in circles. He'd get a new pair of cleats for being so wise.

I had no choice, I'd tell Paula.

Paula loved me. She wouldn't go to California without me.

If we stayed, then ten years from now he couldn't hate me for tearing him away from the girl who made him smile, or for ripping his team apart, or for handing his fragile pale skin over to the blazing California sun. "Good, then this is where we'll always stay— you and me."

Owen tore his eyes away from his ice cream. "I'm not staying here forever."

My brain tingled "But this is home."

He rolled his eyes, then dug his spoon into a heap of syrup. "I'd rather live in California."

His maturity slapped me across the face and flung me into the brick wall of reality. I wanted a free-thinker. I got one. I tossed my half-eaten ice cream cone in the trashcan and gulped.

The only thing left to do now was pray that she didn't get the job or come up with a good way to convince her not to take it.

* *

Paula tested the spaghetti sauce one more time. With a steady hand, she sprinkled more garlic powder into it. She could've been cooking for a group of her kids, she looked so at ease.

At first, I flat-out refused Aziza's absurd request to invite her and Tania over for dinner. But then, Aziza reminded me that if I ever wanted to see her outside of work again, we'd better get the unavoidable over with at some point. The two just celebrated their two month anniversary the other day. In Aziza terms, she and Tania were practically married.

When I asked Paula about inviting Tania, she didn't even hesitate to say yes. Not even five minutes after I hung up to tell Aziza, she started to plan the menu. She decided on Italian sausage with meaty marinara sauce, a side of ceviche, and a homegrown salad.

Tania's favorite.

"You seem more excited than I thought you'd be to have them over," I said to her when we drafted our shopping list.

"If Aziza's really serious about Tania, then we can't serve her peanut butter sandwiches. We have to show an effort."

So, off we went shopping, piling our cart with noodles, bread, cheese, and anything else it would take to keep Tania smiling.

The whole rest of the day I stressed. I prayed we all could keep the conversation rolling that night. Nothing sucked more than silence. I ran through topics of conversation I could start if Paula or Tania started commenting on how lovely the weather was in New England in late summer. What else could two former lovers talk about? How they've improved their sexual techniques since being together?

I could talk about Owen's goal over the weekend on his summer soccer team and how he shot the ball straight through three defenders. Or I could bring up the success of my garden. My tomatoes had doubled in size that year, and even though Aziza didn't agree, the scraps of hair I sprinkled over the soil did, too, help. If a strand of hair running wild in a plate of food grossed out Tania the way it strangely did Aziza, then I better scratch that topic. I still couldn't bring myself to dine at Luciano's since Aziza's embarrassing outburst a few months back. I couldn't understand why the strand of hair Aziza dug out of her gravy caused her to scream like she pulled a rat off her mushy pile of mashed potatoes. Does a surgeon faint at the sight of blood? Duh?

Even with her idiosyncrasies, Aziza meant well. This whole weird dinner party proved her maturity had reached whole new heights. No way would the old Aziza have ever suggested such a ludicrous idea. She must be in love. What else could account for her confidence?

I peeked up at the clock in my kitchen. Ten minutes until they arrived.

211

I drew a deep breath to relax my pounding chest. Tangy Italian seasonings filled my kitchen. Candles flickered and crackled. Jazz melodies floated through the air.

Paula handed me a glass of wine, and then I followed her out onto my patio. We stood staring out at the lake in silence.

She sipped a glass of wine, easing into the night ahead.

* *

Tania had the prettiest smile. When she laughed, her skin glowed just like an Avon model. That's exactly how Aziza described her to anyone who would listen. Under the golden light of my dining room chandelier, I had to admit that Tania did have gorgeous skin. Why would Paula ever break it off with such a beautiful woman?

She was perfect, well aside from the six smoke breaks she took before dinner. Every time she and Aziza stepped out onto the porch patio, Paula wrinkled her nose up in disgust and reminded me how glad she was that I didn't smoke.

Meanwhile, I longed after them, jealous they could puff away together without criticism.

We both looked out at them and their glowing cigarettes. "She didn't used to smoke like this," Paula said.

"Maybe she's under stress?" Why was I defending Tania to her?

"She should just run or something. We used to run the Boulevard all the time."

A tinge of envy burned through me. I imagined Paula in a whole new Californian life, some hot blonde in a ponytail jogging beside her.

Tania opened the sliding door and yelled to Paula. "Do you remember the name of that place we stayed in Maine? You know that bed and breakfast that had that cat that laid all over the bed and dining room table?"

I downed another gulp of wine. Great call, Aziza. Just invite the two ex-lovebirds to reminisce about their old romantic days. I snapped my eyes up at Aziza who blew smoke up in the air, creating a halo around Tania.

I curled my arm around Paula, claiming her.

"Bennigans Landing," Paula said. "Why?"

"That *is* the same place where I stayed," Aziza said, smacking Tania in the back. "How weird is that?"

"It's such a cool place," Tania said. "They have the best muffins I've ever tasted." She turned and crushed out her cigarette.

I wanted to throw up. How could Aziza act so cool with the whole Tania/Paula thing? I hoped they choked on their cigarettes.

Tania and Paula talked about her tours the entire time we ate dinner. I kept shoving dishes in front of them. Meatballs, sausage, spaghetti, bread, even a can of olives at one point, anything to shut them up about this great city's nightclubs and this great city's trails, blah, blah, blah. They even rode motorcycles cross country to Denver just so they could have their pictures taken in front of the Coors Brewery Plant and use it as a Christmas card.

Why didn't they just start making out together and I snap a photo for that year's card? For that matter, maybe Aziza could just sneak right up to them and I could take a picture of the three of them smooching. Aziza seemed just fine with their chummy relationship. Since when did she sprout a layer of confidence?

"Wow, what haven't you two done together?" I just had to ask.

"Well, a lot happens in eight years." Paula's eyes glazed over for a momentary walk down memory lane.

Aziza smiled, joining in the happy moment.

I seethed. I grabbed my plate of half-eaten food and retreated to the kitchen for more wine, straight from the bottle.

Paula followed me in with the other three plates. "Dinner was yummy, wasn't it?" she asked, as relaxed as if we'd just finished eating a casserole with grandma.

"So, exactly what did Tania do to piss you off, then?" I wasn't about to take an ounce more of this bullshit standing up.

"What?" she asked with the innocent confusion of a toddler.

"It's a legit question, isn't it?" I asked.

She put her arms around my waist. "Everything okay?"

"Yeah, I'm just confused." I said wriggling free of her grip and gulping another mouthful of wine. "You sound like you had a great life together. What happened?"

Aziza came into the kitchen, her white teeth flashing. "We're set for dessert! I made strawberry sorbet. I planned to top it off with whip cream and a drizzle of chocolate syrup."

"Aziza, get out of here," I said.

"What's wrong with you?"

"I'm just not in the mood."

She cocked her head. "Oh come on. The sorbet will make you feel better."

Light the pilot on the stove now and they'd all be fucked with the voltage running from me.

"Fuck the dessert!" I said loudly. I turned around to see Tania standing in the doorway holding the empty spaghetti bowl.

"I'm sorry, Tania," I said even though I wasn't. "I've just had a bad day." I clearly wasn't about to reveal my vulnerable insecurities and crushed dreams to the Avon Model of Folk Rock.

"Look, I'm sure we all knew this would be kind of weird," Paula said, not feeding into my attempt to sweep the awkwardness under the rug. "We're all adults here. Maybe it's better we just stop ignoring the big pink elephant in the room and talk openly about this."

Tania sighed first. "Yeah, I think we should. We've got nothing to hide. And, I certainly don't want to come between Aziza and Lauren."

"Yeah, no kidding," Paula said. "We don't want to be scalped at our next haircut."

"Yeah, I've seen Aziza bleach the hair right off one poor lady," Tania said.

Aziza laughed, then Tania. Before long, the three drunk amigos barreled over in laughter, holding their bellies and wiping their tears.

"Okay, I'll tell you what happened between us. Turns out she's a serial killer," Paula finally said.

I unfolded my arms and cracked a half smile.

"Yeah, luckily Aziza is cool with it." Tania hugged Aziza. "Don't piss me off, hon."

Aziza cracked up. "We're a perfect match. What do you think happens to all those customers who mysteriously never return to the salon?"

I broke out into a grin, in spite of myself.

"But seriously..." Paula started, looking to Tania, who then nodded.

"Aziza knows," Tania said. "You can say it."

"I want kids, and she doesn't," Paula said. "Simple as that."

"We just want dogs," Aziza said. "Deogie is so easy. I don't have to worry about diapers, birthday parties, teenaged drama, just scooping up poop and sharing my bed with him."

"So, that's it?" I asked not seeing the big deal.

"We want totally different things in life," Tania said. "I'm a night person. I crave the music scene. I thrive on touring and hotels and new cities each week. And it's not just that I don't want kids, but I really don't like being around them at all. It was a big point of contention with us. She lives for kids, as you well know. We don't share the same dreams. We had fun while we were young and unfettered. But we're on different paths now. We would have resented each other in the long run."

Soon, the four of us friends sat around the couch, laughing and cracking jokes. We played Pictionary and I learned the one talent Paula didn't have. A two-year-old could draw better than she.

Before long, Aziza yawned, signaling she wanted to go. As they gathered to say goodbye, Paula's phone rang. When she looked down at it, her face reddened. "It's California."

I turned numb.

It rang again.

"Well, answer it." Aziza's voice sailed much higher than natural.

Third ring. Paula looked up at me. "Are you ready for this?"

I dug deep for my voice. "Answer it."

She flipped open her phone and walked onto the porch. I froze, unable to lift myself from the chair. Aziza scurried over to me, placing her hands on my shoulders.

Our life could be changed in a matter of seconds. Would I be celebrating Christmas in snow or in sand?

Within two minutes, Paula flew through the sliding door right into my arms. She swung me around in circles and screamed. "They offered me the job!"

She ran out to the porch wagging her smile like a dog who was about to go for a hike up a mountain. She slinked from one end of the porch to the other not even caring that she bumped into the table and a pile of ash and cigarettes fell on her sneaker. She stopped for a second to catch her breath. Then, she launched herself in the air and tapped the roof with her fingertips. She landed on a hoot and then scooped me up into a tango stance before unraveling me right into Aziza'a arms and high-fiving the air. "We have to celebrate." She latched onto my hand and pulled me out onto the patio and down the stairs towards the lake. "Let's go swimming."

I flapped around behind her like a shirt caught in the door of a speeding car. "In that lake?"

Paula let go of my hand and charged towards the water, peeling off her shirt, shorts, and sneakers right before hitting the water. I dropped my jaw and winced when Paula slammed her naked skin into the slime of the lake.

"Whoooo hoooooo." Paula's voice echoed off the condos.

In all the years me and Owen lived in the lakefront condo, I never once stepped foot in that disease infested water. As lore had it, snapping turtles grazed the shoreline for their evening snack. I happened to love the way my feet fit into my shoes just the way they were, thank you. I wasn't about to go waving them in front of some hungry, foot-sucking turtle.

Behind me, Aziza's cackle pierced at my ears. She and Tania ran by me, boobs flapping around like a couple of water balloons, bare down to the crotches. They hooted and splashed and soon the water rose around the three of them like a geyser. Three naked women splashing around like a family of dolphins, loving life and embracing Paula's defining moment. And there I stood like a statue.

Screw it.

I kicked off my sandals and ran towards the lake, pulling my dress up and over my head and unlatching my bra right before hitting the water. "California, here we come." I splashed straight into Paula's arms. Slime and all, Paula's lips never tasted so yummy.

"We're Californians!" Paula dipped me backwards.

Soon, the four of us embraced in a slippery hug, shrieking and hollering. Tania was the first to speak in normal tongue again. "I'm so happy for you two."

I would bet all my toes that Tania actually meant it, too.

I just wished I could've felt the same.

* *

When I nodded for Paula to move forward with our plans, she wasted no time shifting our new lives into gear. The next morning, with credit card in hand, she booked our flights online. Owen stood beside her and pressed the submit button. "Two weeks to go," he said, whizzing past me to retrieve the receipt from the printer.

The scrambled eggs and bacon I had just shoveled into my mouth tangled up in my belly like a pretzel.

I had decided too fast. I should've told Paula that I needed time to plan this move correctly. But no. Throw a couple sets of boobs in my way and I lost all sense. The choice needed picking instantly, and in my drunken stupor, I plucked it right up without blinking.

I looked down at the dust piled up under the fridge door. I had meant to clean that for months. Two weeks from then, someone else would have to worry about it. Aziza suggested that Maggie, the nail tech, sublet my condo from me. Maggie would never scrub the floor with her inch long daggers.

The night before, the four of us had sat dripping at my kitchen table discussing the best way to tie up loose ends in less than two weeks. Aziza had volunteered to help me pack, organize a yard sale, and even contact the state Board of Health to initiate the transfer of my hairdressing license. How sweet of her. Why didn't Aziza just place a full page ad in the *Providence Journal* advertising her immediate opening for a new best friend?

Action needed to be taken. That afternoon, after bagging my groceries, I walked by the community bulletin board and finally tore off the last strip of number hanging on the poster for Providence Phobic Flyers Group. I had stared at that poster for months. Time was no longer a commodity.

Within two hours, determined to fix my problem, I sat on a metal folding chair in the community hall of Saint Louis Church, sipping bitter coffee and munching on a sugar cookie. Owen sat beside me, determined to help.

About the only thing I accomplished in those ninety minutes was how to recite the alphabet backwards. Like that would help save me from my nose diving nerves thirty thousand feet up. Owen urged me to concentrate and wrinkled his eyebrows up when I scoffed at how ridiculous this crazy group's tactics were. No wonder none of them boarded an airplane yet. Focusing on the design of the seat in front of me? Squeezing my earlobes? Journaling as the plane careened down the runway? So ridiculous.

I dragged Owen out of the room. "I'm not staying in there for another thirty minutes to listen to these idiots."

"Mom." He tilted his head, upset like I had just stolen his stash of video games.

"Oh, relax," I said, snapping my words out at him like a whip. I clenched my jaw. "I'm calling Chuck instead."

**

I hadn't spoken to Chuck since that day at the gym. I avoided him, burned up by his harsh departure. But, I needed him now.

I parked at the far edge of the airport an hour before I was scheduled to meet him. I needed some downtime before hopping a flight to South County and back. When I woke that day, a stroke of confidence had flashed through me. If I could get through this one flight, I'd be en route to a life most would envy.

I sipped my water and decided I'd better not drink. I certainly wasn't about to crack the door of the Cesna and pee over the Atlantic Ocean. I fiddled with my radio and bypassed one sappy song after another. Finally I just shut the damn thing off and rested my head back. I hoped Chuck would be serious with me. The last thing I needed him to throw at me was a joke or foolhardy attempt to scare me.

I opened my eyes and watched a family of Canadian geese land on the grass by a pool of murky water. They pecked at the grass and hopped around on their little legs, happy to be alive and in such good company. Good for them.

I got out of my car and dug in my trunk for the emergency pack that Owen begged me to prepare after 911. I could've sworn I tossed a package of crackers in it. I grappled with the zipper, twisting it around until it finally opened for me. I plucked up a bottle of hand sanitizer. Lot of good that would do us if stranded on the highway amidst a sea of other evacuees. I untangled some cord from a roll of duct tape and bypassed an emergency blanket before spotting a box of animal crackers.

I chuckled when I opened them and discovered crumbs. *Welcome to my life.*

I enjoyed the next forty-five minutes feeding the hungry geese, amused at how they gobbled down the stale crackers with glee. I wondered if they even had Canadian geese in California.

Later, Chuck filled me in on this answer right before he removed the wheel stops from in front of the tires. "Don't know about California, but Hawaii's state bird is an evolutionary descendent of the Canada goose."

By then though, I didn't care. I just stirred up small talk to keep my head on straight. I hadn't even touched the airplane and my stomach already rolled with nausea.

"Here put this on." He tossed me a headset.

"Why do I need this?" I'd rather have had a parachute, a flotation device, and a helmet.

"It's the only way you're going to hear me talking up there. In case an alien aircraft fires its laser beams down on us."

My throat burned. "I can't do this, Chuck." I handed him the headset back. "I can't get up in that air with you in this thing that looks like a goose could topple it over."

"You've got to face this head on," he said, sauntering up to the nose of the plane with a can of oil. He poured some into the propeller.

"Why are you oiling the propeller?"

"Normal stuff. Don't worry."

I tapped the flimsy body. "Who chose this color anyway? It looks like someone threw up all over it."

He dipped to check under the nose. "Yours truly. Paula and I painted it drunk.

That's why there are a few spots where you can still see the duct tape that we used to hold the wings to the body."

I scoffed. "Don't be an ass."

"Relax, I promise you'll be the one feeling like an ass when you discover how much fun you've been missing out on all these years."

"How do you find this fun?"

He rose back up and twirled the propeller around a few times. "How do you find cutting hair fun?"

"The same way a painter enjoys creating a masterpiece when he sticks his paint brush in a can of paint. I get to play all day, creating works of art that people can walk around with."

"I get to play all day, too. I get to zoom around the globe anytime I want to. If I want good chocolate, I can fly to Switzerland and eat a truffle while breathing in the crisp air of the Alps if I care to."

I'd settle for Hershey bars from Walgreens. "I'd rather change someone's hair color."

"Yeah, well, if you don't get up in the air, you'll have time to fill all your nights and weekends with dye jobs, too." He climbed into the driver's seat and propped open my door. "Get in."

I braced one foot on the step and kept the other one pressed into the tarmac. "Can't we just ease into this with baby steps?"

"What do you want me to do? Taxi around in circles all day?"

"Well, yeah. We could start there and see where we end up," I said.

He shrugged. "Or we could just sit here and watch the planes take off."

I climbed in. "That sounds perfect."

"I was joking."

He revved up the engine.

"What are you doing?" I slapped his hand.

He threw his head back laughing, while the engine idled higher. "Getting ready to fly a plane."

"Stop making the engine run so high like that." I slapped his hand harder, over and over again until he stopped laughing.

"Put your headset on." He secured his under his chin. "Seriously. We're just going to taxi."

I fastened my headset, yanking it so tight I coughed.

"That's not going to save your ass if we crash. It's not a car seat for your head."

I smacked his arm this time, and winced when my hand hit his steel bicep. "You better not take this thing up in the air until I tell you to. If you do, I swear, I'll kick you in the balls so hard that you'll never be able to produce baby Ambers."

He cracked up. "The world might be better off that way."

"Just stop talking. I need to concentrate," I said, securing my trembling hands under my legs.

He eased on the gas and we jerked forward. My heart landed somewhere in the backseat. He played around with the buttons and murmured something into his mouthpiece to the controller in the tower. He pushed a button and they lurched forward. I gripped the seat and squeezed my eyes shut. "Oh shit."

"Relax, that's normal."

"We're just taxiing, right?"

"Right."

My teeth chattered like I'd just stepped inside a sub-zero freezer. He started to taxi the plane. We rolled down the aisle of aircrafts all safely parked with wheel stops in place.

He stayed off the main drag and weaved in and out of aisles, down the side of the metal fence and to the far end of the runway where birch maples buffered the surrounding neighborhood from noise.

"How are you doing?" He peeked over at me.

"Never mind me. Keep your eye on what you're doing." He wasn't driving his Mercedes down Main Street for crying out loud.

"We're safer in the air, you know," he said.

I looked up through the window at the clouds that hung like mashed potatoes. My heart raced ahead of me. I held my chest to slow it down. This was not how I wanted to live my life. I could learn to deal with life as a lonely lesbian better. I was sure.

"What does it feel like to take off in this thing? Is it like a big plane?"

"It's better."

Of course. I supposed he'd agree that jumping ten cars with a motorcycle was, too.

We passed some shrubs before he turned the plane around to go back the way we came. "Ready to tiptoe a little more?"

Before I could answer, he sped up, and instead of following our path, he veered sharp off towards the runway.

"Slow down," I screamed.

"Again, relax. The only way you're going to get over this is to face it head on. I'm just offering you the push you need."

The engine powered up and the faster we sped, the more the plane shook. The next thing I knew, the plane zoomed forward and its nose tilted upwards. My mouth dried up like a field of cotton. I tried to talk, scream, anything, but the air underneath my feet sucked the life out of me like a super-powered vacuum. I balled up like a fetus, trying desperately to catch a breath, which proved difficult in the small jack-in-the-box space I had crammed into. When the back tires lifted, I dug my nails into his arms and screamed. The plane sank. I wailed like a newborn taking my first breath, flinging tears here there and everywhere.

The plane bumped around the air like a car driving over railroad tracks. Chuck lifted us higher above the trees. I clung to his arms, pleading him to take us down, for the love of God.

Horror took over his face. "I will. I'm circling back around. Just let go of my arm so I can steer this thing."

I rolled up in a ball again, burying my face in my knees. My heart raced like a galloping horse en route to claiming my Triple Crown. Suddenly, the plane dropped, bucking around like a bronco. I screamed like someone was scalping me. My belly rolled. The plane tilted from side to side, like a nervous squirrel not sure if it should cross the street. "Get me off this thing," I begged.

"I am. I am. I'm trying."

Finally, the tires hit ground and we rolled to a stop.

Before he could even drive off the runway, I jumped out of the plane and ran off the tarmac towards the building. The last thing I heard was Chuck calling out after me-something about my pocketbook.

Not until I reached my car did the gravity of the situation sink in. I was grounded for good. Grounded to a life that would never include Paula McKenna.

Chapter Fifteen

I trudged into work all groggy and defeated from my restless night's sleep. When I fled from the runway the day before drenched with fresh tears and moving with the unsteadiness of a Parkinson's patient, I determined I wouldn't get another good night's sleep unless Paula turned down her job or at least six months passed after we broke up. Either way, my future sucked.

I had exhausted every means open to man. Books, magazines, Internet advice, therapy, group support, even the highly-regarded, in-your-face method, and still I wasn't one step closer to freeing myself from the panic shackles that choked me.

"You look terrible," Aziza said to me.

"You try sleeping with a twelve-year-old in the next room yakking away all night to his girlfriend." There I went again, using poor Owen.

"Someone's got some serious PMS," she said.

I hurried past her so she wouldn't see my chin quivering and the broken dam ready to release a raging river down my face. "I just need some coffee and I'll be fine."

"I tried to call you to tell you your morning canceled out on you."

I sighed and dug for my cell. It was turned off. "Well that could've saved me a boat load of grief this morning." I had run a red light, dodging a near collision with a carpet truck, and to really piss me off as I had raced by the coffee shop to get to the spa on time, a freaking cop pulled me over and gave me a ticket.

"You look fried. You should really get some sleep."

I dropped my lunch pack and tote bag at my feet. "I'm not going back out in that traffic. I'll just clean." Clean Aziza's salon. Her floors. Her sinks. Throw her towels into her washing machine and then into her dryer.

"Why don't you go home and start packing?" She scooped up my bags from the floor and draped them back over my shoulder. A worried frown crept across her face.

The room started to tighten its steel hands around my throat. The smell of perm solution and bleach danced together forming a nauseating cocktail. The track lighting seared harsh wedges of heat and glare into me. I needed to leave. Maybe I'd drive to Galilee and hang out with the seagulls. I could toss clam cakes into the water while I sat on a pointy rock and sulked.

I hoisted the straps of my bags higher up on my shoulder and walked over to the receptionist desk. "Let me see how much time to I have until my next one."

She rode on me tail like a car hugging a semi down the highway to save gas. "Well, you see what I did was—"

"What the hell?" I rifled through the appointment book, and when I looked into my column, nothing but ruled, blank lines stared up at me as if laughing, mocking me that even my clients didn't see me fit. From that day forward, my entire column of loyal customers had vanished. Erased and relocated to another column. "Why does Ashley have Ms. Davis and Ms. Roberts today? Why is everyone in her column?"

She patted my back like I was a child who skinned my knee and needed a band aid. "I just thought you'd want to spend your last two weeks here doing fun stuff."

Cutting hair charged me. How could someone like Aziza, who screwed up every head of hair she touched, get that, though? She should've just signed that modeling contract back when she starred in the Providence Fashion Show ten years back and left the hair industry to people who actually cared about it. So not fair. She pranced around her salon all day acting important and bossy and now erased my career away with the back end of a stubby pencil.

I backed away from the book. Salty bile rose up in the back of my throat, threatening a mutiny of its own. "Put my clients back."

"You're foaming at the mouth like that Yorkie who attacked my ankles last year."

"They're my clients," I said. "I earned them. What right do you have just feeding them off to Ashley's greedy little hands?"

"Take it easy." She backed away this time. "Go take a Midol and chill out."

"Just get out of my way." I pushed her out of the way and charged towards the door.

"Is this how you plan on spending your last couple weeks with me?" she asked. "Like a bitch on steroids?"

I plowed towards the door, catching my foot on a basket of magazines and spilling them out onto the floor like a deck of cards. I bolted out the door and yelled out over my shoulder at Aziza, and for that matter anyone within a two mile radius, "I'm not moving to California."

* *

I drove straight to Paula's house. Her driveway was vacant. Her front door folded up into the door jamb like a new pack of t-shirts. Neat and untouched. She had taken Owen for some special bonding time, and I had no clue where they were. Mother of the Year. I snuck in around the back gate, half-expecting them to jump out at me and blast me with squirt guns set on the highest stream. But, only the morning glories greeted me, opening their petals so wide they could swallow me up whole and still smile towards the sun under the stench of my rotten mood.

Next I circled the Boulevard, where a group of people of all different shapes practiced Tai Chi on the lush grass in front of the mansion with the gigantic Elvis portrait on the front room wall. A grave sin against interior decorating. The first time I caught a glimpse of the utter tackiness, I nearly got myself killed. Luckily Paula had grabbed me by the shirt and yanked me back on the grass before the yellow Volkswagen Beetle could run me over. What if some other weirdo in one of the many mansions lining the well-manicured street decided to hang up a picture of Audrey Hepburn with that cute little bun in her hair? Who would save me then?

I coasted the road at a turtle's pace, skimming the sidewalks with bleary eyes. I studied the tops of bushes for a tuft of Paula's golden hair. I scanned the park benches, past the teeter-totters and around the water fountain. I darted back towards the Tai Chi people, jealous of their peace. They danced their arms and legs around like wings, unaware of the negative force field passing to their right side in a Beemer. Not until they disappeared in my rear view mirror did I finally exhale, afraid I'd somehow snuff out their good spirits just by breathing their same air.

I drove on down Hope Street back towards the East Side of Providence and passed Apsara restaurant. Paula had introduced me to the shoebox-sized restaurant. That first night, we waited in line for over an hour. I had just finished a twelve hour shift at Bella and my feet throbbed. Each time I shifted my balance to ease the needle-stabbing pain, Paula had assured me the Nime Chow would erase the aches and pains the moment my teeth sunk into the fresh wrap stuffed with rice noodles, basil, bean sprouts, lettuce, and shrimp dripping in peanut sauce. Nime Chow had now replaced Advil for good.

My head throbbed as I traveled closer to downtown Providence. And, only one thing could soothe the knocking in my head. I pulled into the crowded drugstore parking lot just past the string of "mom and pop" shops hugging the street. Once inside, I marched right down to the candy aisle, which was filled with treats beckoning for my attention like puppies in a shelter. I walked down a little further to the single chocolate bars and sought out my favorite. A Hershey bar. I reached for one and plied open the wrapper with my teeth. I devoured it in three bites, then folded the torn wrapper and made sure to hold it high enough for the camera to see, so anyone peeking at me wouldn't think I'd set out to steal it. Next to flying, my other nightmare was jail.

I hunkered down to the tampon aisle and passed an elderly woman with blue hair. I wanted to kidnap her, tie her to a chair at Bella, and make her over. The lady peered up at me and offered a weak smile. She looked at me with a glimmer of pity and concern before hobbling away, stamping her cane into the ground with each wobbly step.

I folded my frown into a half smile, hoping the gesture would actually inject me with some peace. But, it just felt phony like I'd taped my lips up at the corners.

I grabbed a box of tampons and then hunted down the card aisle. I surveyed the topics and scoffed when I saw that some card maker actually approved cards for breaking up with someone. *Although we shared many good times… If only we could agree more than disagree… I only wish I could have been the person you needed me to be…* What about *I'm sorry I'm such a freak?*

I had to find Paula now and tell her that it was over; that she deserved more than I could give her; that I would just waste her precious time and eventually she'd end up hating me.

I checked my cell again. Still nothing.

I called her again. This time she answered in a breathless giggle.

"Where are you two?" I asked.

"We're at the mall. Want to meet us for an ice cream break?"

My smile spread naturally this time. One more night of faking it wouldn't kill them. "I'll be right there."

I shuffled down the aisle, shoving the wrapper in my pocket and tossing the box of tampons on a shelf in between a can of almonds and a box of granola bars. I passed a worker wearing a blue apron and a smiley face pinned to his chest. His name tag wilted to the side. I handed him a five dollar bill on my way past. "That's for a candy bar I ate. Keep the change."

* *

I remembered when the Providence Place Mall first opened. I was decked-out in a gorgeous, sequined cocktail dress I had dug up off the floor under a clearance rack at Macy's. Aziza had wrapped my hair up into a messy crop at the base of my head, and doused me with a healthy squirt of Design Beautiful perfume before I headed out the door. The city's top dignitaries and VIPs had attended. I had landed the shot to schmooze my way into a conversation with the head of the Department of Health, which totally made my life at that point because, after forgetting to pay my licensure fee, my cosmetology license had been voided. I could no longer practice as a licensed hairstylist legally, and the little bitch at the other end of the phone line at the Board of Health just snickered when I had started to cry. Well, thanks to an opportune conversation with Jacky Pullman, the daughter of the CEO of the construction company that built Providence's new pride and joy, I had been able to meet the head honcho of the health department and resumed cutting hair the legal way.

Now, almost a decade later, the mall teemed with back-to-school shoppers whose children probably were not even alive at the time of the mall's grand opening. One mother tangled at least ten bags from her arms, mangling her wrists with their strings as she dashed towards the escalator towing a few scrawny kids behind her. Another kid mouthed off to his mother because she wouldn't buy him the sneakers his friend Billy just bought. Thank God Owen wasn't a brat.

I cut through a line of people shuffling up the escalator towards the movie theater. Even from one floor below, the smell of buttery popcorn circled the air and compelled children and adults to raise their heads up and breathe it in deeply.

People zigzagged through the crowded aisle, stealing a pace here and there by cutting off unsuspecting shoppers. Children attached to bungee leashes pulled their parents along, while others snuggled up to blankies in their strollers and stared up with bright eyes to the pretty lights above.

By the time I finally rounded the corner to the ice cream shop, I had elbowed two people, stepped on a man's toe, and cut off an elderly woman on a scooter. Why was everyone out to get me that day?

I peeked inside for them and only saw a cook wearing a white folded cap leaning back from a blow of steam and a young waitress with a ponytail dangling half way down her back, wiping a table clean. The smell of brownies and waffle cones melted into a sweet aroma and masked the slight scent of greasy French fries.

When I turned around, Owen jumped out in front of me and beamed. A ring of chocolate traced his mouth. "Hi, Mom!"

Paula hugged me immediately.

"We have matching shirts," Owen said from behind us.

My face squished up against Paula's chest, I snuck a peek at their shirts, which were as breezy and southern Californian as one could get. "We bought you one, too," she said, releasing me to take in the full view of their bright, colorful shirts. The belligerent patterns partied together, spilling all sorts of noise and chaos around them. She handed me the shirt.

My head hurt. "Thanks."

"Look, Mom." Owen stepped up and handed me some brochures. "We picked up some info on California! Coach said if you say yes, I can go parasailing with her!"

I glanced down at the picture of a man flying through the air with an over-sized kite attached to his back. He would hate me in a few days.

"We'll see." I patted his head. "How about we get that ice cream?"

* *

Later that night, with Owen shuffled safely off to Jake's house for a night of movies, popcorn, and endless rounds of video baseball, I knocked on Paula's front door and entered. I heard her clanking dishes in the kitchen. I passed four towering stacks of brown moving boxes each labeled in Paula's neat print. Office, bedroom, basement, patio.

I gulped.

She scooted around the kitchen island as though on hockey skates, shuffling from one plate to the other, stopping to garnish, to sprinkle, to toss. She looked up at me with those almond eyes and smiled.

"Hey, beautiful," she said, now pouring olive oil over the salad without looking.

Her kitchen smelled like a pizzeria. Garlic and mozzarella melded together. My stomach growled. "I thought we were just ordering delivery."

"I thought I'd surprise you with something more special."

She stuck a pot holder the shape of a chili pepper on her hand. When she opened the oven, the sweet and fruity smell of pineapple swept over me like a teasing summer breeze—its pleasantry short-lived, but nonetheless powerful and lingering. A cruel reminder of what was about to unravel.

"I made California-style pizza. Oh, and I also made, just a sec..." She placed the steamy pizza on the stovetop and tore her mitt off. She ran over to the fridge and pulled out a coconut with two straws peeking out the top of it. "Home-made piña coladas!"

"Oh, wow," I said, stepping back, beating the nagging pulse at the back of my throat down so it wouldn't hurl up and ruin the moment.

She cupped the coconut and brought it to me. "Take a sip."

Circling my lips around the straw, I sucked up a mouthful of the milky sweetness. It trickled down my throat, coating it in a comforting layer of all that was perfect with Paula.

The tips of her fingers traced my cheek. I latched onto the love welling in her eyes, knowing any second that love would be replaced with something bitter, regretful, angry.

I nuzzled my cheek up to her hand, savoring the last few crumbs of love I'd surely ever feel again in my lifetime.

One last time. I deserved one last time with the woman I loved.

Pushing the coconut aside and clearing the spatula and bowls of salad from the counter, I leaned into her and kissed her. Hungry, impatient, blood pumping through my veins like a freight train late for a delivery, I pressed my lips against hers with force, afraid if I lightened up my touch, she would slip away out of my grip and go tumbling down the side of the mountain without me. Without me.

One last chance to make love to her. To feel her breath against my face, my neck, my breasts.

She lifted me on the counter, but I slid down and urged her body up instead. I needed to taste her and bottle her memory airtight in a private pocket in my mind so I'd never forget her aroma, the tangy, the sweet, the salty, the delicious combination of her.

She obliged. She pulled down her jeans and lifted herself on the counter. I poured my love into her, caressing her, guiding her to that special place that only we could get to together.

After she came, she laid back against the cold granite countertop, next to two salad bowls overflowing with lettuce and avocado and a crispy oven-baked pizza fattened with chunks of pineapple and mushrooms, exposed, vulnerable, and completely clueless about the real cause for the tears streaming down my face.

* *

The hours passed. The pizza long since devoured. The coconuts bone dry. We curled up side-by-side on the sofa and took naps. At least she did. I just laid there wondering at what point would be most appropriate to destroy our lives.

The monologue I had prepared earlier that day traveled off somewhere else. I couldn't even remember the first sentence, let alone the whole ten minute preamble I had rehearsed over and over again. I searched my mind for a way to break into the relaxed smile on her sleeping face.

Maybe in an hour? Another day? At the airport?

I shifted to rise from the couch and she woke. Her eyes bloodshot, her face groggy, yet as peaceful and content as a vacationer far away from anything reminiscent of everyday life. "Hey, where are you going?"

"To get a drink of water." I lied. I didn't want anything to wash away her taste from earlier.

She stretched her eyes open. "Are you crying?"

I felt my throat clamping shut.

I needed air.

I walked over to the picture window and cracked it a few inches. The fishnet air coming through was humid, not refreshing at all. Smelled just like the moldy dust of the vacuum bag after sucking up Deogie's fur at the salon.

I breathed it in anyway, struggling to get it past my throat and into my lungs. My lungs burned and only allowed a small amount to squeeze through. But enough to keep me alert, and unfortunately in the moment; in the moment I dreaded since that first day she told me about California.

I could fool others into believing I had the power to face my fears. Not myself, though. Leading up to that point, every time she asked how my treatments were coming along, I laughed and pretended to be over it, figuring maybe I could be eventually. I should've known better.

Now, riddled in guilt, I hurt just looking into her trusting eyes.

She placed her steady hand on my shoulder. I turned to face her and drank in that last bit of understanding and concern.

"What's going on?" Paula asked, her voice sputtering out, as though she already knew.

I just shook my head. The inside of my mouth dried up like a desert, all scratchy and parched, cracked into crevices that swallowed my essence whole. I scrunched my face up into a wince not sure how to begin.

Nagging questions circled my head like an annoying bee.

Maybe we could have a long-distance relationship?

Two thousand eighty eight miles.

Maybe I'd be alright once up in the air?

Thirty thousand feet.

What's the worst that could happen?

Turbulence. Death. Worse, burning alive.

I wanted to go back to the Brown quad, to our first kiss, to watching her dance and sing to a crowded audience, to that first night on the beach under the moonlight.

All my life I ran from fear. I let it wrap its nasty daggers around my throat and strangle me, dooming me to a lonely, pathetic life. I crouched in its shadows and turned my back on its evil pranks. I stood back and allowed it to steal from me. Steal my fun, my dreams, my chance at rising above the cowardice I'd always been chained to. My dignity. My son's pride in me. And, now Paula's faith in me to be who I'd pretended to be these past few months.

She searched my eyes. "What's bothering you?"

I struggled to remember my speech. Even a word. Nothing. All I could do was blurt out, "I can't do this. I can't go to California with you."

And just like that, my world crumbled down around me. Not from a scream, or a harsh accusation, but from one single truth-induced, biting statement. "I can't believe you're just giving up," she said, backing away.

I stared into her disappointed eyes. Pity loomed. A much different look of pity than the one my parents drenched me in year after year whenever they'd travel on vacation in our van instead of a plane.

Anger would've been easier. I wanted her to yell, lunge, curse, spit, anything but pity me.

"I'm sorry I turned out to be such a disappointment for you," I said, choking back the sadness that clogged my lungs.

She closed in and cupped my face in her hands, touching her lips ever so slightly to mine. "You should be more worried about disappointing yourself."

Then, she walked away towards her hallway, turning back one more time. "I hope someday you can summon up the courage to do something really wild and crazy just to spite your fears. I think that's the only way you'll ever understand how great it is to be alive."

I kept my eyes glued to her as she left, drinking in what would most likely be the last sight of her, the most remarkable woman I'd ever met.

I wished I could be that woman she thought I was.

* *

A few minutes after I pulled out of her driveway, I drove around the bend from her house and pulled off to an empty church parking lot. I angled my car against a grove of trees towards the back of the parish hall and jammed my car into park.

Then, I sobbed.

Chapter Sixteen

The time leading up to D-day stretched one agonizing hour after another. After a week and a half, Owen finally acknowledged my presence when he bumped into me in the hallway on his way to the shower that morning.

I couldn't blame him for hating me. He said I ruined his future. We merely coexisted. He huffed by me, slammed cabinet doors, locked himself in his room, and even skipped Tuesday night ice cream two times in a row, which was the most serious indicator to me that forgiveness was far off.

Thankfully after I sidestepped out of his way, he stopped to say thank you, which as far as I was concerned, opened a real doorway to peace talks. He even managed a smile before walking out the door an hour later.

"Owen's finally coming around," I told Aziza, who sat across from me in our favorite back row booth at Frank's Diner.

She studied my face. "You look like shit."

"I don't care." I buttered my biscuit, then tossed it back onto my eggs, disgusted with eating, drinking, breathing. It all required too much effort. Effort I just couldn't face.

"How are you *really* doing?" she asked.

"She's leaving tomorrow and I haven't heard from her." I stirred my black coffee. "How do you think I'm doing?"

She curled her hand around mine. "I know it's tough. But, I promise it'll get easier."

I yanked my hand away. "I don't need your pity."

"That's it." She paused to swallow a mouthful of scrambled eggs. "I'm going to cancel my day tomorrow. We'll go shopping, have lunch, and I'll even treat you to new shoes."

"Don't bother. I've already made plans."

"Oh?" She creased her eyebrow. "Doing what?"

"Getting my teeth cleaned."

She scoffed. "No way. We're going shopping for shoes and getting you out of this funk. No arguing."

"I don't care about a new pair of fucking shoes." I slid against the slippery seat and climbed out of the booth. "I just need to be alone right now."

* *

D-day arrived. I scanned the bins at Lee's Beauty Supply for shampoos that would protect my new auburn color from spilling down the drain too soon. The night before, tired of feeling lonely and numb, I doused my blonde hair in bonfire red and prayed the change would lift my spirits like it used to in my hairdressing school days. After I rinsed and blow dried, a fiery blaze of tangled strands toiled together. When I looked in the mirror, I didn't recognize myself. The red dye ran down my elbows and splotched across my shirt. The tears welled, and I dropped to the ground to clean the dye from the grout in my bathroom floor. Even the red blotches on my knees afterwards didn't hurt me. Nothing did. I felt empty as a black hole, sucking everyone into my bottomless abyss of misery.

I picked up a bottle of Color Save and checked it out with the young girl at the counter who chewed gum and didn't bother to look up at me. When the clerk handed me the receipt and bag without as much as a thank you, I stormed out and yelled over my shoulder, "You're welcome." Then muttered, "bitch" as I hammered the pavement with my heeled boots.

Was anyone happy anymore?

**

"Just call her," Aziza said ten minutes later when I called her from my car and whined.

"She's done with me. She hasn't even tried to contact me since we broke up. I wish she would've just yelled at me. I hate this silent treatment."

"Then be the one to end the silent treatment," she said.

"And say what? She's leaving. I'm staying. What more is there to say?"

"You'll cave and call her eventually, so why not just get it over with?"

Within five minutes of hanging up with Aziza, and a few hundred attempts to press send, I finally did. I drew a deep breath and braced myself.

A beep pierced my ear, and then an automated message told me that Paula's number had been disconnected. Someone honked from behind, another person swerved on the side of me and chucked the bird. I just stared at my phone. I pressed send again to make sure I called the right number.

"Drive your freaking car, lady," someone screamed at me.

Sure enough, I had called the right number. The message repeated again and again. My chest burned when I drew in air. Brakes screeched behind me. More horns honked, and people screamed all around me. Suddenly my car jolted up over the sidewalk and collided with a set of wrought-iron table and chairs outside Sam's Café. My face vaulted off the steering wheel.

People ran out of the café and stared, their mouths gaped open so wide I could stuff a loaf of bread in their mouths, and they'd still have room to breathe. A man in an apron dashed over to my side. He smelled like donuts and French vanilla coffee. He offered me a napkin to wipe the blood trickling from my cheek. The gash pricked, like a dull razor blade against the back of my ankle.

One woman flagged a waiter and asked him to fetch a blanket or tablecloth. "She might be in shock. We need to get her warm," she said to the young guy with spiky hair and a stud perched on his upper lip. The color faded from his face and, when he turned to escape, he whacked his knee on the leg of a table sticking up in the air.

I still clutched my cell phone in my right hand, staring down at it, willing Paula to pick up her disconnected phone.

"Are you hurt?" the man asked.

I wriggled my legs free and climbed out. "I'm fine."

Sirens blared in the distance, people whispered, a dog snuck in to get a sniff, waitstaff tossed broken hunks of metal off to the side, another person swept the glass from the sidewalk. My car still idled on the curb, the backend sunk into the street below.

The man helped me over to a chair that I managed not to destroy. "Let me get you some water," he said and ran off.

I stared at the drops of blood on my jeans. Paula didn't want me to find her. No note. No email. No call from her new cell. Just a frayed phone line.

I searched my contact list for Chuck. I'd beg him to hand over her number.

I called him. And when his phone beeped and told me he had disconnected too, my stomach wretched into a tight ball. I bent forward, swallowing fast and hard to keep the bile down. But it rose faster than I could swallow and I threw up. I lost it, right there on the sidewalk, on my boots. Even the compassionate lady ordering the spiky-haired guy to help swaddle me in a tablecloth backed away, sickened and pale.

Maybe I could persuade Aziza to call Amber for me.

Yes. Aziza would call her. She would know just how to ask for the number so Amber would actually hand it over to her. Hopefully Amber had given me the correct number back in D.C.

I called Aziza. She didn't answer this time. I stole a glance at my watch. The countdown to Paula's flight had begun. Time was running out. I needed to call her. To talk to her. To see her one last time.

Screw it. I'd call Amber myself. I'd be quick, to the point. Eat the frog. Eat the frog. In those first two rings, I promised God that if Amber answered, I'd donate half my shoe collection to the Veterans' Shoe Drive that year.

"Hello," Amber said.

Okay maybe not half. Maybe a quarter of my shoes, but only the ones from last season. "Amber?"

"Yeah?"

"Thank God!" I smiled. Damn it, my cheek hurt. "Listen I need to ask you a favor."

"Who is this?"

I padded my cheek with the bloody napkin and winced. "It's Lauren."

An ambulance pulled up alongside the chaos, bleating out one last siren blast before a team of paramedics rushed over to me.

"What do you want?" she asked.

"I'm sorry to call you like this, but I need to ask you a favor."

"Ma'am, my name is Mike," a medic said. "Are you hurt?" He was a handsome man with thinning hair and sharp hazel eyes, and a dimple set on his chin.

I nodded him off and continued. "Amber, it's really important that I get in touch with Paula. Both she and Chuck disconnected their phones. Do you have their new numbers?"

The medic wrapped a blood pressure cuff around my arm.

My arm shrunk under the pressure.

"Chuck broke it off with me two days ago," she said with a voice that sounded much too small and feeble to be hers.

"He did?" I managed a smile. "So, you don't have his number, either?"

"Obviously not."

The medic pumped the cuff and released it slowly, watching the dial.

I sighed. "So, he broke up with you and decided to disconnect his phone?"

"He decided to move to California with Paula. I'm guessing they got new calling plans and didn't want us bothering them."

Me and Amber were kindred spirits. How fitting.

"Ma'am, I'd like to ask you a few questions," the medic said.

I nodded to the guy. "Amber, I have to go." Before I hung up, I decided to add, "I'm really sorry."

"I'm sorry, too," she said with a sincerity that reached out and tugged a little.

I ended the call and lay my head back against the gurney, paralyzed by a new fear.

What if I could never find Paula again?

* *

With a fresh line of stitches running across my cheek, I barged into the wax room at Bella. Aziza was slumped over Gretchen Hoskins' eyes, plucking away at her Godzilla brows. "You have a sec?" I asked her.

She waved me off, not even looking up. "Not now. I'm running really late."

I couldn't wait. I needed her now. I needed to hear her soothing voice, her words of wisdom, her direction. "I'm in crisis mode."

Aziza sighed. A dramatic, *give-me-a-break* sigh. "You're always in crisis mode." She combed Gretchen's brows.

Gretchen stretched her eyes up at me and offered a half smile. "Eww, what happened to your face?"

Aziza whipped around to look at me and shot off the stool. "Oh my God. What happened? And what the hell is with your hair?"

"None of that's important right now," I said. "I really need to talk to you."

"How many stitches are there?" She counted. "Twelve? Did you get in a fight with that bitch at the supply shop?"

I shook my head and sat on the stool. "She's leaving in three hours and I can't reach her. I can't reach Chuck, either. They've disconnected their phones already."

"Really? Disconnected?"

I broke out into full blubber. "Is she that pissed at me?"

She hugged me, and Gretchen just lay there watching our drama unfold before her like a passive television viewer.

I cried into her shoulder. "She hates me."

"She doesn't hate you," Aziza said.

"She used to admire me."

"She still admires you."

"Then why did she shut me out of her life?" I asked, sniffing back tears.

"Baby, *you* shut her out."

A fresh cascade of tears poured out of me. She was right. I wanted Paula to say no to the job, not just because I didn't

247

want her leaving me, but because I wanted her to scoop up that scared little girl inside me and tell me it was okay for me to be afraid. I craved what I'd always been so used to receiving. No one ever made me face my fears before. I resented her for that in a way. But, loved her more for it at the same time.

"What should I do?"

"You need to figure this out on your own."

I cried like a two-year-old pitching a fit after my mother just yanked my favorite doll out of my hands. "Please tell me. I need you to tell me what to do."

She just hugged me tighter. "Not this time."

* *

I left Bella's and the security of Aziza's arms, and headed straight to my condo, charged with superhuman adrenaline. I didn't need Aziza to knock me over the head with the great answer to it all. There was only one way out of this whole mess.

Up.

I ran through my front door and called for Owen, then continued toward the desk in the office. I rummaged through the top drawer and dug out our airline tickets. Our flight took off in two hours.

"Owen," I hollered. "Did you hear me?" I knocked on his door then opened it to find him curled up in front of his television with a headset on. I shook him by his shoulders, and he screamed.

"Mom, I told you not to do that anymore!" He turned towards me and gasped when his eyes landed on my stitches. "What happened to your face?"

"We don't have time to get into it right now." I plowed over his sneakers and a plate littered with pizza crusts and reached for the backpack hanging over the edge of his bedpost. I tossed it at him. "Get packed."

His face lit up. He hopped to his feet. "Are you serious?"

"Get packed before I change my mind."

He charged around his room flinging underwear, t-shirts and bathing suits into his bag, releasing little pig squeals. "What about all of our stuff? How will we get it there?"

"That's what Auntie Aziza is for. She'll ship it out to us when we tell her to."

I flew to my bedroom and prepared a carry-on bag, too, and within five minutes, the two of us landed in the front seats of the car, panting like two rabid dogs who just escaped our death cages.

Flying on auto-pilot, I weaved in and out of traffic. I managed to hit every red light and when they'd turn green, I'd spin my tires and accelerate like I was sky-rocketing my son to the moon. We passed a sign that told us we had five miles to go. "We're going to make it in time," I said to Owen who bounced his knees up and down like he had to pee really badly.

Then, to my horror, we rounded the bend and as far as my eyes could see, there was a sea of brake lights. Cars snaked the interstate, crawling, inching forward ever so slightly.

"Call Coach and tell her, Mom. Tell her we're on our way. Maybe she can make them stop the plane for us?"

I would've if that were still possible. "We'll make it."

Horns honked. People stood outside their cars. One man jumped on his hood, craning his neck at the red-lined horizon. More people gathered outside their cars. Someone walked by my car cursing, muttering something to someone else about a tractor trailer dumping thousands of cases of sugar up ahead.

"Un-freaking-believable." I punched the steering wheel. "We're never going to make it now." I gripped the wheel until my hands turned white.

"Call her, Mom."

"I can't call her." I snapped at him then softened my voice. "She disconnected her phone."

Owen dropped his face and shoulders and just let them hang like a lumpy sack of potatoes over his legs.

"Let's not give up," I said. "We still have time."

* *

Surely the airlines have held planes for people before. The gate couldn't be too far out of our reach. I ran up to the ticket counter, breathless from our jaunt across the short-term parking lot. "Excuse me, sir."

A man with glasses punching a keyboard looked up at me and smiled. "Hello, ma'am. How may I help you?" His smile spilled onto his face and didn't move.

"We're running late for our flight and I was wondering if there was any way we could ask the pilot to hold the plane for us?"

"Do you have your tickets?"

I threw them at him, pointing my eyes at his hands, willing them to move quicker.

"Oh, this flight is taking off in ten minutes. You'll never make it to the gate on time. They've probably already filled your seats with standby passengers."

"Well, can't you call someone and tell them we're here?"

"Even if your seats are still free, the chances of you getting through that long security line in any less than thirty minutes would require a miracle. Sorry."

"Sorry?" I shook my head unable to comprehend this man's lack of human compassion. Couldn't he see that my life hung in the balance? "There was a traffic jam. Sugar spilled all over the roadway. We couldn't move."

"It doesn't matter, ma'am. I can't hold up a full plane for you."

"Then can you get a message to one of the passengers for me?"

"I could try to call the gate and ask them to relay it to the flight attendants." His face softened into a natural smile. He picked up the phone and dialed. He lowered his eyes. He tapped his fingers. He waited. His twisted his mouth to the side. He hung up. "No one's answering."

I dropped my head in defeat.

"We could try and get you on the next flight if you'd like that?" he said.

That'd be great except I'd have no way of telling Paula I was actually in California. "It's no use if I can't get a message to the passenger."

"Well, there is one other thing we could try." He tapped his fingers on the keyboard. "Let me try and send them an instant message. What do you want to say?"

"Tell Paula McKenna that Owen and Lauren are here and will miss the flight. We're taking the next one. Tell her I'm ready to pay back my bet from the Brown quad and take on that marketing class now." I nodded to Owen who grinned. "Oh, and add that I'm not even nervous, yet."

I felt Owen pat my back.

"It's worth a shot," he said, typing away.

"So when's the next available flight for us?" I asked, blinking away the sudden panic that began to swell.

"Let's see." The man scrolled. "I have one taking off in three hours."

"Three hours?"

"It's nonstop."

"No. You don't understand. Three hours isn't going to work."

I needed to do this now.

"Well, there is one taking off in forty-five minutes. You should be able to get through security and down there in time. Coach is filled, though. First class is wide open."

"Okay, first class then. Whatever." I pulled out my wallet.

"Ma'am, the cost is four times that of a coach ticket."

Owen tugged at my shirt. "I'll mow lawns, mom. I'll clean pools. I'll walk dogs. I don't care what it costs." I handed him my credit card. If we had to eat Ramen noodles for a year, then we would.

Within two minutes, he handed us our first class tickets, and we sprinted to security. My throat knotted up like a pretzel, and my heart throttled, but I took off my sandals, laid my bag on the conveyor belt and walked through the scanning machine, shaking on the verge of convulsions, but still walked through nonetheless.

* *

The only way I could get through the security checkpoint with my wits somewhat intact was to play out my reunion with Paula over and over again. I imagined the message got through to her in time. Then, I pictured her walking towards us with a big, goofy grin on her face. She'd be waiting for us at our gate in California with an armful of Hershey bars, ready to welcome us to our new home. We'd throw ourselves at each other and make out in front of anyone who dared watch.

Instead, when Owen and I approached the gate, we looked out over what appeared to be an indoor campground of scattered luggage, business men curled up on the carpet, children weaving through mazes of connected chairs.

As we got closer, I noticed that the people wore long faces, painted with irritation and hostility. Couples snapped at each other. Kids whined.

I looked up at the board next to the gate. This was Paula's plane. It hadn't taken off yet. The gate worker spoke into the microphone. "We just need a few more volunteers to take another flight and we'll be able to leave."

I scanned the three lines, desperately searching for her. I tapped an older lady's shoulder. "Excuse me, Ma'am, what's going on?"

"Our plane is too heavy. They spent all this time boarding us, then moving us off the plane, then weighing the plane. Apparently they need some people to give up their seats before we can take off."

"Mom, what's going on?" Owen asked.

"Honey, this is Coach's plane," I said beaming. "It's still here."

His face beamed like he had swallowed the sun.

"Do you see her?" he asked as he continued to search the crowd.

Just then, the gate worker spoke again. "Okay, we've got a family willing to give up their seats, so it looks like we'll be able to start boarding." The crowd cheered. "Please have your ticket stubs ready to show me."

The first line started to move.

What happened next stopped me dead.

"There she is," Owen said, pointing to the back of the first line.

Sure enough, I stared right at the back of her head. Her hair was freshly cut, which stung me for a second.

Owen lunged forward, then, what we both saw, struck us down faster than lightning. Paula wrapped her arms around a woman and hugged her. I recognized her from that night in the bar when she sang. She was pretty and had this wild, wavy strawberry blonde hair. Her tight shirt pushed her boobs together like a couple of plump cantaloupes. All of a sudden visions of Paula shaking her face in between them popped into my mind, wrestling any of the faith I had in Paula right out of my heart. Less than two weeks and she already latched onto someone else, invited her to move to California, and forgot about me and Owen just like that?

"I'm sorry, Mom."

I bit my lip to ease the blow. I had messed it up for myself. My stupid fear. My selfish little stupid fear had fucked up both our lives.

I stood and watched the made-up whore follow Paula past the gate worker and down the ramp, laughing and carrying on like a couple of giddy teens en route to a homecoming dance. If Owen hadn't dragged me away, I'd have hit someone, anyone, just to get rid of the pain strangling me. He led me back down the concourse towards security checkpoint, holding my hand the whole time, squeezing it when I sniffed or coughed away a cry.

"Let's go home, Mom."

How many more times could I disappoint this boy?

Before we crossed the point of no return, I pulled him back. "Wait."

"Mom, she's moved on." He rolled his head side to side as if trying to sway me to get the hell out of the place before I made an even bigger fool of myself.

In his twelve years, Owen had never left the east coast. Washington D.C. was the furthest he'd ever ventured. My fear ruined his life, too. I grounded him to a life he didn't deserve. No more. No more pity from him. No more giving into this fear. No more keeping my two feet on the ground safe in a place I didn't want to be safe in.

I pulled him back towards our gate. "We're going to California. You're going parasailing. You're going scuba diving. And we're going first class."

"Mom, you don't have to do this for me."

I stopped and looked right into his eyes. "I'm doing this for me, too."

We ran for our flight, which would leave shortly after Paula's. We ran so fast I doubted my feet hit the carpet. My bag waved behind along with my loose waves and giggles. I outran my fear, my sadness, my regrets and hoped what I'd find on the other side of that flight would somehow heal my wounded soul.

* *

I would have no big airport moment where Paula would scoop me up in her arms and profess her undying love for me. Instead, I faced a dreadful six hour flight to the west coast alone with sad thoughts circling around my head. I wouldn't be moving 2,800 miles away. I'd return to Rhode Island, to my condo, to Bella, to all I knew.

When we boarded, I let Owen take my window seat. I plunked down in the over-sized leather seat disappointed, defeated. We watched the passengers pile on. No one looked panicked or scared, just nonplussed, bored even. I braced for the panic to set in. But the only thing that survived the burning sight of Paula a few minutes ago was a numbness that enveloped my body's sensors. Crashing would be more humane at that point, maybe even a relief. I shook my head at the irony.

The sight of Paula with her arms around that other woman cut through me. More tears leaked down my face. I just let them roll as people walked past me, studying my pain.

I watched the flight attendant tidy up the kitchen area, tend to the coffee, put dishes away, fold a blanket, then answer the phone. She was a short lady with a starched bun. She spoke into the phone and darted her eyes around the few people in first class and hung up. Then, she walked over to us with a soft smile.

"I know this is going to sound strange, but you need to look at your cell phone."

"Huh?" I sat up straighter.

"I just got a call from our captain upfront and he was informed that a passenger on another plane has sent you a message. Well, actually, he was asked to transcribe the message, but he refused, so the passenger sent you a voice message instead."

New life pulsed in me. My heart raced. My fingers felt like my fingers again instead of plastic nubs. I could swallow again without that lump getting in the way.

I bent forward to get my purse and Owen had beaten me to it. He turned the cell on already. We stared at the phone as it came to life. Then, Owen called my voice mail and pushed the phone up against my ear.

Teamwork.

Paula's voice broke the agonizing silence. *"I got your message, and I can't believe we missed each other. I never should've disconnected my phone so soon. Call me a sore loser. Chuck is giving me the eye that I have to finish this up. So, I have one thing to tell you. I love you. And I'll be waiting for you when you land. My friend, Alisha, is with me and Chuck. She came along to help us get settled. I think she has a crush on Chuck. Okay, now Alisha is punching my arm and Chuck is turning red. I have never been happier, Lauren. I'll see you in a few hours. I love you."*

"Well? What did she say?" Owen asked me when I hung up.

"Her friend isn't gay."

"That's it?"

I leaned my head back with a smile. "Oh, and she loves me."

Owen raised his hands up in the air and released a winning hoot. Then, he bucked around in his seat like a wild horse wanting to get the race over with.

The engine revved and the flight attendants prepared for takeoff, ensuring everyone's seat and tray tables were in the upright position.

I tucked my hand around Owen's and swallowed. My stomach tossed and turned, rolling over in quick somersaults, a combination of thrill and death defying adventure. "I'm a little scared, Owen."

He squeezed my hand tighter. "Think of something good."

That would be easy. I had a whole lot of good things to think about now. So many, I'd need a closet the size of my condo to fit them all in. "I'm ready."

The plane raced down the runway, and as it lifted off the ground, the fear disappeared in a poof.

I came alive.

* *

Three months later, me, Paula, Owen, Chuck, and Alisha stood outside the airport security gates waiting for Aziza and Tania to bolt through at any second. Owen spotted them first. We strolled towards them, arms linked around each other. When Aziza saw me, she ran towards me and we launched ourselves in the air, laughing, crying, screaming out in joy like it had been years since we'd last laid eyes on each other.

"I have a surprise for you," I said to her as we strode away a half an hour later with their collected luggage.

"Is it something western?" she asked. "Or is it food? Did you bake me macadamia nut cookies?"

"Wait and see." I reached out for my best friend's hand and led her to our car.

Paula drove while Aziza looked out with her mouth open. "This place is dripping in beauty. What an adorable place to shop. How do you manage to keep from going broke here? Look at these designer stores!"

"This is my hometown. Can you believe it?" I asked, cuddling up to my best friend in the back seat.

"I want to see where you work. Take me there," Aziza said.

Paula drove faster. "We're almost there, actually."

"Oh my God. You work around here?"

I could barely breathe; the intensity bubbled in me like a geyser. I pointed a few hundred yards to a vacant building on the corner. "There are my new digs."

The sign, prominently hanging in the front window next to the building permit notice, still sent chills down my spine when I saw it.

Bella II.

Aziza looked from the sign to me at least a dozen times. "You finally ate the frog."

"Swallowed it up whole," I said.

The group exited the car and stood in front of the empty storefront. Aziza curled her arms around me. "How does it feel?"

"Like I'm finally free."

Printed in Great Britain
by Amazon.co.uk, Ltd.,
Marston Gate.

NOTE FROM THE AUTHOR

As with all of my books, I enjoy giving a portion of proceeds back to the community by donating to the NOH8 Campaign www.noh8campaign.com and Hearts United for Animals: www.hua.org. Thank you for being a part of this special contribution.

A SPECIAL REQUEST

If you enjoyed reading this story, I'd be so grateful for your favorable review of it. Just a sentence or two saying what you liked about Two Feet off the Ground will help others discover it and help me to serve you better with future books! (www.amazon.com/author/suziecarr)